#FollowMe
for
Murder

#FollowMe for Murder

A Trending Topic Mystery

Sarah E. Burr

LEVEL
BEST BOOKS

Author Photo Credit: Doug Walters Photography

First edition

ISBN: 978-1-68512-073-3

This book was professionally typeset on Reedsy.
Find out more at reedsy.com

To Mom, Dad, and George for always believing in me

Praise for #FollowMe for Murder

"*#FollowMe for Murder's* sleuth Coco Cline is confident, chic, and cool. The book is fun, and I enjoyed spending time with the characters. Coco's breeziness and style reminded me of the Agatha Raisin in the TV series. I'll definitely be reading the rest of this series."—Lane Stone, author of the upcoming Big Picture Trilogy

"Author Sarah E. Burr does a great job of bringing the seaside town of Central Shores to life and of introducing her engaging, youthful characters. Coco Cline is a wonderful protagonist—likable and smart and timely. I found the details of her job as a social media PR expert to be fascinating and the mystery she solves to be engrossing. Highly recommended."—Carol E. Ayer, author of The HSP Mysteries

"Ms. Burr has her finger right on the pulse of the generation who grew up with technology and with the Internet a single click away. Coco uses her phone and tablet hand in hand with her keen intellect and sharp eye for detail to unearth clues and identify suspects. Who knew you could learn so much about people by digging into their social media footprints? Coco sure does, and she uses that skill to find clues, spot liars, and bring the murderer to justice."—J.C. Kenney, author of the Allie Cobb Mysteries and Darcy Gaughan Mysteries

Chapter One

"It's the difference between life and death."

As Hudson's smirking lips parted to reply, I held up my hand, intent on him not interrupting me. "For their business. Choosing the right filter is crucial for a promotional post. You don't want the graphic to look too artsy and standoffish, yet it also needs to be eye-catching and fun. I should never have given Olivia the password to their account." I tossed my iPhone onto the marble countertop, giving Hudson my best pouty look. "I should know better by now."

He leaned over the kitchen island, giving me a kiss on the forehead. "Well, now you *really* know better." His handsome smile melted away my frustrations. "I'll get out of your hair while you deal with this PR nightmare. Need to stop by my place to grab a fresh shirt before work. I think I left one there in case of emergencies." Grabbing his keys that dangled from the small shelf shaped like a lighthouse, he called over his shoulder, "I'll be home after the six p.m. taping." His smooth voice was cut short by the screen door snapping shut.

I thrummed my fingertips against my yellow coffee mug, watching my boyfriend's shadow retreat down the flagstone pathway that led to the garage underneath my feet. I'd plainly heard him call my condo "home." Even after four years of dating and a year and a half of living together, Hudson still insisted on keeping his apartment in Milton, where a few of his belongings still roosted. He claimed it made for the perfect crash pad when he worked late nights at the station and had to be back in the newsroom early the next morning. In the last six months, I could count the number of nights he'd

1

slept there on one particular finger, yet he still refused to give up his lease. While he was all but moved into my two-story, seaside condo, it irritated me to no end when he had to stop by "his place" to pick up some type of necessity.

Although, today's pit stop was my fault, and Hudson had been considerate enough not to call me out on it. I'd been the one to drop the ball on having his button-ups laundered. When we'd moved in together, Hudson and I reached a verbal agreement: laundry was my domain, while Hudson's was garbage and dishwasher duty. In my eyes, Hudson got the short end of the stick, but that was because I always waited until the laundry hampers were bursting to do anything about them. I'd never allow Hudson to slack off with the garbage or the dishes the way he let me with the laundry. Resigned to doing my chores, I took my steaming cup of joe with me as I ambled down the hallway into the master bedroom that overlooked the tossing whitecaps of the morning.

Taking a few moments to enjoy the view outside, I smiled as I then gazed over the impressive interior space, adorned with a king-sized bed, a small loveseat covered in clothes, a vintage vanity, and a large flat-screen TV pinned to the wall. The ocean-themed wallpaper paired nicely with the bright yellow comforter on the bed, beckoning me to crawl back under the covers. *If this coffee doesn't start working its magic, I may have to.* I wandered over to the doors of the large walk-in closet that Hudson and I shared. While I was proud that my myriad of clothes and shoes only took up one side, leaving Hudson with more than enough space for his own items, the closet *was* the size of a small bedroom. It was one of the reasons I'd bought the place to begin with, as silly as it sounded. I'd fallen in love with the open kitchen looking out over the water the moment I stepped into the condo, but I'd been looking at beachfront properties all day. It was the size of this closet that sealed the deal.

Its stunning location and various condo association amenities had put this spot at the top of my price range, but I decided to treat myself and had not regretted it a moment since. This condo exuded what I'd been telling my online followers all along: *your world, your bliss.* And considering how at peace I felt in my home, the splurge had been worth it. Not that I didn't have the money to spend at the time.

The reason I had been house hunting in the first place was to invest the windfall of cash I'd received when my college startup company, LiveIt, was bought out. Memories of those whirlwind days made me swell with pride. Five friends and I sitting around a dining room table, fresh from commencement, developing the lifestyle app we always wished for to help us navigate the latest beauty trends, online shopping sales, and endless celebrity gossip inundating our social media feeds every day. It only took a few penniless months after graduating from Bayside University before LiveIt and my lifestyle blog, *Trending Topic* (the flagship content of the mobile app), took off. LiveIt was the one-stop-media-shop the online world had been waiting for. Our team had designed an easy-to-use program, using smart, technical search engines and algorithms, that allowed users to see entertainment news filtered to their interests, cultural events based on their likes and hobbies, and online discounts for their favorite stores, all in one place. With a tap of an app, you could catch up on celeb drama, discover what was happening around you, and get a notification that the must-have Fendi Baguette bag you'd been eyeing at Bloomingdale's was finally on sale. All users had to do was fill out a quick preferences survey upon downloading and signing up for LiveIt, and the online world was at their fingertips, all in one sleek newsfeed.

Since I had next-to-zero coding experience, you might be wondering where I fit into this picture. While my tech-whiz business partners were rolling out crazy computer code to house all this information, I got to have a bit more fun. During the development phase of LiveIt, my friends decided that we wanted the app to offer original content in addition to the curated newsfeed, and thus, my *Trending Topic* blog was born. While my colleagues waded through garbled C# code, I created fun videos and on-trend posts about topics ranging from how to get glorious Blake Lively-lookalike waves to dining room decorating tips that would impress your in-laws. In the blog's infancy, I let users vote on which topic I would tackle week-to-week. I had my favorites: reviewing books and films, fact-checking celebrity gossip, and decoding the latest fashion obsession. I always struggled when users wanted material featuring dieting tips or elaborate recipes made easy. While I had some gourmet triumphs in the kitchen, I had also shared some pretty epic baking disasters, which only had *Trending Topic* followers begging for more of "Coco's Cooking Capers." They even started sharing pictures of their own baking fails in the comments section, giving birth to the #FlawlessFails hashtag, which I still bust out to this day. Luckily for me and my poor oven, once I'd established my voice in the blogosphere and become a social influencer in my own right, I got to be more selective with my content, narrowing *Trending Topic*'s focus primarily to fashion, beauty, and wellness, entertainment news, and home décor.

Overjoyed with LiveIt's initial success, our team rented a small office space in Dover, Delaware, and built our headquarters from there. Within our first year, *Trending Topic* amassed over three hundred thousand followers and our app was downloaded from the Apple and GooglePlay stores over two million times. By year three, we were at over ten million downloads and one million blog subscribers. Our success was staggering for such a competitive field. There had never been such a popular social media app—or any app, for that matter—developed and managed entirely by women. Because of the "Women in Leadership" creed LiveIt embodied, industry giants wanted to ride our coattails, all the while getting their hands on a nifty piece of tech. You know the old story: two birds, one stone. In the bidding war that ensued, Facebook ultimately won the prize by offering us forty-two million for our relatively small, upstart company.

Our whirlwind adventure didn't stop there. After news of the acquisition broke, my colleagues and I were booked on *Today*, where we were billed as "tech industry leaders" by Savannah Guthrie and Hoda Kotb. Throughout the surprisingly down-to-earth segment, Hoda continually praised us as role models for young women; we'd broken the glass ceiling, finding huge success in a field dominated by men. I'd felt a bit like a fraud for basking in the glow of her compliment because I really had nothing to do with the technical aspects of the LiveIt app. Yet, as my teammates frequently reminded me, it was the original content I delivered through *Trending Topic* that kept our users returning and wanting more. My face greeted our eleven-million-and-growing users every time they logged on to check their curated newsfeed, making my name synonymous with the app and its success.

Thinking back on it now, I still can't believe how in over our heads we were. If my business partners and I had known better, we would have pushed for way more money, considering the insane profits Facebook eventually made from integrating the LiveIt tech into their platform. But try proclaiming patience to a group of twenty-five-year-olds. I had the good business sense to ensure that *Trending Topic*, still one of the main attractions to those using the original app, came with me as my intellectual property. Facebook countered that I could keep my blog, but the value of the company would drop to thirty-eight million, since all they'd be acquiring was the curated newsfeed algorithm. Not wanting to shortchange my friends, who had poured so much of their own IP into LiveIt, I agreed I would walk away from the sale with rights to *Trending Topic* and three million dollars, while the others cashed in at a cool seven million.

Three years later, I still got annoyed at my twenty-five-year-old self for not being savvier or for not hiring a better lawyer to navigate the acquisition negotiations. At twenty-eight years old, I certainly wasn't living paycheck to paycheck but, considering I foolishly blew a chunk of my three-million-dollar payout as soon as it hit my bank account, I certainly couldn't afford to retire at a little over a quarter-century into my existence. *Trending Topic* still brought in a steady income from advertisers, but if I was going to live the lifestyle of the rich and fabulous for the rest of my days, I needed to come up with another lucrative business idea.

Since my job experience and skillset amounted to online networking and promotion, I decided to stick with what I was best at, and thus, Center of Attention Consulting Services was born. My reputation as a lifestyle blogger boosted my social media influence once I made my Instagram account public. With all my followers and, pinch me, fans, I could use my internet fame and expertise to help other small businesses achieve the commercial success that I had at such a young age. Center of Attention, or CoA, worked with small business owners to promote their stores by increasing their social media presence. At two thousand dollars for a standard engagement, I worked with clients remotely, training them on everything from catchphrases to hashtags, all aimed to grow their clientele through online means. I even guaranteed a five percent increase in customer growth after the first year or I refunded the client one thousand dollars. To this day, I was proud to say that had yet to happen. For clients that wanted a more personalized experience, they could hire me for five thousand dollars and I would come onsite to work alongside them. Right now, this portion of my business was limited to folks within one hundred miles of my hometown of Central Shores, Delaware, but it had still been pretty prosperous thus far.

My discarded iPhone was proof of CoA's growing success. While pouring my cup of morning coffee and scrolling through my Instagram feed, I'd come across a post from a business in town that had recently solicited my services. Once Used, Twice Buy was a new consignment shop opening along Central Shores's beachside strip, where most of the prominent local businesses rented or owned storefronts. Central Shores was what I would call a Florida beach town with an old New England twist, even though Delaware wasn't a part of New England. I'd spent enough time visiting family in Massachusetts and Maine to realize that the hardy attitudes of folks along the New England coast mirrored those in my little town of two thousand and sixty-two residents.

When I was a teenager, I would have thought you were crazy if you'd told me I'd be back in Central Shores by the time I was twenty-eight. My childhood dreams involved moving to New York City after college, working for a fashion magazine, and living in an artsy apartment in SoHo. But as luck would have it, life had other plans for me. In the early days of LiveIt, to save money, my friends and I had all roomed together in a rented, two-bedroom apartment in Dover after graduating from Bayside University. As our app grew more popular and generated more revenue, we were able to branch out and get our own digs, but we still decided to keep our home base firmly rooted in Dover. With our headquarters in a small city, we strove to maintain a down-to-earth, startup image, even as our company's footprint grew. It wasn't long before LiveIt's popularity skyrocketed and *Trending*

Topic began to be compared to blogs like Meghan Markle's *The Tig,* Gwyneth Paltrow's *Goop,* and Perez Hilton's infamous celeb gossip page. Things really took off once the LiveIt-Facebook acquisition hit the news cycle. *Trending Topic,* in particular, garnered tons of media attention through the process, and I spent the next few months in the blazing spotlight as LiveIt's unofficial spokeswoman. Fame was something I had always dreamed about as a kid, but as they say, be careful what you wish for. Having my picture snapped at my local Food Lion grocery store or while leaving a hot yoga class in sweats and no makeup wasn't as glamorous as I had thought it would be as a teen. I loved developing the content for *Trending Topic,* and promoting my brand across social media platforms, but not at the expense of my everyday privacy. Skirting the paparazzi just to grab a pizza slice grew old real quick, and I found myself yearning to return to my roots. Surprising even myself, I decided to retreat to the comforting embrace of my former life. I loved the peace and tranquility Central Shores offered me. Although, some days, the small-town gossip often wore me down the very same way being in the public eye did.

Placing my coffee mug on a small end table, I leaned down to grab the laundry hamper buried in the back of the closet. The aftertaste of the bland, off-brand K-cup had me yearning for the real thing. Yet, my ears still rang from the buzz of the local coffee shop yesterday morning, when I walked in to grab a caramel macchiato, my ring-less finger on display for everyone to see. Earlier in the week, I had unwisely mentioned to a few chatty locals that Hudson and I were celebrating our fourth anniversary that Monday night. He had taken me out to a lovely dinner, and we'd had a wonderful time, but part of me was disappointed that he hadn't used the occasion to propose. The barrage of coffee-shop whispers Tuesday morning revealed Central Shores's disappointment, too. Hissing comments of "What is he waiting for?" and "Maybe he doesn't want to make the commitment" still bounced around inside my head. Thank goodness none of them knew about the apartment Hudson still kept near his workplace, or that would've fueled the fires even more. You'd think I'd be used to criticism and gossip, considering my livelihood was tied to social media, where people were free to comment however viciously they wanted, but reading vitriol online wasn't the same as hearing it float through your ears. Confident that what Hudson and I had was the real deal, I pushed the memory of the snide remarks aside and focused on the task at hand.

Scowling at the overflowing laundry hamper, I realized it had been a while since I'd been home long enough to clean the house. While Hudson and I had the spare income to hire a cleaning service, I wanted to keep our seaside haven hidden away from potential busybodies and the like. I honestly enjoyed cleaning, and part of *Trending Topic's* continued success was due to the fact that I was more down-to-earth and relatable than most celebrity influencers out there. Believe me, nothing kept you more grounded than folding your boyfriend's boxer briefs.

My gaze trailed longingly out the window. Today would have been the perfect day to wade through my growing list of chores, but now I had to deal with the fallout over this Once Used, Twice Buy Instagram post. Instead of our quick, scheduled touch base to approve the grand opening special invite list, I needed to have a longer, more serious conversation with the Chens about my role as their consultant…again. This wasn't the first time Olivia Chen had gone rogue, and I doubted it would be her last. As smart and shrewd as she was, Olivia had totally violated the agreement we had regarding Once Used, Twice Buy's social media account usage. All Center of Attention contracts stated that during the first thirty days of a consulting engagement, I managed their social media postings exclusively. Usually, if the client had an existing Instagram or Twitter account, I changed the password and didn't give it to them until the thirty days were up. But Olivia had asked for the passwords yesterday because she needed them in order to link the accounts to their website, so pictures and tweets could be displayed on the Once Used, Twice Buy homepage. I made a mental note that I would take over account linking for all social media sites during future CoA engagements.

A little while later, my iPhone hummed against the countertop in the kitchen. Always one to prefer a text to a phone call, no one called me unless it was important, even my clients. I taught them that texting was a good way to prepare themselves for communication management through Twitter, where everything was tied to a few select characters. Lucky for me, they bought it as all part of the CoA program, not just my dislike for talking on the phone.

Leaving the half-emptied hamper by the washing machine, I hurried into the kitchen. Hudson's name glowed from the screen. Frowning, I picked up the phone. "Is everything okay?"

Hudson chuckled on the other end of the line. "I almost bet Cynthia here that you wouldn't pick up. I was prepared to leave a message."

Cynthia Yates was Hudson's eighty-year-old next-door neighbor and landlord.

"Did you lose your keys between your car and the front door?" I tried to imagine why Hudson would be interacting with his landlord.

"No. There seems to be a leak in the bathroom ceiling. I was just showing it to her, but that's not the reason why I called." I heard shuffling in the background as Hudson scooted along through his bachelor pad. "I forgot to invite you to a fundraising dinner the station is sponsoring. I found a Post-It on my fridge just now, reminding me. Must have left it here last week when I stopped by to grab an extra Xbox headset."

Yet another reason why Hudson's apartment remained a thorn in my side. This wasn't the first time he'd left a note for himself there and forgotten about it. I'd suggested countless times that he let the apartment go and settle in here, but he always mumbled some excuse before changing the subject. In recent weeks, I'd decided to bench my nagging and wait for Hudson to come to the realization on his own. I didn't want to make my boyfriend feel like I was forcing him to live with me, but I also didn't understand why he refused to let go of the last piece of his bachelorhood. If I dwelled on it too long, it made me a bit wary.

"When and where is it?" There was no point in chastising him for the error.

"At the Milton Botanical Gardens...tomorrow night." I could sense nervous vibes coming through the phone. Hudson was steeling himself against my wrath at the short notice.

I took a deep, calming breath, not wanting to argue over the phone. Who threw a big, boujee event on a Thursday night?

"Fine." It was not fine. "I'll plan to meet you there after work. I need to get going. I'm in the middle of doing laundry, trying to finish up before heading out to confront the Chens."

Hudson must have realized he had escaped within an inch of his life because he exhaled loudly into the phone. "Perfect. Knew I could count on you, babes."

Closing out the call, I checked the swarm of new Twitter and Instagram alerts filling my screen, finding a text notification from Sean Chen, Olivia's husband and business partner, buried among them.

You probably saw Liv's post. Sorry about that—I know we're not supposed to be doing that ourselves, yet. Told her to take it down. Only had two likes when she did. Still on for lunch meeting at the store?

I said a silent prayer thanking God for Sean's sensibility and influence regarding his wife's actions. At least some good had come from this little snag. Sean's text told me he'd paid attention to the number of likes the photo had garnered on Instagram before deleting. One of my teachings was that it was pertinent to review your online portfolio and eliminate posts that did not show any audience engagement, whether it be likes or comments. Quality over quantity was my social media philosophy. I'd rather have an account with five photos with seventy-five likes each than an account with sixty photos with three likes here and there. Not that I considered seventy-five likes to be a successful post. Once I opened my Instagram account up to the public as *Trending Topic*'s content creator, I averaged roughly fifteen thousand likes on an off day. First thing this morning, I'd launched Instagram and uploaded a candid photo of the scenic beach view from my living room window. It had been live less than two hours and the post had already been liked eleven thousand three hundred eighty-two times. Not to mention the number of DMs I received, asking me for some type of beach product sponsorship. But for a small-town business just starting out, anything over twenty-five likes would be considered a win in my book. Texting Sean back,

I responded:

Saw the post. Will need to speak with Olivia about contractual 30 days again once we confirm the opening invite list. I'll grab wraps from Zaddick's and see you both at noon.

I'd had been working with the Chens for about three weeks, long enough to know their favorite order from Central Shores's most popular deli and takeout spot. Glancing at the minutes blinking away at the top of my phone, I calculated that I still had enough time to make a dent in the laundry and a few other chores before having to leave for my midday meeting.

Checking my other unanswered text notifications, I winced at a message from one of my best friends, Charlotte Whittaker. She had been trying to arrange drinks with Hudson and me for the past two weeks to meet her latest beau. Not that I didn't love spending time with twenty-nine-year-old Charlotte, whom I'd befriended since moving back to Central Shores three years ago, but her nonstop cycling in-and-out of boyfriends was exhausting to keep up with. In the three years I'd known her, she'd dated at least fifty different guys. How she managed to continually find new blood in a town this small always amazed me. The internet not only worked wonders for my professional life, but for her personal life as well. Of course, her stunning good looks might have also been a factor. Charlotte was one of those rare people who had both incredible beauty and a lovable personality. The first time I saw her behind the counter of Brewed to Perfection, I tripped on the welcome mat, blind with envy at her beachy amber waves and hauntingly, clear gray eyes. Being the sweetheart she was, Charlotte rushed over to help me up off the floor and offered me my drink of choice on the house. As she made my favorite coffee beverage, a caramel macchiato, she trilled on in her singsong voice how she'd just opened Brewed to Perfection after moving here from South Carolina. She'd chosen to drop out of college and get her business degree online to save the money needed to open her own business. At the time, I'd just moved back from Dover, ready to start the next phase of my life, and, after hearing her struggles trying to increase foot traffic, I asked her to be CoA's first client. A social media campaign that had customers arriving in droves to try Brewed to Perfection's custom caffeine creations bonded us for life, and we'd been as close as sisters ever since. Which meant that, while I was always happy when she found someone who made her smile, I knew deep down he would likely break her heart. As much as I urged her to take things slow, my pleas fell on deaf ears.

Looking at her invitation for dinner now, I bit my lip trying to figure out how to answer. Not having to prepare a meal would free up some of my afternoon once my meeting with the Chens wrapped up, so my fingers hovered above the iPhone's keyboard, tempted to say yes, even without asking Hudson first. Considering how he'd ambushed me with the fundraiser tomorrow night, I figured he owed me one. **Hudson will be home around 7. Where do you want to meet?**

Charlotte's response was almost immediate, a slew of heart emojis preceding her words. **Yay! Jasper coming, too. Meet at The Pearl at 7:30, if okay?**

Sighing dramatically, I quickly sent a note that we'd see them all tonight. My other best friend, Jasper Hastings, worked and lived in Dover, and The Pearl was our typical halfway meeting spot for dinner gatherings as a group. The only downside was that it was roughly thirty minutes away with traffic, and, with the upcoming fundraiser, I didn't feel like being out late two weeknights in a row. I silently cursed Jasper for choosing to live so far from the rest of us.

Ours was a storied friendship. Jasper and I met when we were in second grade. His family had recently moved to Central Shores, a few blocks away from my parents' house. We first laid eyes on each other at the neighborhood bus stop. Our parents tried to get us to say hello, but we both childishly refused to acknowledge the other's presence. Maybe our eight-year-old psyches sensed we were fated to be rivals for the spotlight. It wasn't until we got on the bus and sat across from each other that I pulled out a copy of *People* I had stolen from my mom's bedside and he pulled out his parent-purloined copy of *Us Weekly* that we realized we were destined to become besties.

Growing up in Central Shores wasn't exactly super thrilling for two larger-than-life personalities, but we survived, thanks to our mutual love of all things celebrity. In college, I visited Jasper at NYU to see Broadway musicals and crash movie premieres. I even offered him the opportunity to be a partner in LiveIt, but he turned it down in typical Jasper fashion. He wanted to "create news, not repost it." To this day, he complained that I didn't try hard enough to woo him onboard, considering the payout and notoriety LiveIt ultimately received. But even though he pretended to be upset, there was nothing that would have taken Jasper away from *Divulge*, Dover's one—and only—society magazine. It still cracked me up that Dover even had a society to write about, but it was all thanks to Jasper, who transformed a failing gossip rag into a competitive piece of journalism. Most of what he and his team wrote about focused on Hollywood and high society news, but they always spotlighted the Dover area events as if they were comparable to the Oscars. He single-handedly created a culture of wannabe starlets, using *Divulge* columns and events to boost and promote social influencers who wanted to play the game with him. When Jasper had started at *Divulge*, it had been on the verge of bankruptcy; now, he cultivated Dover's high society and a media empire from his fourteenth-floor corner office.

Promising myself I would soon put my phone down and concentrate on making my home look presentable, my thumbs danced across the screen, texting Jasper. As Editor-in-Chief, he also oversaw *Divulge's* fashion spreads and could often borrow designer pieces featured in their shoots. I wanted him to bring me some jewelry to showcase at the fundraiser tomorrow, since I'd be hobnobbing with the studio's elite sponsors.

Jasper sent me a girl-power gif of Beyoncé in a confirming reply.

Setting my phone down on the granite kitchen countertop and severing ties with the outside world, I spent the morning cramming in as much cleaning as time allowed. Upstairs was a full bathroom and two guest rooms that went unused for months at a time, so I left the second-floor chores for another day. With my office, bedroom, living room, and kitchen all on the first floor, I tended not to venture upstairs unless I needed to grab something from the linen closet. My parents lived in town, and Hudson's parents lived only thirty minutes away near Milton, so we didn't have many reasons to host guests overnight. Sometimes my sister's triplets, my four-year-old nieces and nephew, stayed the night, but my lack of maternal instincts and busy lifestyle made their sleepovers a rare occasion.

By eleven fifteen, I finished putting away the last piece of laundry, a checkered blue-and-white shirt of Hudson's. Glancing at the clock on his side of the bed, I had to make waves toward Zaddick's before the lunch crowd descended. Popping into the en suite bathroom that shared a wall with my lovely closet, I assessed my appearance. I sported one of my favorite dresses, a sleek black number that hugged my curves in the right places, giving the world the illusion I had a trim waist. It wasn't the most appropriate outfit for housework, but one never knew when a photo might be taken. The material was also super comfy, which was mainly why I wore it.

My outfit might not have needed adjustment, but my hair certainly did. My long, strawberry champagne-dyed locks hung loose, plagued with ratty tangles. My hair was naturally mousey brown, but growing up, I'd pined for a beautiful shade of red circa Nicole Kidman in the movie *Moulin Rouge*. I blew my first big paycheck from LiveIt on a salon visit, where I discovered *Little Mermaid*-colored locks were nearly impossible to maintain. The following months were filled with additional salon trips, trying to find the right shade for me. I might not have been born a redhead, but in my soul, I felt like one. Eventually, I'd found the perfect, shimmery hue that blended together blond and rosé tones, and I'd been nurturing it for years.

I quickly went to work on the frightening knots, fiercely weeding them out with a hairbrush so much so that my eyes grew a bit teary. There were many days I wished I could chop my hair into a shoulder-length bob, but I had secretly vowed not to cut it drastically until after my will-it-ever-happen wedding when I would no longer require long hair for an intricate up-do.

Pressed for time now, I swiped some espresso eyeliner over my lids, smudging the liner with my pinky until a flawless smoky eye emerged—an easy technique and one of my favorites to remind my followers about. I loved developing *Trending Topic* content about the power of eye makeup because out of all the things on the beauty spectrum, it came easiest to me. My sea-green eyes were hands down my best and most alluring feature. Changing shades as often as the tide, my irises always fascinated people,

14

and I'd learned a ton of tricks to really play them up. While they usually remained somewhere in the realm of blue-green, the precise hue varied depending on the color palette I was wearing that day. Complemented by the earthy tones of my Stila eyeliner, a seafoam gaze stared back at me.

Satisfied with the reflection in the bathroom mirror, I waltzed my way into the kitchen and snatched up my phone. Another flurry of Twitter notifications greeted me. Last night, I'd tweeted out a movie recommendation to the online cosmos because as an influencer, I have a duty to influence. In less than twenty-four hours, the tweet had hit fifteen thousand retweets. Even one of the movie's minor, supporting actors had jumped on the retweet train, praising my excellent taste in sci-fi romance movies. I'd even gotten a follow back from him. Burying my inner fangirl, I snoozed all social media alerts for the moment, Googled Zaddick's, and placed my call with a simple tap of the number on their website.

"Hello, Zaddick's. What can I help you with?"

Even without introduction, I knew Mr. Mendez's voice right away. He'd been my third-grade teacher before quitting to open his own deli, and, because of this, I still called him Mr. Mendez rather than Bill.

"Hi, Mr. Mendez! I'd like some wraps for pickup," I said cheerfully, hoping I wouldn't get tongue-tied placing the order like I normally did when speaking on the phone.

"What'll it be?" His gruff tone was all business.

"Two blue crab and veggie, broccoli salad on the side, and one Italian combo with chips." As much as I despised the smell and taste of seafood, the Chens loved it, and I always aimed to please my clients. Blue crab season had also kicked off three weeks ago at the beginning of April. It would be a crime to deny them the chance to enjoy the Delaware delicacy.

"We'll have it ready in fifteen. Who's the order for?"

"Coco Cline." I smiled as my snappy moniker rolled off my tongue.

"Coco Cline? You related to Cordelia Cline? I had her in my third-grade class a long time ago."

I rolled my eyes at the joke I'd heard a thousand times. I could practically see Mr. Mendez grinning a toothy mouthful through the bushy beard he always sported. "Yes, we're one in the same, sir, as always."

He chuckled, and I said goodbye.

When I was fifteen and rebelling against everything the world threw at me, I decided I would no longer go by my childhood-given name, Cordelia. To me, it sounded like a grandmother from the 1800s rather than an attention-seeking, fashion-forward teenager. After much debate between my friends and I in late-night OG Facebook Message chats, I rebranded myself "Coco," a name that, in my opinion, exuded sassy sophistication. It was an uphill battle getting everyone in town who'd known me as Cordelia for my whole life to call me Coco, but with LiveIt's rising popularity and *Trending Topic* somewhat of a household name, as I grew older and more established, so did my rebranded moniker. Only my parents continued to resist. To them, I was still affectionately known as Delia.

Rummaging through my purse for my favorite tinted lip balm, I dabbed it on my lips as I puckered them in the mirror. Looking presentable enough for a client meeting was one thing, but I needed to remember to leave enough time to swing back home to prepare for the looming dinner outing tonight. Around Charlotte's effortless beauty, I always had to go for glam, or I'd be invisible the entire evening.

Grabbing my keys from the shelf rack, I locked the front door behind me and followed the mossy flagstone path down to the two-door garage situated underneath my free-standing condo. This particular seaside development shied away from traditional connected townhomes, so my closest neighbor was on the other side of the spacious one-acre lot. The Huntingtons were seasonal residents, making the annual trek to Central Shores to escape the Florida heat during the summer months. As it was only late April, Hudson and I had the shared yard all to ourselves.

Entering the garage through the side door, I walked by Hudson's vacant spot, taking in the sight of my baby, Jolly. Nicknamed by Jasper as the "Jolly-wagon," I had purchased the two-door convertible, British-racing green Mini Cooper with a portion of my three-million-dollar buyout. While I had never been one to care about cars, having driven my parents' hand-me-downs for most of my life, when I set eyes on Jolly, I knew he was going to be mine. The compact car also gave me the perfect excuse for not offering to drive my friends and family around. *I* preferred to be the one chauffeured when the option was on the table.

Sliding into the leather driver's seat, I started the car as I waited for the garage door to lift open. Zaddick's was down by the strip, meaning I could park in the residential parking lot for the remainder of the afternoon and walk to the Chens' from the deli. As much it miffed me to put a tacky parking sticker on Jolly's back window, not wanting to pay for metered parking won out in the end. Due to the influx of tourists Central Shores had in the summers and falls, the mayor's office had surrendered to the locals' demands for private parking a few years ago. My mother, a member of the town council, had been instrumental in organizing the protesters. Led strategically by my father, the protestors convinced the rest of the council that Central Shores needed a residents-only parking lot. There hadn't been a Thanksgiving since where my parents hadn't regaled their heroic deeds in tandem.

Backing out of the garage into the searing spring sun, I was surprised to see that the information panel on Jolly's dashboard read seventy-six degrees. Unusually warm for late April, but I wouldn't complain. My lightweight dress would keep me cool while I walked around town, and, thankfully, the Chens' store had central air.

Zipping along the oceanside road, I drove out of the Sunny Shores residential development. Noticing the welcome sign in my rearview mirror, I rolled my eyes at the marketing director who'd approved "Sunny Shores at Central Shores." It was one of the newer, high-end housing complexes in the area and had been met with a lot of resistance by the locals. As much as it thrived on tourism, Central Shores valued being a small, tight-knit community, something harder to maintain once more people moved into the area. To the town's benefit, the Sunny Shores development team went bankrupt two years into the project, resulting in only a handful of completed condominiums. The Huntingtons and I owned the largest of the beachfront properties, while Charlotte had purchased one of the smaller units set farther up the cul-de-sac, away from the beach. The other six homes lining the private road were in various stages of for-sale to sale-pending.

I hoped the Sunny Shores condos stayed that way—I adored having this slice of heaven practically all to myself. I had moved back home to seek refuge from the chaos of city life, and I'd certainly found it here. Some days I missed the youthful, fast-paced energy that pulsed through the urban jungle, but I loved the sense of quiet contentment I felt by the beach. Nothing bad ever happened here.

Chapter Two

The drive up the coast took me ten minutes due to a stop sign fender bender impeding traffic. I glanced at the flashing police lights at the scene as I safely pulled around, catching a glimpse of each driver, angrily waving their phones in each other's faces. I could guess what had happened. As much as I valued technology and what it had contributed to my way of life, I had no tolerance for people who stared at their phone screens while driving and caused accidents because their attention was diverted elsewhere. I'd seen one too many articles about lives ripped away due to texting and driving. My phone remained tucked away in my purse whenever I drove Jolly, my Bluetooth activated.

Minutes later, I slid into an open spot in the strip's residential lot. As I put the car into park, my nose wrinkled at the unsightly, unmanicured backings of numerous brick and cement shops. What a drastic contrast they were from the charming and picturesque exteriors lining the main street. The lot had been tarred behind the Central Shores strip, or "the Boardwalk," as the town council had tried rebranding it, in hopes of making it sound more sophisticated and classier. It hadn't worked with the locals. Old habits die hard, and the strip was the strip. Only wealthy newcomers and tourists called it the Boardwalk these days.

Hopping out and locking Jolly, I hurried down the alley between Jewel's Ice Cream and Harper's Pub that served as a shortcut for folks who didn't want to walk all the way down to the end of the strip to get out of the parking lot.

Catching a whiff of loaded potato skins from Harper's almost made me

19

double back and request an order, but I briskly strode past the rowdy joint. Even though it wasn't yet noon on a Wednesday, Harper's was already serving up fried food and craft brews to the early boozers.

I was always impressed, even as a kid, by the variety of attractions Central Shores boasted on its coastal strip. Over the years, some businesses had come and gone, but a majority of the storefronts had been around for as long as I could remember. Growing up, I spent my days at the beach with Jasper and my high school friends, taking breaks from the sun to duck into Story's End Bookstore or The Blackout Arcade. As a family, we frequently walked from my parents' house down to the strip for dinner at Beauforts, then for dessert at Jewel's Ice Cream. On Sunday mornings, my mom sent my sister and me on our bikes to get pastries from Flakier than Thou, where we dallied a bit in front of Mystic's Cards and Games to gush over the adorable Pokémon characters or Beanie Babies displayed in the window. Of course, there were the boring places like the Central Shores Chamber of Commerce and Golden Gates Credit Union, but due to the town's need to attract visitors, businesses like the laundromat and grocery store had been opened farther inland near the elementary and high schools so tourist attractions could dominate the beachfront property. Some of the newer places had only popped up since I had arrived back home, like Squeezed the juice bar, and Quincy's Finds, a cute little dress boutique. Charlotte's coffee shop sat at the southern end of the strip, as well.

Glancing at the time on my phone, I picked up my pace and headed toward the line billowing out of Zaddick's. Mr. Mendez designed the deli to have a curbside service window so folks could order directly from the sidewalk. Tourists were happy to remain out in the sun, while Mr. Mendez was happy to not have them tracking in sand. Opening the glass door, I headed to the inside counter to pick up my carryout order. Inside the bustling restaurant, there was limited seating, and what was available had already been scooped up for the lunch hour. I waved at a few familiar faces but quickly engaged myself in a pretend phone call so I wouldn't have to make small talk. As much as I thrived off attention from my online followers, I was much warier about dealing with people in person. When responding to comments online,

I could take my time to craft the best reply, but when people approached me in person, I had to think on my feet, which flustered me pretty easily.

The freckle-faced teen manning the register saw me making my way toward the front of the line and reached under the counter to look for my bagged order. "Got everything right here, Ms. Cline. We charged it to the card on file." The trembly young man held out my sandwiches.

Graciously accepting the bag, I thanked him. "Glad to see you got approval for your work-study, Jonah."

A senior at Central Shores High, Jonah normally worked for Mr. Mendez after school and on the weekends. However, due to his impending college bills and stellar grades, he and the other senior class officers started a program a few months ago allowing their classmates to work for local businesses during free periods to teach them good work ethic and allow them to save some extra money for college tuition. I had featured their initiative on my blog, using it as an example of how kids today could give back to their community, all while benefiting themselves. I knew that a portion of my online audience consisted of Gen Z's who needed motivation and mothers who wanted to motivate them, so I figured the piece was a nice way to inspire my generational followers. The traction the post got online all but secured its success when it came to the school board vote.

Jonah's smile seemed more like a cringe, his skin glowing beet red. He had been my student liaison while writing the article, and I dared say he had developed a little crush on me. "Thanks again for your help, Ms. Cline. We couldn't have gotten the proposal passed without your help."

"Please, call me Coco," I reminded him for what felt like the hundredth time. Secretly, I was a bit tickled that I left the younger Central Shores generation starstruck. LiveIt had hit the national news cycle just as Jonah and his peers were signing up for their first social media accounts. They'd been introduced to me through the LiveIt app, YouTube clips, Snapchat, Instagram Stories, and *Trending Topic*.

With a perky wave, I backed away from the counter and the swarming sea of hungry lunchers. Glad that I had called in my order ahead of time, I ducked out onto the sidewalk and headed down the strip, passing the bookstore and the arcade before arriving at the darkened storefront of Once Used, Twice Buy. Reaching for the door handle, I pulled back and found it locked. Checking my phone again, I saw that it was eleven fifty-five. The Chens technically weren't late for our meeting, but it was unlike them to not be at the store already. With all they had invested in this venture, Once Used, Twice Buy was their whole world.

When Sean and Olivia originally pitched their idea to me, I was skeptical of how successful a consignment store that catered exclusively to dishware could be in Central Shores. Yet, once they explained that a majority of their sales would be brokered online and their storefront would serve as a mini shipping center, I began to see the potential. It also helped that Olivia had amazing taste and had accrued gorgeous china patterns from all over the world, giving their selection an avant-garde edge that would no doubt draw affluent buyers. With her style requests in mind, Sean spent much of his time combing through garage and yard sales all over the state, cultivating stock for their initial launch. Once the business was fully operational, they would also allow customers to sell their own used dinnerware through the company's webpage, after taking a small brokerage fee for themselves.

The grand opening was set to happen next Saturday and, looking at the empty shelving units through the window, a lot still needed to be done in ten days. The store's impending launch was why it was strange that the Chens weren't already here.

My phone vibrated, and I saw a text from Olivia.

Running late. Sean and I getting coffee. Long line. Feel free to let yourself in.

Fumbling for the spare key Olivia had given me at the start of our engagement, I fiddled with the lock before twisting the door open. A blast of AC-generated air hit me with surprising force, chilling the line of sweat forming under my bra band. Brushing aside the shiver running down my spine, I peered out the large bay window facing the beach. With temperatures climbing into the high seventies today, there would no doubt be a herd of diehard beachgoers intent on braving the freezing Atlantic. I looked longingly at the dark blue waves crashing onto the dusty sand, wishing I were outside instead of in this dark and somewhat creepy store. I hoped the weather would stay this nice through the weekend. I wanted to put my access to the Sunny Shores private beach to use soon.

My gaze trailed around the main showroom of the store. I was still impressed that the Chens had managed to snag this coveted piece of real estate. Whenever there was a vacancy on the strip, a bidding war ensued. If I remembered correctly, Sean said they'd beat out a chocolate store and a gourmet popcorn shop. As much as I adored my clients, I would take chocolate or popcorn over dishes any day, so if the Chens' business ultimately failed, at least there was a silver lining…for my stomach.

Sean had been working on setting up the display shelving for the last two weeks, while Olivia and their assistant, Stacy Lockner, worked on inventory. I would never have pegged Sean as the rugged handyman type, but he'd done an amazing job. I walked around inspecting the room, wondering if it would be rude if I started in on my lunch. I hadn't eaten any breakfast before diving into my chores, and my stomach roared its disapproval.

Thinking it might be better if I ate now so that I could talk uninterrupted during our meeting, while Sean and Olivia stuffed their faces full of crab, I maneuvered past a tower of boxes over to the small break room behind the glass counter. Olivia's sleek, new iMac sat on top of the display, acting as their cash register and accounting system. The Chens' seemingly endless budget allowed for top-of-the-line purchases to enhance the luxury vibe of their store.

Putting our lunches on the countertop, I turned and opened the door to the break room, hoping to find some paper plates and napkins from our last catered meeting.

"Oh my God!" I shrieked, my knees giving way as my wide eyes focused on the sight in front of me.

On the rustic wood floor, a crumpled figure lay in a dark pool of blood. A gruesome gash to the side of the head marred blond ringlets, the pretty strands caked in crimson. Recognizing the small figure, I rushed to Stacy's side to see if she was breathing. Fumbling with her wrist, slick with blood, I attempted to find a pulse, but my shaking hands were of no use. Panic drove me backwards, although I was unable to tear my gaze away from a gaping wound above her ear. Nausea boiled in my stomach. What on earth had happened here? My thoughts flailed for only a moment. Snapping into action, I dove for the landline the Chens had installed in the back. Dialing 911 with bloody, trembling fingers, I tried to calmly demand that help be sent to the strip.

"We have an ambulance and a police car on the way, ma'am. Please remain calm." The voice, which sounded too much like a robot for my tastes, urged me to take deep breaths. "Have you checked for a pulse?"

I clutched the phone desperately, the rusty smell of blood beginning to make me feel lightheaded. "I tried. I'm sorry, I'm not sure I did it right. I couldn't find one." I'd never taken any kind of CPR or first aid training before. Maybe I hadn't been doing it right. For Stacy's sake, I prayed that was the case.

"It's all right, ma'am. You did the right thing by calling for help."

Her reassurance reminded me that I'd wasted precious seconds sitting on the floor in shock. "Please, hurry. There's a lot of blood."

"Help is on the way, ma'am. You sound a bit shaken. Try taking some more deep breaths with me."

A bit shaken? You think? I bit back my sarcastic comments, knowing the emergency operator was only doing her job. "Okay." I did as she instructed, inhaling and exhaling loudly enough for her to hear through the phone.

"Excellent. Good job," she praised me with more familiarity now. "Are you alone, ma'am? Are you somewhere safe?"

At the operator's words, I froze. It hadn't clicked until now, but there was no way Stacy's wounds could be self-inflicted. Someone had attacked her. The front door had been locked when I came in. Had Stacy left the back door unlocked? Was that how her assailant entered? Had they even left? Was I sharing air with a violent maniac?

"Ma'am, are you all right? Are you still there?" Concern seeped into the operator's monotone voice at my silence.

"I'm still here." For the first time since finding her, I summoned the courage to turn around. The sight of Stacy's body greeted me. *I'm certainly not all right, and neither is Stacy.*

"The police just radioed in. They're waiting for you outside the building."

I said a silent thank you that the Central Shores Police Department was located only a few miles inland from the strip. "I hear their sirens outside. I'm going to hang up and let them in." I was the one who now sounded like a robot. Inching away from Stacy's battered body, I used my blood-soaked hands to steady myself on the counter as I backed away from the horrific scene that would likely haunt me for the rest of my life.

With the front door unlocked, a handful of policemen greeted me in the main showroom. "Ma'am, we received a call about an unresponsive woman," one of them announced. "Are you the one who called it in?"

In my dazed state, it took me a moment to recognize Gavin McInnis dressed in his crisp lieutenant's uniform. I didn't know who I was expecting. Our local police force was only eight officers strong, including the police chief, Lloyd McInnis, Gavin's uncle. It also seemed it took Gavin a moment to recognize me, as well.

He was a year younger than me, but we had been friends in high school. "Coco?"

The mention of my nickname confirmed this was, in fact, real life. I grimaced weakly. "Yes, I'm the one who found her, Gav. It's Stacy Lockner. I felt for a pulse, but…"

Two EMTs hustled to the back room, disappearing from my line of sight.

Gavin shifted uncomfortably on his feet, clearly uneasy at the sight of me, and I couldn't blame him. My hands and arms were covered in Stacy's blood, as were my bare legs from where I'd knelt to help her. If my dress hadn't been black, he also would have seen rivers of red smeared on that, too.

He took a notepad out of his breast pocket, his hazel eyes watching me with concern. "Why don't you take a seat and tell me what happened?" He motioned to a nearby chair.

Nodding, I collapsed onto an old wicker rocker Olivia had put out last week in preparation for browsing customers. "Well, I arrived a bit early for a lunch meeting with the Chens." I motioned over my shoulder to the sagging bag of Zaddick's wraps sitting on the glass countertop next to my purse. I caught a glimpse of the wall clock while doing so. Where were the Chens, anyway? Charlotte's café was popular, but the line for coffee couldn't have been *that* long.

"And?" Gavin's question prompted me to focus.

I shrugged. "Olivia texted me that she and Sean were on their way and that I could let myself in. I have a spare key to the front door, so I unlocked it, came in the store, and found Stacy in the back."

Gavin squatted down to his knees so we were at eye level. "What time did you arrive here would you say?"

"Eleven fifty-five. I remember because I looked at my phone just before Olivia texted me that I should let myself in."

"And did you notice anything out of place when you entered? Did you hear anything suspicious?" Gavin prodded my recollection further.

I shook my head. "No, nothing. The Chens are planning their grand opening for next week, but we've yet to set everything up, so it all looks a bit chaotic and out of place. But nothing caught my attention until..." I went to bury my face in my hands, only to jerk away from the bloody stains staring up at me. The memory of Stacy lying in a pool of her own blood tortured my mind. "Please tell me she's alive, Gavin," I whispered, my eyes brimming with tears. I couldn't believe we were having this conversation. Just last week, Gavin had stopped by our table at Brewed to Perfection to consult Hudson on his fantasy baseball team.

Gavin glanced back toward the break room, the sounds of flurried activity coming from the other side of the closed door. "Sit tight, okay?"

I almost asked him if I could go wash up, but my words died in my throat when the break room door swung open and another officer emerged, giving Gavin a grim look as he approached. Gavin mumbled a few covert sentences into his shoulder radio before turning to the other two officers assembled around him. Straining my ears to hear their conversation, I listened to Gavin's words intently.

"The chief is on his way down. He's made the call into the county medical examiner, who should be here in thirty minutes. Meanwhile, we need to take pictures of the scene, but be mindful not to disturb anything. A few techs from the crime lab are on their way as well."

My knuckles went white as the small group dispersed. A medical examiner and crime scene techs? That could only mean one thing. I hadn't screwed up when checking for her pulse. Stacy Lockner was indeed dead.

Chapter Three

After Gavin finished doling out orders to his men, he turned his hazel eyes back to me, taking careful steps toward my shivering figure.

"Not sure how much you overheard just now, Coco, but we're going to need to keep you here at least until the crime scene unit can speak with you and take some pictures."

My eyes widened. *I* was a part of this crime scene.

"We'll have you out of here and back home as soon as we can. We don't have any fancy forensic equipment here in town, so we're calling in the county crime lab to help us with evidence collection. Do you mind if we borrow your keys for a moment? We'd like to unlock the back door so the EMTs can load the ambulance in the alley, away from prying eyes." He snagged his fingers through his uniform belt loops.

"They're in my purse. The Chens' key has a pink sticker on it." I held my blood-soaked hands up, indicating he was free to grab them himself. "What about my meeting with the Chens?" I asked blankly, not even realizing until the words escaped my mouth how grossly out-of-touch I sounded. And where were Sean and Olivia? They should have been at the store by now.

Gavin met my gaze with sympathy, suddenly looking much older than his twenty-seven years. His eyes flickered over to the other officer left in the room. "Officer Riley here will be posted out front, and Frank Thompson will be at the back door. Either way, they'll let the Chens know what's going on. I'm sure they'll understand why you'll need to reschedule." With pink ears, he rummaged through my purse.

"Have you ever encountered something like this before?" I croaked, my throat parched.

Signaling Officer Riley with a wordless request, Gavin handed him the keys and sighed as Riley vanished into the break room. "No, can't say as I have. Usually, it's speeding drivers and drunken brawls for our crew. I don't know if Central Shores has ever had something like this happen before."

A few moments later, Riley reappeared with a bottle of water and dropped my keys back into my purse. He handed the Poland Springs bottle to Gavin, who promptly offered it to me.

I cradled the bottle in my trembling hands. Silence blanketed the room as Officer Riley disappeared out the front door and Gavin headed to the back of the store.

I sipped the water, cringing at the ominous murmuring and shuffling going on in the break room. Outside, I could have sworn I heard Olivia's screech and Sean gasping, but I couldn't see the storefront windows clearly from this angle, with all the free-standing shelving blocking my view. No doubt, they had finally arrived for our thwarted meeting and had been greeted by the stoic policeman out front. I checked the clock on the wall with a moody glance. Geez, it sure took them long enough to get here.

Left by myself in the dark showroom, I stared blankly at the floor, trying to un-see my arms and legs covered in blood. Stacy's blood. Oh God, how had this happened?

A few anxious moments passed before Riley came back inside, his clean-shaven face looking a bit slack. "Mrs. Chen would like you to reach out at your earliest convenience, Ms. Cline. She voiced her concern about how this incident might affect the store's image." His voice was as smooth as his dark brown skin.

I could tell he was unimpressed with the Chens' reaction to a death in their store. "Thank you, Officer. I will." I wasn't familiar with Officer Riley, and I didn't know his first name. Even in a town as small as Central Shores, there were always new faces popping up in the area, and I definitely didn't know everyone by first and last name. "I'd introduce myself and shake hands, but you probably don't want to." I motioned to the dried blood that would have soiled my firm grip.

"My name's Adrian." He offered a wave instead. "I transferred here from Dover about two months ago with my wife. After she had the twins, she wanted to make sure my line of work didn't take me away from my family prematurely, if you get what I'm saying." He raised an eyebrow. "We decided to move to a place with a lower crime rate." Adrian folded his arms, glibly staring at the break room doorway. "So much for that, I guess."

Despite my skyrocketing anxiety, his candor put me at ease. "My sister has four-year-old triplets. My brother-in-law had to find a job that allowed him to work from home."

Adrian grinned, perhaps because he'd become desensitized to gruesome scenes like this while working in a big city. "The things we do for family, right?"

Before I could respond, Chief Lloyd McInnis barged in through the front doorway, looking like someone had set fire to his prized flower beds.

"Riley, what in God's name happened here?" Clearly not spotting me in the corner, he marched his towering six-foot-something frame within inches of Riley's shocked face. "There's no crime scene tape out front. People are just moseying along the sidewalk, trampling evidence!"

Riley cleared his throat, trying to motion to my hunched figure in the chair. "Chief, uh, we determined the assailant used the shop's back door to enter and exit the premises. Gavin and Frank are back there now, making sure the perimeter is kept clear."

My muscles tightened upon hearing confirmation that a vicious crime had been committed a few feet away from where I now sat.

"Set it up out front, anyway." Chief McInnis crossed his beefy arms, not bothering to apologize for assuming incompetence. "Is the county crime unit here yet? We need to get this place processed. I don't want some jury to acquit a lunatic because we let evidence settle too long." The middle-aged man grumbled, still not acknowledging my presence. "This is why I wanted to get some techs hired and trained up."

Riley looked at the police chief with skepticism. "You were expecting this to happen?"

Chief McInnis nearly hacked up a lung sputtering. "Good Lord, no. But those city boys you're used to running with will never let us live this down if this goes poorly. The department can't afford any bad press right now. The station is already in enough jeopardy."

At his begrudging use of the words "bad press," I perked up somewhat, the squeaking wicker chair announcing my presence. "Chief McInnis, I'd be happy to help rehabilitate the department's image, if you're in need of a PR consultant." My shocked state did nothing to dampen my entrepreneurial instincts.

"Sweet Baby Jesus. Cordelia Cline?" Not bothering to answer my proposition, Chief McInnis shot another heated look at an abashed Officer Riley. "What is she doing here?"

"Ms. Cline was the one who found the victim. She called nine-one-one and made the report," Riley explained. "We're holding her here until County can process her."

McInnis's stormy eyes narrowed in on my blood-soaked appearance. "Well, then, *Ms. Cline...*" His tone suggested he abhorred addressing me like an adult. As a teenager, I'd been a thorn in his side—once or twice—and it sounded like he hadn't forgotten. "I'm sure my officers have informed you that while this is an ongoing investigation, your discretion regarding this incident is warranted."

Raising my eyebrows, I resisted scoffing at the thinly veiled threat against exercising my right to free speech. "Don't worry, sir. Posting about murder really isn't my style."

The chief's cheeks reddened, apparently not pleased with my retort. "All we know for certain is that a young woman lost her life today. We don't need people running around retweeting, or whatever it is you do, that there's a murderer on the loose."

"As I said, Chief, I don't post about grisly things like this." I narrowed my gaze, not caring if it seemed disrespectful. "Social media is already a big enough garbage dump with all the horrible crap out there. I certainly would never want to add to it." As much as I loved social media, I was well aware of its giant pitfalls. More and more these days, it seemed the internet ran on negativity rather than connectivity.

Riley's dark eyes widened in overdue recognition as he grabbed my purse off the counter and placed it on the floor by my bloodstained shoes. "Oh, wow. You're that famous blogger, aren't you? My wife, Lana, loves your site."

I smiled at Riley with genuine appreciation, pleased to be known as a "famous blogger," even with all the horror going on around me.

"We don't care what your wife loves, Riley. Why don't you go outside and wait to direct the county folks around back? They should be arriving any minute." Chief McInnis sent his officer away with his metaphorical tail between his legs. "You'll continue to sit right there, Ms. Cline." With that, the chief thundered into the break room, where everyone else, but me, was allowed to gather.

Watching the minutes tick away on the wall clock posted over the counter, I listened to the incessant humming of my phone vibrating in my purse. Not wanting to contaminate any more of my personal belongings with poor Stacy's blood, I anxiously tapped my foot, hoping that the notifications were people just checking in on me, and nothing more serious.

At nearly five minutes to one, an hour after I'd first arrived, a gaunt woman emerged from the break room, her smart gray suit highlighting her sharp shoulders and long legs. Her presence startled me as I hadn't seen her come in through the front door. She must have used the back entrance Riley had unlocked.

"Ms. Cline? My name is Detective Harriet Forester, and I'm from the Sussex County Crime Lab." She stopped in front of me and placed a large duffle bag on the ground between us. "I'd like to ask you a few questions, as well as take a few pictures for our records. I have various articles of clothing that you can change into once we conclude so that we can take your shoes and dress back with us."

"Will I be able to pick up my dress—" Shocked by my own materialistic concerns, I immediately went to clamp a hand over my mouth, only to stop myself at the sight of Stacy's blood on my fingers.

If she thought any less of me, Detective Forester didn't show it. "It's

32

evidence, so I'm afraid not, ma'am. I'm sorry."

I felt near tears once more. "God, no, that was completely insensitive of me to ask. I'm sorry. I think I'm still trying to wrap my head around things. I can't believe Stacy is dead."

The detective pulled out a small notepad from her breast pocket. "Did you know the victim well?"

I shook my head. "Not really. I primarily interact with the Chens when I'm here. I'm a social media consultant, so I usually work with Olivia Chen, while her husband, Sean, coordinates the setup of the store with Stacy." I paused, taking a controlled breath, racking my brain for other details I could provide. "Olivia was in the process of training Stacy to manage their online orders and in-store inventory, but that's really all I know about her work. I rarely spoke to Stacy other than in passing. Our conversations usually involved me asking her where I could find Sean or Olivia."

Detective Forester nodded as she finished writing her notes. "And did you ever see Ms. Lockner outside of business hours? Central Shores is a relatively small place. Did you see her out and about?"

My face heated as I tried to formulate a tactful answer. "No. I don't really socialize with a lot of folks in town these days." With my crazy schedule, I spent my free time at home with Hudson or meeting Charlotte and Jasper somewhere closer to Dover for dinner.

"You're saying that Stacy was a bit too small-town for you?" There was no judgment in the woman's voice, but it still made me feel guilty.

"No! I'm just saying we didn't run in the same circles." I hoped I didn't sound too defensive.

"Do you know anyone in her circle of friends that we could speak with?"

"No, I'm sorry, I don't. I really didn't know much about her personal life outside of the store." I stared at my hands, ashamed of my uselessness. "I think her parents still live in the area though, so you'll probably have better luck with them. I only know her as the Chens' assistant."

The detective then asked me to walk her through my discovering Stacy step-by-step, only interrupting me a few times to ask clarifying questions. Satisfied I'd given her everything I had to share, she finished our session by photographing my arms and legs to capture the bloodstains. Her examination felt like an hour, but, in reality, the wall clock revealed we'd only been together for fifteen minutes.

"All right, Ms. Cline. That's all we need right now." Detective Forester tucked away her notepad. "Unfortunately, the restroom in the back is sectioned off for our investigation. I'll escort you to the establishment next door so you can change and wash up."

My heart plummeted into my stomach, not looking forward to the attention I was bound to receive emerging from Once Used, Twice Buy covered in blood. That wouldn't be good for my wholesome, fun image, should any pictures end up online.

Detective Forester must have seen the expression of dread on my face, for she leaned down to pick up the duffle bag of clothes and grabbed my purse for me. "The owner of the arcade has closed down the place at our request, just to help widen the perimeter to allow our team more space to move around in, away from prying eyes." She pushed open the front door and handed me her suit jacket. "Here, put this over your head. You'll thank me."

Having the sense not to argue, I threw the coat over my head, and the world disappeared. The detective's strong hand guided me out the door, her body shielding me from the boisterous crowd that had gathered. Through an open flap in the jacket, I could just make out that someone had put up caution tape on the sidewalk between Once Used, Twice Buy, and The Blackout Arcade, so we were able to move into the next building without interruption, and, amazingly, without me being recognized. I hoped no one had snapped a picture of us, though. Even if they didn't know it was me under the coat, it would still be unnerving to know proof of this debacle existed on someone's cell phone.

Ripping off the jacket and racing through the black-lit arcade to the restroom, I shoved my hands under the faucet, bursts of scalding hot water spitting out. Seething at the motion sensors for not realizing I needed a bucket of water dumped on me, not a trickle, I scrubbed furiously at my hands and arms for nearly ten minutes before I decided they were clean enough. Taking a damp paper towel, I went to work trying to cleanse my legs but gave up after a few minutes. My attempts to scrub away the blood without soap had been mostly in vain. The whole time, Detective Forester kept a close eye on me from the doorway. I was evidence after all. She gave me a sympathetic shrug as she handed me the duffle bag of clothes once I'd cleaned myself up enough. I began to rifle through the assorted apparel, deciding on a pair of old, baggy sweatpants with "Juicy" written on the butt, sparkly flip-flops, and a pink T-shirt that showed off way too much cleavage for my liking. After this, I planned to go straight home and jump into the shower, so I changed quickly and handed my dress and shoes over to the detective. I chided myself for the tiny ache in my heart as I watched her bag them. A woman was dead, and here I was upset over losing my favorite little black dress.

"Thank you for your cooperation, Ms. Cline. After you've cleaned up, we'll need you to come down to the police station and make a formal statement." Detective Forester checked her watch. "I'll meet you there in forty-five minutes to walk you through the process. We'll also need to take your fingerprints, now that the blood has been washed off."

I looked at her flabbergasted. Forty-five minutes? She expected me to be finished rubbing my skin raw in less than an hour? "Detective, may I please have a little more time? The police station is on the other side of Central Shores from where I live."

The detective's warm brown eyes softened just a bit, but she remained all-business. "I'm sorry, Ms. Cline, but we want to get a formal statement taken down as soon as possible. Every minute that passes creates room for misremembering."

I knew she was the expert here, but I still felt completely overwhelmed by the ordeal. I simply nodded my acceptance and followed her to the back door of the arcade, which dumped me out only a few rows away from Jolly.

"Drive safely, Ms. Cline. I'll see you soon."

Giving her a feeble wave, I rushed away from the nightmare I'd stumbled into, holding myself together until I was buckled securely inside Jolly. My hands were shaking. "Get a grip, Coco." I gritted my teeth as I clung to the steering wheel. As soon as I started the car, my phone connected to Bluetooth, and my mother's personalized ringtone burst through the speaker system.

I reluctantly answered the call. "Hi, Mom."

"Delia! Thank goodness. I've been trying to get in touch with you for nearly half an hour!" My mother's hysterical voice filled every inch of Jolly as I maneuvered my way out of the parking lot. "Your father heard about an attack at that store you're working at on the radio. Is everything okay?"

For a moment, I was confused why the local radio station was already reporting on the incident at Once Used, Twice Buy, but then I realized this was my dad we were talking about. Simon Cline took early retirement from accounting to become a volunteer firefighter, meaning he was never far away from a police scanner. "I'm fine, Mom. I really can't talk right now, but I'll stop by later and explain."

For once, my mother didn't push for more details. "Have you eaten? Do you want me to save you some lunch? We're having macaroni salad."

I thought back to my untouched salami wrap on the countertop, my bloody handprints marring the glass around it. "Sure. I'll take whatever's left." I didn't want to alarm my mother by passing up her homemade salad. While I knew I should be hungry, my stomach was too in knots to care.

"Okay, honey. We'll see you in a bit." Mom sounded as if it was killing her to not pry further into what was going on.

Grateful for the quick, painless call, I sped home, the skin on my legs feeling like the lingering blood might burn it off. I had less than an hour to make myself presentable for my formal statement with Detective Forester. I hardly took a moment to enjoy the safety my home offered as I entered the front door. Careful not to touch anything, I rushed to the master bathroom and blasted the shower at full strength, hopping in, clothes, shoes, and all. Removing all evidence of the traumatic afternoon, I stripped off the secondhand clothes and scrubbed my skin senseless with every bar and gel I had available in the walk-in shower, even the ones normally reserved for Hudson. As my loofah ripped over my arms and legs, leaving a raw, red trail behind, my mind began to conjure ghastly images of Stacy's crumpled body sprawled across the break room floor. But, as the gruesome scene assaulted my thoughts, I had a hard time remembering the details. What had she been wearing, lying in that pool of blood? Had it been blue jeans and a T-shirt or a dress? Was her purse nearby? What about her cell phone? I couldn't even recall if I'd seen anything that looked like a murder weapon lying around. I couldn't believe I was in the shower, thinking about murder weapons. Wincing, I cursed at my obliviousness. How was I supposed to help the police if all I could remember was the sight of Stacy's mangled, matted blond hair?

Despite the steamy shower, I couldn't get warm. I just stood there, numb to the feeling of hot water cleansing my skin. Shivering, I turned off the stream of water and reached for my bath towel, enveloping my tall frame as I stepped into the mirror's line of sight. I was overreacting, but my skin looked impossibly pale, and my eyes had darkened, as if the thoughts haunting my mind affected their gloomy color.

Since I was pressed for time, I twisted my wet hair into a messy bun. I then pulled on a khaki skirt and bright teal blouse, deciding to forgo applying any makeup. As I stepped into coral flats, I knew I was being irrational, but the thought that I could do something as normal as apply bronzer made me feel guilty, considering what had happened to poor Stacy.

Walking out of the house and back to the garage, I finally pulled my iPhone out of my yellow Coach purse. I had sixty-seven missed texts and thirteen missed calls. A majority of the texts were from Sean and Olivia. The evolution of their knowledge of the crime became evident as I scrolled through them. Their questions went from **What's going on in there? Why can't we come in?** to **OH MY GOD, how did this happen?** Sean's responses seemed more concerned about Stacy than Olivia's did. Her main complaint was about their store's bottom line and how this was going to affect business and the grand opening. And now that she'd put the worry in my head, I couldn't help but feel anxious about Once Used, Twice Buy's grand opening, too.

Charlotte and Hudson were among the flurry of messages from my clients and my mother. Charlotte had likely seen the police cars gathering around at the northern end of the strip, and her coffee shop would no doubt be Grand Central for gossip. I texted her quickly. **Long story short, I'm OK. Fill u in @ dinner.**

The earliest of Hudson's messages had just been checking in to see how my day was going. He must have come across the police report at the television station only a few minutes ago because his everyday comments now transformed into words of concern. **I'm fine**, I texted him, knowing he and his fellow news anchors would be gearing up to report this breaking story, **I'm a bit shook, but I'll be OK.**

He immediately responded back.

Boss filled us in. Coming home early whether u want me to or not. Tori will fly solo without me tonight. Should be leaving here no later than 3:30. Be safe, babes.

A strangled sob escaped my lips. Hudson planned to drop everything to come home and comfort me. As much as I fought to contain my anxiety, I didn't want to be alone right now. Steeling myself for what lay ahead, I drove out of Sunny Shores and hung a left inland, taking the road toward the town's municipal buildings. About two miles west of the strip, there was a small town square situated just across the road from the elementary and high school. The library was the largest of the four buildings surrounding the quiet park, with the aging town hall, police station, and fire department rounding out the cluster of brick. They were beautifully constructed, albeit a bit rundown, old colonial-style architecture that had been forgotten as the Central Shores strip became the main focal point of the town's interest and financing. While the library did its best to rejuvenate attendance with weekly book readings and children's activities, with the advent of online book lending and e-books, there was a debate on how much longer it would remain open.

Moments later, I pulled into the small parking lot in front of the town hall and walked across the Central Shores Commons, the grassy park that blanketed the middle of the square. In my day, the Commons had been the designated hangout spot for us after school, cliques facing off from their strategically-claimed park benches. Nowadays, there was a shuttle bus ferrying kids from school to the community center, which was on the southwest outskirts of town. The community center hosted afterschool programs for kids and teens who wanted a place to socialize until their parents picked them up. It was situated near the majority of Central Shores's residential homes so the commute wasn't out of the way for families coming home from jobs in Milton or Dover.

The police and fire stations always reminded me of oversized garages, the town's one firetruck and the three police cars normally gathering dust. Today, the cruisers were nowhere to be found, likely still helping the crime scene techs from County. Walking in through the side door that led into the main part of the police station, I gave a weary wave to Maude, the daytime receptionist. Maude Longford had been the watchdog of the precinct since I was a young girl. The years had been kind to her, with only a splattering of wrinkles and gray hair showing the passage of time.

"Ms. Coco, I was told to let you on back," she greeted me in her typical no-nonsense manner. "Detective Forester is waiting for you in the chief's office." Maude pushed a button on her desk, buzzing me past the metal door separating the outside world from the inner sanctum of the station.

Being one of only three doors in the hallway, I found the chief's office with relative ease and knocked before entering at the detective's summons.

"Thank you for coming, Ms. Cline." Detective Forester urged me to sit down in the spare chair across from the chief's desk. She pushed a stray strand of brassy brunette hair back from her face. "I promise this won't take too long. I know you've suffered a great deal today. That being said, I would recommend making an appointment with your doctor as soon as possible. With the amount of foreign blood you were exposed to at the crime scene, it's better safe than sorry."

I froze at what she was implying. If Stacy was carrying any type of disease, I could very easily have been exposed to it. My mind started going a mile a minute, manufacturing wild health-related nightmares like I'd just Googled symptoms on WebMD. My panic must have been apparent to Detective Forester as she jumped in to explain, "The medical examiner has already done a preliminary exam of the victim and obtained her healthcare records.

While I obviously can't share any specifics with you, Ms. Lockner didn't have any serious issues reported during her last checkup just a few weeks ago. I just advise visiting your doctor to cover all the bases."

Sinking back into the wooden chair, I breathed deeply, saying a silent prayer and cursing my overreactive imagination at the same time. Just to be certain, I would stop at the local urgent care clinic on my way home from my parents' house. "Thank you, Detective, I'll arrange for an appointment. Now, how do we do this?"

Chapter Four

My formal statement consisted of me telling my story aloud to a digital recorder, as well as signing a written account of what happened. Detective Forester escorted me back to the front of the station in less than twenty minutes, after I'd thoroughly washed my hands to scrub off as much of the fingerprinting ink as possible. She had given me a citrus-based hand degreaser to take into the bathroom, and it miraculously worked wonders wiping away the evidence. A self-serving idea floated through my head as I rubbed my fingertips. *I should feature this stuff in my spring-cleaning posts. Watch out, Mrs. Meyers. You've got competition.* Only a few dark stains marred the ridges of my fingertips. A lovely souvenir of the harrowing process I'd just endured.

"If we have any questions, we'll be in touch. Do you have somewhere you can go where you won't be alone, Ms. Cline?" Detective Forester's dark eyebrows furrowed with concern.

Nodding, I gave her a reassuring smile. "I'm going to swing by my parents' place for a bit until my boyfriend's able to get back home."

"Good. Here's my card if you think of anything else. Even if it doesn't seem important, let me know." The detective handed me a crumpled business card before ducking out of the waiting room.

Waving a dazed goodbye to Maude, I swiped through my phone as I walked across the Commons to my car. I hadn't yet responded to the Chens' attempts at contacting me, so I dialed Olivia's number. She picked up on the first ring.

"Coco!" Her screeching voice almost cracked my iPhone screen. "We've

41

been worried sick about you. Isn't this just the most terrible thing? Stacy was such a sweet and helpful girl. She was putting in crazy amounts of overtime to get the inventory all done. What will we do without her? Are the police even going to let us back into the store? Was there a lot of blood? I've already found a cleaning service that specializes in crime scenes. I guess fingerprint powder is extremely tricky to scrub off. What is this going to cost us? Will we still be able to open next Saturday?"

Amazed that Olivia finally took a moment to breathe, I rubbed the growing pressure behind my temples. She was a perfectionist and hyper-focused, but even this was above and beyond her normal neuroses.

Ignoring her unanswered questions, I lowered myself into Jolly and started the engine. The call immediately switched to Bluetooth. "I'm just leaving the station now. I gave the police my formal statement. I imagine they'll be reaching out to you and Sean to do the same."

Olivia murmured something away from the phone, likely conferring with her husband.

"Why don't you put me on speakerphone, and we can all discuss next steps," I suggested.

After a quick burst of static as Olivia repositioned the phone, Sean's voice rang loud and clear. "Coco, are you all right? I can't imagine how you must be feeling. How horrible. Is there anything we can do to help?"

I smiled, imagining Sean's kind face, his dark hair slightly balding. "I'm a bit shaken, for sure, but I'm heading to my parents' house right now, and Hudson will be on his way home soon."

"Good," Sean replied, only to be interrupted by an impatient Olivia.

"Coco, how are we going to handle this? This is a waking nightmare for the store!" Her shrill voice battered my eardrums.

Drumming on the steering wheel as I waited at a stoplight, I tried focusing on the matter at hand. No publicity was bad publicity, and I was annoyed by Olivia's insensitivity toward the ordeal. "In the long run, this is only going to help promote your store. The news coverage you'll receive is going to be free advertising. We just have to spin it the right way, and make sure we're the ones controlling the narrative."

"How do we do that?" Sean, ever the attentive student, asked.

"We'll need to release a statement about how much you both valued Stacy as an employee and as a person. The sooner we can do this, the better. And of course, we'll have to let the media know you're fully cooperating with the police." I paused, trying to figure out other ways to help the Chens emerge from this brewing media circus unscathed. "I would even go as far as to suggest having the proceeds from your first month go to a scholarship or charity in Stacy's name."

"A month?" Olivia barked. "Are you trying to bankrupt us?"

Sean quickly cut her off. "Liv, we've got enough money to keep us afloat for a while. Remember the rainy-day fund our advisor suggested for emergencies? I think we can spare a month's income if it will help the store in the long run."

Olivia spat back. "I hardly think our financial advisor was referring to someone being killed in our shop as a rainy-day emergency. What happens if there's a fire or the place is robbed?"

Sean sighed. "That's what insurance is for. I agree with Coco. We need to make sure we appear supportive to the investigation and cooperate with the police."

I jumped in. "That means you will not reach out to the investigators, bugging them with questions as to when you can have your store back." My warning was clear if a bit blunt.

Luckily, the Chens didn't argue. "Coco, we'd like you to be our official liaison for this matter. You're right. We can't be seen bothering the police about this or it will play badly for us, especially in a small town like Central Shores," Sean said, and I could almost picture him silently begging Olivia to agree. "And since you and I both know how stubborn my wife can be, I'd suggest drawing up an amendment to our contract saying there will be a financial penalty for us if we reach out to the police without your approval, otherwise Olivia will be too tempted to butt in."

Dollar signs danced in front of my eyes before I fully comprehended Sean's potentially lucrative proposal. "While I appreciate your faith in me, interfacing with the authorities in criminal investigations isn't part of my

PR skill set. I'm here to boost your customer base through social media campaigns."

Somehow, Sean had fully tamed his wife for he continued to lead the conversation. "We know that, and we know we're asking a lot of you. Unfortunately, our customer growth is tied to how successfully we navigate this situation. We're going to need you to step up your game."

"How severe of a penalty would be enough to ensure you both remain out of the police's way?" Coming to terms with this new challenge, I grimly accepted my new role.

The line was quiet for a moment before Olivia spoke. "Five thousand dollars for the first incident. A thousand dollars more is added to the fine for every subsequent violation."

Balking at the number, I almost wanted them to break their promise. If Olivia bothered the police behind my back just three times, I'd make eighteen thousand dollars. "Are you sure? That's a big chunk of change."

A long pause followed. I wish I had pulled the car over and taken this call over FaceTime so I could witness the silent debate on the other of the line between husband and wife.

At last, Sean cleared his throat. "Yes. It's necessary, Coco."

My heart fluttered against my chest, followed by a rush of guilt. It felt wrong to potentially pull in a major profit from Olivia's incessant meddling. "I'll have my lawyer draw up the necessary paperwork and send it over to you to sign."

"Bring it tomorrow in person," Olivia snapped. "We need to have a face-to-face meeting to plan out next steps and what our formal statement to the press should be. Can you be here by eight A.M.?" Her request came across as more of a demand.

The Chens lived in the old money part of town, even though they themselves were new to the area, having moved to Central Shores only two years ago when they bought the old Eldrich place. Town mover-and-shaker Montgomery Eldrich passed away at the ripe old age of ninety-six, leaving a huge estate in the care of his seven offspring. Deciding to sell the property rather than hold onto it for sentimental value, it had been on the market for a cool six point three million for four years. Olivia bragged to me when I first visited their stately manor that they purchased the property for four point seven million, as the Eldrich offspring were desperate to unload the house onto someone due to the children quickly spending their father's inheritance.

"I can be there at eight." I forced myself to contain a sigh of frustration. It would only be a twelve-minute drive to their side of town from my condo, but I'd have to wake up early to make sure I was prepped and in the right headspace. Getting up before seven A.M. was never something I did with much enthusiasm.

"Fine. We'll see you then." Olivia ended the call before I had a chance to bid the couple goodbye. She was no doubt ready to ream Sean out for his suggestion of a penalty clause in private.

Putting in a quick call to my attorney, who promised to send a PDF of the amendment via email by four this afternoon, I pulled into my parents' driveway. My childhood home was nestled amongst a row of craftsman houses. My mother had insisted on adding a gorgeous extended porch after my parents bought it, their home putting the rest of the neighborhood to shame. My dad, ever the handyman, had successfully maintained the exterior of the house for over thirty years, and my mother's blooming gardens completed the cozy look of the picture-perfect homestead. It looked as though it had stepped right out of my childhood memories. The only recent major change to the house was the stunning sunroom my parents had installed two years ago. When I'd received my big payout from LiveIt, I insisted on treating my parents to something special. At first, they had resisted by telling me not to spend my earnings all in one place, but eventually, they had let me fund the home renovation project they'd been dreaming about for years.

I parked behind the bright orange Jeep sitting smack dab in the middle of the driveway, blocking any opportunity to have two cars parked side-by-side in front of the garage door. Leave it to Dorothy to be so wrapped up in her own life that she wouldn't even leave room for me to park.

Wondering how my younger sister managed to fit three car seats comfortably in the compact SUV, I dragged myself out of Jolly and walked along the stone pathway to the storybook front door. Just as I was reaching for the brass handle, the door snapped open and three little figures dove at my legs.

"Auntie Coco!" The triplets' shrieks broke through my foggy haze. Chocolate ringlets and blue eyes gazed up at me, toothy smiles aglow.

"Well, hello, my little munchkins." I bent down to be at their level. "How are my favorite nieces and nephew doing today?"

Parker, Blake, and Taran sent secret looks to each other as if telepathically conferring with one another.

"We're getting a kitty cat!" Blake finally shrieked, her hands clasping her chubby little cheeks in excitement.

"No, we're not." My sister appeared in the doorway, crossing her arms disapprovingly at her offspring. Three years my junior, Thea had married her college sweetheart the summer before her senior year and had the triplets nine months after her honeymoon. Even though she had bags under her blue eyes, she still looked radiant. The trials of motherhood clearly suited her. Her tight ship of a homestead was praised daily by my mother. "We're only looking after the poor creature until we can find it a home," she explained to her children, her exasperation apparent. "Please go help Mimi with the cookies while I talk to Auntie Coco."

Taran, Blake, and Parker disappeared down the lengthy paneled hallway toward the back of the house, likely heading for Mom's enviable baking kitchen. "Sorry they ambushed you. I couldn't contain their excitement. It's been a while since you've seen them." My sister gave me a stiff hug. We didn't have the most affectionate sibling relationship.

"I know." I rubbed the back of my neck to alleviate the guilty tension building up. I loved my little nieces and nephew to bits, but time tended to get away from me these days. "I've been meaning to invite them over, but it's been crazy lately. And now, after what happened at the strip this morning..." I stepped inside the house, away from nosy neighbors. "Thea, you're not going to believe what I've been through today."

The names Cordelia and Dorothy were about eighty years behind the times when we were kids in school. Both my sister and I were teased by our classmates growing up, Dorothy more so than me. The nickname Thea was born out of a twelve-year-old's desperation to not be associated with *The Wizard of Oz* for the rest of her life. Even now, at twenty-five, she refused to let her children call our mother Granny or Grandma, mainly because that was what Thea had been called growing up. I don't know where the term Mimi came from, but Mom didn't mind, and it didn't give my sister night terrors. Thea's childhood bullies were also the reason for the triplets' trendy names. She never wanted her kids to be subjected to the taunting she'd endured.

"Dad mentioned an accident at the Chens' shop," Thea prodded as we wove our way through the house, the scent of Mom's famous cinnamon chocolate chip cookies wafting through the hall.

"It wasn't an accident." I lowered my voice and quickly filled her in on what I'd stumbled into.

"Oh my God. Poor Stacy!" Thea clapped a hand over her mouth in shock. "I would have died right then and there, seeing her like that."

I only then remembered my sister had gone to high school with Stacy. "She was a few years younger than you, right? Were you close?"

Thea shook her head, her ashy blond hair swinging around her shoulders. "She was only a grade below me, but we never really ran in the same circles. You know the story. She was a cheerleader, and I was a band nerd." As if she had said something incriminating, she sputtered an afterthought. "Not that I'm not upset she's dead. What a tragedy."

I nodded in agreement. "When was the last time you saw her?"

Thea's nose wrinkled in concentration. "Gosh, it's been ages. Ever since that new club opened in Cherry Springs, I feel like everyone under the age of thirty who isn't married has abandoned Central Shores for greener pastures."

While she might have been exaggerating a bit, Thea was right. A few months ago, a development company had purchased a bankrupt resort and converted it into a swanky beach club called Cyprus that catered to young singles. I had actually done a *Trending Topic* feature on the place a week or so after it opened, as well as done some free consulting for their Instagram account as a thank you for giving me the inside scoop. Since then, I'd only been to the reformed resort a handful of times with Hudson. We'd been plagued by man-hunting women throwing themselves at him, and, thus, it wasn't a place we frequented.

"I saw Stacy nearly every day for the past three weeks, but I hardly ever spoke with her. I felt like a complete idiot talking to the police." I leaned against the hallway wall, not wanting to face my parents and rehash everything again just yet.

"It's out of your hands now. You've done all you can do," Thea said simply, as if her words alone could put my fears to bed. "I'll get the kiddos out of here so you can talk to Mom and Dad. They'll be beside themselves to hear you're involved in a murder investigation."

I rolled my eyes at her dramatization. "I'm not *involved* with it, Thea. Let me go move my car so you can back out." Before our pleasant conversation turned into our usual sibling bickering, I retraced my steps to the front door and parked my car on the side of the road. Walking back up to the porch, the kids ran past me, shouting various versions of childish good-byes before piling into the Jeep.

I smiled and waved after them. "Love ya, you little goobers." I promised myself I'd spend more time with them this summer. I may have created a college fund for each of them, probably the most sensible and selfless thing I'd done with my LiveIt payout, but money did not buy nor represent the love I felt for them. Time shared and memories did.

"Keep me posted on this Stacy business. I primed Mom and Dad for you." Thea gave me an air kiss.

My sister got in her car and backed the Jeep out of the driveway. The tinted windows didn't quite hide the kids squirming around in the backseat, Thea shushing them over her shoulder as she took off down the road. It was sometimes hard for me to see my little sister as a mother. She'd always been my annoying shadow growing up, unable to take care of herself in the slightest. My parents doted on every little thing she did, coddling her in ways that forced a chasm to grow between us after I went off to college. I hardly spoke to or saw Thea for the next four years. Once LiveIt took over my life, our interactions became even fewer and farther between, and I really didn't make an effort to be a part of her world until I arrived back in Central Shores. By that time, the triplets had already been born, and I realized, as an aunt, I had a lot of time to make up for. There were moments, of course, when my parents gushed over Thea's domestic lifestyle and bitterness crawled up the back of my throat. But I tried not to let it get me down. My parents had expected both their children to walk the normal path of life: get a steady job, get married, have babies, and then make those children have children. Only Thea had willingly obeyed and taken that road, and she was happy to do it. Having someone depend on her was new and exciting for Thea to figure out, and, based on how well the kids behaved, she was doing a pretty good job.

I, on the other hand, was not even engaged, rapidly approaching thirty, and showed no sign of forming any kind of maternal instinct, much to my mother's dismay. Many of my baby-brained friends had said it would come along eventually, and, to put the topic to rest, I usually agreed with them. But I made it very clear to Hudson the night we first met at a dimly-lit bar in Dover that I didn't see kids as a part of my future. I wanted a life of travel and leisure, and, to me, having kids didn't fit into that picture. Besides, I was too self-centered to want to put someone else's needs before my own, although I had never revealed that reason to anyone but Hudson. Lucky for me, he was on the same page and shared my desire to live kid-free.

"There you are!" My mother's voice shattered my reverie, and I turned around. She was waving from the front door. "I thought you might have left with Thea and the babes."

Cringing that Mom's pet name for the triplets was also Hudson's name for me, I obediently followed Mom back into the house, with her ushering me into the kitchen for a late afternoon lunch.

"Ah, she arrives at last. We've been dying to know what's been going on down at the strip. It's all very hush-hush." Dad smiled at me, his blue eyes shining with interest. He was sitting at the kitchen table, poking his fork at the uneaten mound of macaroni salad on his plate. Looking fit as ever for his fifty-nine years, he eagerly rubbed a hand on his stomach. "Sit down and tell us what happened, will you?"

"Goodness, Simon, you didn't even say hello to your daughter," Mom snapped, but her tone was good-natured. She dished me out some salad and sat across from my father. "And for goodness sakes, it's the *Boardwalk*, not the strip." Her stern glare reminded us all of the vigorous rebranding campaign she and the rest of the town council had forced down the throats of the Central Shores community.

Moira and Simon Cline complemented each other in every way, still appearing in my eyes the same as they looked when I was a young child. Sure, their brown hair was shaded with gray these days and both sported a few wrinkles across pale skin, but they still embodied the life and soul of those two young kids who'd gotten married at twenty, absolutely smitten with one another. I could pull out a picture of them on their wedding day nearly forty years ago and still see the same love and devotion in their expressions when they gazed at one another now.

"You look like you've had a rough day, dear." Mom reached out to hold my hand.

I choose to ignore the unintended jab at my worn-out appearance and picked up my fork. I took a few theatrical bites of creamy macaroni to appease her worries. If fame and fortune ever started to go to my head, Mom and Dad's kitchen table was the place to come for a reality check. They were poster children for the Baby Boomer generation, and my influencer popularity was a foggy concept that they just didn't get. In a way, their obliviousness made me thankful. Sitting here in my childhood home, I could just be their daughter. "It's been interesting, for sure." I shot a look at Dad. "You two need to promise to keep this between us until an official statement has been made." I stared them down until they both nodded in agreement.

Now even more confused, worry saturated Mom's expression. "Official statement? What's going on?"

I walked them through my traumatic morning of finding Stacy's body and dealing with the police, leaving them speechless at the conclusion of my story. "It's hard to believe something like this could happen in Central

Shores." I shook my head at the thought.

Dad was the first to recover from the gruesome details. "Are the police sure it was murder? Could something in the store have dropped on her head?"

"I'm having a hard time remembering the scene clearly. I was so focused on Stacy and that horrible gash that I didn't really take a look around." I rubbed my temples, massaging the memory in my mind. "Something must have told the police she was killed intentionally. One of the new cops on the force said the assailant walked right out the back door."

"Oh my God, Delia, you could have been in the shop with him!" Mom gripped her face, her blue eyes widening with tears of fright.

Placing my fork on the table where I had eaten breakfast every morning growing up, I reached for her trembling hand. "I'm fine. A little shocked, that's all."

Neither Mom nor Dad looked convinced.

I glanced at the clock over the kitchen sink, and seeing the time, pushed my chair back. "Hudson will be home in an hour or so. I'd better get going. I need to stop by the urgent care clinic. The county detective recommended I check in."

Mom opened her mouth to protest, but Dad reached over and squeezed her arm. "Be safe, kiddo," he said to me, "and let us know if you need anything."

I gave them both a one-armed hug before heading to the front door, surprised by the lump forming in my throat. Not one to normally show an abundance of fragile emotion, I took a deep breath, trying to calm my nerves. As much as I wanted the horrible image of Stacy out of my head, burying my last memory of her felt disrespectful. Adding to the fact I hardly knew her, yet saw her every day for nearly a month, I was racked with guilt over the whole thing. If I hadn't waited around to let myself in, perhaps I would have thwarted her attacker or at least taken them by surprise. I could have helped her. Saved her. The lump in my throat hardened. Why was she alone at the store to begin with? Olivia and Sean were always there to supervise her work. How did the culprit get in and out of the store if all the doors were locked? As I slid into the driver's seat, I realized I hadn't yet asked myself the biggest question of them all. Who could possibly have killed her?

Chapter Five

Hudson's voice rang out from the entryway of our condo, the door snapping shut behind him. "Babes, I'm home."

"I'm in here!" I called before taking a sip of lemon ginger tea, my feet tucked snuggly underneath me on the massive sectional sprawling across most of the living room. Reveling in a clean bill of health from the local clinic, I figured I'd earned some rest. Nesting in the corner of the large, liberty blue couch, I enjoyed my tea from the best spot in the house. Hudson and I often went to war over who got to sit there while we Netflixed a show on our imposing 70-inch OLED screen. I usually won.

Hudson appeared in the kitchen moments later, his short, dark hair ruffled from the wind, his face a mask of concern. He placed a small paper bag on the island counter that looked like it might contain my favorite jelly-filled donuts from Flakier than Thou before taking tentative steps into the living room space.

"I'm fine." I figured I'd spare him from having to ask. "I really am. It was just…shocking."

He sat next to me, placing a hand on the blanket covering my lower body. "I'm sorry this happened to you. I can't imagine how scared you must have been. We only got a few details released to us from the police at the studio. Tonight, the network will be running a brief story about it."

Gripping my tea mug, I leaned forward, the words spilling out of my mouth before I could stop them. "You're not going to paint the Chens in a bad light, are you? Accuse them of neglect?"

Hudson's jaw hung slack for a moment, surprised by the change in subject, but I saw a lusty sparkle smoldering in his dark eyes. He often told me that my tenacity and passion for my work were among the reasons he had been drawn to me in the first place. Now, undeterred by the gruesome topic of Stacy's death, my mind for business was clearly turning him on. "Tonight's broadcast will just announce Stacy's death and ask for anyone to contact the police with information that might be relevant to this case." He paused, and I knew he was building up the courage to say what came next. "We'll be running a more in-depth segment later in the week. Probably after we've collected some information about Stacy from her family and friends."

"Like a tribute piece? What's so bad about that?" I sensed that Hudson wasn't telling me the whole story as I set my tea down on the coffee table.

"Not a tribute, per se. More of an exposé about how a gruesome murder could happen in such a small town." Hudson averted his eyes from my fuming gaze.

"And I suppose you're going to feature Once Used, Twice Buy as a den of crime and gore?" I jumped off the couch and stormed to the floor-to-ceiling windows overlooking the ocean. I'd always had a bit of temper, and the threat of my clients being portrayed in such a crass way sent me reeling. "This town doesn't need to be scared out of its wits, Hudson. How tacky is that going to appear? Why don't you push for a nice tribute piece?"

Hudson gave me the *you-know-why* look, not afraid to go head-to-head with me on this. "Because fairytales and rainbows don't sell as well as sex and lies, babes." He got up from the couch and joined me at the window, wrapping his strong arms around my shaking frame. "If I could help you, I would, but I'm still too junior on the anchor team to push for something like that. However, if *you* speak with my producer," Hudson whispered in my ear, pulling me teasingly close, "maybe at the fundraiser tomorrow, you might be able to persuade her to go with a different angle for the story. You know she worships you."

I turned and faced him, stroking the blossoming dark stubble already poking through his bronze skin from his shave this morning. "And how am I supposed to convince her of that?"

Hudson chuckled softly, planting a kiss on the base of my jaw, my weak spot. "Offer her an exclusive. You know the game, Coco. Play it."

Roughly an hour later, I buried myself into the throng of pillows encompassing our disheveled bed, my arms draped across Hudson's well-sculpted chest.

"Feeling any better?" His suggestive tone referenced what we'd just done.

"You did keep me preoccupied, for sure." I sighed, my thoughts returning to all that had happened today.

"The police don't seem to have any suspects at the moment." For a man, Hudson had a surprising gift and could often tell the direction my mind had gone. "I'm worried about you being associated with Once Used, Twice Buy, babes. I don't want someone to come after you because they think you saw something." His concern filled me with quiet comfort.

"I think it will be clear during the news report tonight that I gave the police absolutely nothing of use. I was a complete waste." I gripped the eight-hundred-thread-count sheets that caressed my bare skin, anger suddenly flaring at my ineptness. "I couldn't even remember what the room looked like while I was giving Detective Forester my formal statement. All I kept picturing was Stacy's head."

Hudson pulled me closer to him, his silence the reassurance I often needed when crushing anxiety settled over me. I considered myself a perfectionist, and my failure to be of any help to the police gravely wounded my psyche. For most of my life, I'd struggled to process things beyond my control, but Hudson's supportive presence never failed to calm me.

After a few more moments of lounging in bed, I looked at the alarm clock on the bedside table. "Yikes. We need to get moving. I texted Charlotte when I got home that I was still up for dinner tonight. Jasper wants to come along, so we're meeting him halfway at The Pearl." I clawed my way out of the pillows and sheets, moving toward the shower for the third time today.

"Are you sure it's a smart idea to go out tonight?"

I poked my head back into the bedroom. "I need to get out of the house. If we stay in, I'm going to dwell on what happened today and that's the last thing I want to do."

Hudson tossed a pillow at my face in answer.

"So, who's the lucky guy we're meeting tonight?" he asked jovially a few minutes later, joining me for a brief portion of my shower.

"I'm such a bad friend. I don't even remember his name." I wrinkled my nose as I breathed in my honey-scented shampoo. "He's not from around here, and I think he lives up the coast a bit, near Cherry Springs."

"You still up for this?" Hudson asked for what felt like the millionth time as he finished tying his tie.

I zipped up a peach-colored cocktail dress and threw an exaggerated eye roll his way. "Yes, I'm fine. I need to blow off some steam, or I'm going to go stir crazy."

Hudson pulled on a sports jacket, knowing the dress code of The Pearl—swanky and sophisticated. "Just let me know if it gets to be too much. We can leave early."

I squeezed his arm as I strutted past, picking up a shimmering gold clutch to pair with my outfit. "Thanks, babe. But don't worry about me. We need to be in top form to vet this guy for Charlotte."

The ride to The Pearl took about thirty-five minutes. Hudson chose to take the scenic route up the coast, which was surprisingly void of cars. Arriving in the seaside town of Slaughter Beach, it made me a little uneasy to be dining in a place that had such a graphic name, especially after what had happened this morning. It had never bothered me before, but now...it just felt like a bad omen.

Even though we were early, I immediately noticed Jasper's Porsche parked in front of the sleek and secluded restaurant. Glad that we would have a few minutes to ourselves before Charlotte arrived with her new beau, Hudson and I walked inside, spotting Jasper at our usual booth in the corner by the ocean-view windows.

"Good evening. Do you have a reservation?" A chipper, blond young woman in a tight black dress greeted us as we made our way to the maître d's podium. Her eyes widened with excitement as recognition flooded her face. I prepared myself to politely decline any unwarranted advances about appearing as a model on *Trending Topic* when she opened her mouth once more. "Oh, Mr. Caruthers! It's a pleasure to have you dine with us tonight."

My not-so humble comments died in my throat, and my face boiled with embarrassment. I had been ready to give this woman my autograph or possibly even pose for a TikTok video or something, but it had been Hudson whom she'd recognized. When had my boyfriend's fame surpassed my own?

Seemingly unaware of my humiliation, Hudson shook the hostess's hand. "Thanks for the warm welcome. We'll be joining our friend in the back there." He pointed to Jasper, who was watching the scene with a critical eye.

"Are you sure we can't move you to another table?" The hostess scrambled to look at her seating chart, likely seeing whether she could place Hudson and his entourage somewhere we could be put on display.

"The table in the back is fine," I snapped, a bit more forcefully than I meant to.

As if seeing me for the first time, the hostess's eyebrows inched up even higher. "Omigod, wow. You're Coco Cline, right? My mom just adores your little blog."

Little blog? Judging by the way she had plaited her blond hair, the earrings she wore, and the shoes she had on, I guessed Hostess Barbie was also one of the over four and a half million followers of *Trending Topic*. The earrings and shoes had been featured in my "Spring Deal Delights" post, and her fishtail braid had been highlighted in a "How-To" YouTube tutorial I'd made a few weeks ago. "Well, tell your *mother* I say thank you," I gushed with a warmth I didn't feel. What was it with women my age refusing to give other women credit for their achievements?

She must have understood my veiled threat because her cheeks colored slightly. Turning her focus back to Hudson, Hostess Barbie plastered a flirty smile on her heavily made-up face. "My roommates and I loved your sports segments on WMTG. I'm *so* happy I'll get to see you more often now you're a full-time anchor." Her tongue ran seductively over her bottom lip.

At that, Hudson threw a shocked look my way, taking my hand firmly in his. "My girlfriend and I will see ourselves over to our booth, thanks." With that, he led the way past the hostess, who, by the looks of her, knew she'd overstepped her boundaries.

Choking back the burst of jealousy spouting up from my stomach, I flashed a stunned glance at Hudson. "I'm speechless."

"I swear, that's the first time that's happened, babes." He looked disgusted by the blatant flirtation and disrespect the hostess had shown me. "I mean, not the getting recognized. That's been happening a lot more lately, but never has anyone made me feel propositioned like that. Objectified." He shuddered and I could tell he wanted to look over his shoulder, but he resisted. "Should I say something to the manager? Do you want me to say something to the manager?"

I bit my tongue to keep from shouting an abrupt "Yes." Sure, the woman had been shamelessly trying to seduce my boyfriend right in front of me, but I realized, that for me, her flirtatious behavior wasn't the saltiest of her offenses. Hudson was loyal to me, so this random bimbo's flirting didn't bother me too much. What really got under my skin was that Hudson's star power was beginning to overshadow mine, and I was a little afraid of how painful it felt. With his promotion to evening anchor at WMTG a little more than a month ago, Hudson's local celebrity was on the rise and people seemed to already be forgetting I was famous in my own right. No longer was I "Coco Cline, celebrity blogger," but just "Hudson Caruthers's girlfriend." Not that being his girlfriend was a bad thing, not in the slightest; it was just an adjustment for me. I wasn't used to being on the outskirts of the spotlight, even though I'd moved home to Central Shores to evade it. The age-old mantra haunted my thoughts, *be careful what you wish for.* Had I made the right choice?

Chapter Six

"Don't worry about it." I wrapped my arm around his, eager to put the unpleasant encounter behind us. "I can't believe I'm being escorted by such a well sought-after gentleman."

Hudson's frown told me he wasn't completely at ease with my joke, but he squeezed my hand. "Sorry about that, babes. What a basic."

I chuckled at his adoption of a term Jasper and I tossed around daily. We used it to describe people who were void of personality and tended to thrive off popular or mainstream trends. *We have trained him well.*

Arm in arm, we approached my oldest friend, who sat hunched over our table.

His highlighted brown hair was slicked back, his pale face illuminated by the screen of his iPhone. Considering I made my livelihood through social media, it always was a bit humbling to know that, regardless of how much time I spent online, hooked to my phone, Jasper Hastings was ten times worse. Since he began rebranding his magazine *Divulge,* I didn't think I'd ever been with him for more than three minutes without him checking his cell, even at a theater during a movie. Anyone else, it would have been annoying and disruptive, but Jasper had finessed his movements so much over the years that now, I hardly even noticed it happening. He was dressed in fine clothes, his ever-changing wardrobe always a secret envy of Charlotte's and mine. Even though designers often sent me new, exclusive items to feature on *Trending Topic*, like the all-purpose clutch I had brought along tonight, I could never hope to match the fashion closet Jasper had access to at *Divulge*. Jasper's gray suit was tailored to fit his tall, broad physique. The shadows flickering from the candles on the table gave the illusion that his massive arms were about to burst from his jacket. It seemed that any time Jasper wasn't devoting to *Divulge*, he devoted to his bodybuilder-esque physique. At first glance, he appeared to be a sophisticated heavyweight champion, not the head of a brilliant media empire. He certainly made for a unique individual.

"I can't believe I beat you both here," Jasper greeted us. "I thought I was going to get creamed in traffic, but I took off from the office a bit early to speak to my agent and managed to get out of the city unscathed." His sly comment poked fun at my neurotic obsession with being early. If I was on time for something, I was late.

"Agent?" Hudson slid into the booth, silencing any chance for me to snap a biting retort.

"*Real estate* agent." Jasper steepled his fingers together, as if ready to dish some delicious gossip. "I'm thinking about buying one of the condos in Sunny Shores."

I nearly choked on the glass of water I'd just sipped.

Jasper's icy blue eyes narrowed. "You don't seem too enthused to have me as your neighbor, Coco."

"I know I told you I wanted you to move closer, but isn't that *too* close?" With Jasper, I wasn't afraid to speak the truth. "You know I love you, but are you sure you want to be on top of us?" Jasper was forever mocking my "lovey-dovey" relationship with Hudson. He was a perennial bachelor.

Jasper's well-groomed eyebrow arched comedically as he conceded. "You're right. I hadn't really thought about what it would be like living next door to Mom and Dad."

Hudson chuckled at the pet name Jasper had graciously bestowed upon us a few months after we'd started dating. I had been living in Dover with Jasper as my roommate when I serendipitously met Hudson at a hole-in-the-wall bar LiveIt had rented out for an office holiday party. I'd practically floated home that fateful night, and poor Jasper had to listen to me gush on and on about the dreamy guy I'd met while scarfing hot wings and drinking watered-down margaritas. In the early days of my relationship with Hudson, it was common practice for all three of us to go out together, a little family of sorts. Since I had relocated to Central Shores and Hudson had eventually moved in with me, our outings as a trio had become fewer and farther between.

"What about a place in Cherry Springs? With the new club there, it might be a fun spot," I suggested with hope, as I did want my best friend to move closer to my home base.

Jasper stared at me for a beat before whipping out a bright red folder from his blazer. "I'm seeing a few places there on Sunday. Want to come with?"

Checking my calendar on my phone, I nodded. "Yeah, I shouldn't be doing any damage control by that point."

Jasper's brow furrowed, intrigued by my dramatic statement. "Do tell, please." Since his world revolved around places other than Central Shores, I wasn't surprised he hadn't heard about Stacy.

I shook my head and took another long sip of water. "I'm waiting to spill the tea until Charlotte gets here. I only want to go through today's ordeal once more."

With a pouty look that didn't belong on his angular face, Jasper crossed his arms and sat back, looking around the restaurant in appraisal. "What do we know about this latest catch?"

"Nothing, at least, not that I can remember." I opened the drink menu as our server arrived, and ordered a Midori sour. I loved the sugary flavor of the sweet, tangy melon liqueur cocktail. "She met him a few weeks ago, I think."

Our waitress interrupted the conversation with a squeal of recognition. "Oh wow, are you Hudson Caruthers?"

Hudson's bronze skin darkened a few shades. "Yes, that would be me."

"Oh my god. I love your TV segment. You've made watching the news hot again." With a wink, she bounced over to the bartender with our orders.

Jasper and I nearly doubled over in silent laughter as Hudson's face collapsed into his hands.

"If I was with anyone else, this wouldn't be as horrifying," my rising-star-of-a-boyfriend moaned through his fingers.

"You know that girl was blowing smoke up your ass because watching the news will never, ever, be 'hot' again." Jasper mimed sassy air quotes. "Just goes to show you how shallow the dating pool is out here."

Hudson gave Jasper a deadpan look. "Did you ever think that my suave delivery actually *does* make the news hot?"

This time, all three of us dissolved into a jumble of laughs, Jasper wiping tears from his eyes by the time he'd regained control of himself.

"What were we even talking about before we were so rudely interrupted?" I reminded my two dinner companions we had more important issues to discuss.

"Charlotte and her new boy toy." Hudson accepted his whiskey and ginger from a passing waiter.

"Do you know where she picked this guy up?" Jasper asked.

I shook my head. "No, she's been unusually quiet about this one. I can't tell whether that's a good or bad sign."

"Well, looks like the tall drink of water has arrived," Jasper purred over the top of his menu.

Looking toward the front of the restaurant, I immediately noticed Charlotte in all her glory. Her impeccably windswept amber waves cascaded down her back, her sun-kissed skin glowing under the pale turquoise sundress that fit her God-given curves like a glove. Even after knowing her for three years, her effortless beauty still left me green with envy.

Tongues wagged as she glided with grace past a table full of businessmen, hardly noticing their crude and undressing looks. She only had eyes for the guy beside her, who I finally shifted my focus to assess.

"Wow, girl's done good this time around." Jasper whistled suggestively.

I had to agree with him. Charlotte usually put whomever she stood beside to shame, but her newest beau seemed to be able to hold his own quite well. He was well over six feet, with sculpted muscles visible under his button-down shirt and tailored khakis. His shaved head made his fiery hazel eyes illuminate against his ebony skin. White teeth beamed from his full lips as he nervously approached the table.

"Guys, I want you to meet Deacon." Charlotte squealed as she reached the booth. "I'm so glad you all were able to make it tonight!" She leaned in and kissed me on the cheek. "I know it's been a wild day for you," she whispered so that only I could hear. But considering the curiosity swirling in Jasper's eyes, he'd heard her too.

Hudson stood to shake Deacon's hand, looking slightly relieved to have another outsider at the table. Whenever the four of us went out, Hudson tended to be on the fringe of our conversations, considering how close Charlotte, Jasper, and I were. "Nice to meet you, Deacon. I'm Hudson."

Deacon gave us all a hearty, warm greeting as Jasper and I also stood to shake his hand. "Char has told me lots about this little gang. I'm honored to be in your presence." His voice was smooth and lilting.

Always one to cave at flattery, Jasper fanned himself jokingly as the couple scooted into the booth. "Well, we're certainly interested to learn more about the latest guest star in *Charlotte's* ongoing romantic comedy of a life."

Charlotte punched Jasper from across the table, giving her date a mortified look. "Don't mind him. My so-called friends think it's funny to tease me about my dating struggles."

Deacon took her hand in his and laughed. "Mine are the same way. It means they care."

"Yeah, Charlotte, we care," Jasper mimicked, drawing an elaborate eye roll from me. I loved him, but boy, he could be annoying at times.

"All right, that's enough from you," I shooed Jasper's antics away. "We have more pressing matters to talk about. First, tell us all about yourself, Deacon, and how you met Central Shores's resident glamazon." I folded my arms on the table and leaned in for the story.

Deacon looked at Charlotte for the okay before sharing. "Well, I grew up in Dallas with my mom, dad, and two older brothers."

Ah, that explained where the smoky twang in his speech came from.

He continued. "Went to Temple University for college, where I studied forensic medicine. Got a job in New Jersey after graduation and only just recently moved to Cherry Springs. I now work for the Sussex County Crime Lab."

My eyes widened in surprise. "Well, isn't that a coincidence. Do you know

Detective Forester?"

Charlotte and Jasper both shot me a confused look, wondering how I'd pulled that name out of thin air.

Deacon, however, smiled in acknowledgment. "Indeed. It seems like we just missed meeting each other earlier today. Harriet mentioned she was on her way to interview a 'Ms. Cordelia Cline' when I arrived at the shop with the rest of the team." He paused, scanning the posh restaurant with perceptive eyes. "Although, I'm glad I got to introduce myself here and not over a dead body. Not sure how great of a first impression that would have been."

Charlotte held up a hand. "Okay, I'm going to graciously turn the spotlight over to Coco so you two can fill us in on what the heck you're talking about." She sent a threatening look my way. "Although, we're going to come back to how Deacon and I met before this dinner concludes."

"Honey, if it involves any type of online matchmaking, we really don't need to hear it," Jasper whined, taking a sip of his dirty martini. "Now, spill the deets," he directed at me.

I gave Deacon an uncertain look. "Am I allowed to talk about it?"

At that, both Jasper and Charlotte looked like they might combust in their seats.

Deacon gave me a quick nod of affirmation. "The incident is already being reported tonight on the local news, so you're free to share your involvement with your friends. I'd just advise your version of events not to leave this table."

With his blessing, I unloaded my discovery of Stacy and how the police believed she was murdered right in the Chens' store. My friends were understandably speechless by the time I concluded with my interview with Detective Forester down at the police station.

Deacon steepled his fingers together once silence settled over the table. "Now, I'm not officially allowed to discuss this case, but, Coco? You need to be careful. The police aren't making it public that you were the one to discover the body." His gaze was intense. "Our lab has yet to turn up any conclusive evidence, so, with the culprit at large, he or she might think you're the only link investigators have if word gets out about your involvement."

His sternness left me unsettled. Up until now, I hadn't seriously considered that my own safety could be in jeopardy due to this harrowing incident. I'd been primarily concerned about my clients' reputation and financial well-being...and of course, who had done this to Stacy. "Okay, I'll be mindful of that, Deacon. Thank you." I shared a worried look with Hudson, who sat tensely at my side.

I thought about my conversation with my parents and sister and quickly sent a text message in our family's group chat reminding them to keep what I'd shared about me finding Stacy a secret. My parents weren't ones to gossip, but Thea...I breathed a sigh of relief when she instantly sent back a lips-are-sealed emoji.

"My God, I can't believe Stacy Lockner is gone. She came into Brewed to Perfection for a latte only just this morning," Charlotte murmured. "Everyone on the strip saw all the cop cars swarming around during lunch, but no one knew what the hell was going on."

"Let's hope it remains that way," Deacon said. "In a small town like Central Shores, it's vital to keep details of the crime under wraps until the appropriate time. Gossip destroys cases like these."

"What do you mean, cases like these?" My curiosity was piqued by his sour expression.

"Small-town crimes of passion. If rumors and lies circulate long enough, people begin to believe them and report them as fact. It muddles the integrity of the investigation for law enforcement." Deacon fiddled with the straw protruding from his Rum and Coke. "We caught a break given that no one has yet to tie you to the scene, Coco. With your connections and background, it could turn into a nightmare if any media outlets got wind of your involvement in the case."

His words reminded me of Thea's earlier admonishment about being involved in a murder, and I bristled. Chief McInnis had already expressed his displeasure that there was a chance news of Stacy's death could go viral, since a celebrity (i.e. me) was embroiled in the case. I was content to fly under the radar. No one in their right mind would want to stir up this kind of fame. "Well, I certainly don't plan to tweet about it."

Charlotte batted her absurdly long, natural lashes, stroking her boyfriend's arm. "You really can't tell us anything more, like what Coco may have left out?"

He patted her hand. "Why don't you tell your friends how we met?" He skillfully navigated the topic of conversation away from the confidential information he harbored.

I tried to listen attentively to Charlotte's story about how she and Deacon had met each other at the Sussex County Humane Society. Charlotte had been there volunteering on the one afternoon a week her coffee shop was closed. Deacon had been looking for a dog who liked to go for long runs and needed a good home. As fate would have it, he ended up with a new Labrador mix *and* date with the Tuesday afternoon dog walker. As much as I wanted to gush about their "meet cute" story, my thoughts drifted back to Stacy. Deacon had said the police didn't have much to go on, meaning this investigation could take a lot longer than the Chens were expecting. I hated that my mind went to the business repercussions over concern for Stacy's murder, but the Chens' success was tied to mine. If their business failed, it would tarnish Center of Attention's sterling reputation, no matter how much of it was out of my control. I decided that, after my meeting with the Chens tomorrow morning, I would go to the police station and see what could be done to ensure the Chens had their store back in time for their grand opening.

With my thoughts preoccupied for much of dinner, Jasper unceremoniously guided conversation throughout the meal. When it came time for us to pay the bill, he nudged me in the side. "As much as I love being the focal point of an evening, it felt weird not competing for it with you. Everything okay?" he asked, his voice low and unheard by the others as they got up from the table and began saying their goodbyes.

Leave it to Jasper to know something was wrong by the simple fact I wasn't vying for the spotlight. "Just have a lot on my mind right now. I'll be back in top form by the time we go house hunting, I promise."

Turning to Charlotte and Deacon, I gave them each a hug. This had to be the first time that one of Charlotte's boyfriends had earned my seal of approval. "Let's get together again soon, without the fifth wheel." I jokingly threw a look at Hudson. The good sport that he was, he held his hands up in defeat.

"Deacon's a nice guy." Hudson pulled Jolly out of the parking lot a few minutes later. "Charlotte seems happy with him."

I nodded, genuinely thrilled for her. "He's definitely a million steps up from the skeeze balls she normally finds for herself. How cool is it that he works in a crime lab?" I leaned my head against the back of the seat. "I wish he could have told us more about what's going on with Stacy, though."

"I don't want you any more entangled in this than you already are. You heard what Deacon said about you becoming a target, right?" Hudson reached over and squeezed my hand. "This isn't an episode of *Mare of Easttown*, babes. You need to be careful. Even if it means stepping away from the Chens."

"What?" I screeched. "I'm not dropping my clients. A PR consultant who bails at the first sign of a scandal? That would torpedo my business."

Hudson maintained his cool and collected tone. "I'm just saying, you've got your blog and all your social media sponsorships—why don't you stay focused on that? With my promotion to evening anchor, it's not like we need the money."

I folded my arms, stewing with anger. "It's not about the money, Hudson. It's about doing something I love. *Trending Topic* is great and all, but I don't want to spend the rest of my days posting contouring tips and office décor ideas. CoA is new and exciting and *fun*. Why would I want to give that up?"

"Because your life could be at risk!" Hudson's calm façade uncharacteristically crumbled. "I don't want anything to happen to you, okay?" He shot a quick, pleading look my way, not taking his eyes away from the road for too long. "Is it so hard for you to believe that I need you to be safe?"

His very real fear forced me to take a deep breath. "Of course not, you big goon. I'm sorry. As usual, I'm only thinking about myself." I took his right hand, stroking his long fingers. "I promise I'll be careful. I won't leave the

Chens hanging, but I also won't go around town touting that I'm the one who found Stacy. People may know I'm working for the Chens, but really, anyone could have gone into the store and found her." I shuddered as the horrific memory penetrated my defenses once more. "I honestly want to forget about this whole thing and pretend like it never happened."

I could tell from his tight jawline that Hudson wasn't completely satisfied with my compromise, but he didn't push back further. He respected me to make my own decisions, something I greatly treasured.

The rest of the car ride continued in silence, the vibrating of my phone the only interruption. Charlotte wanted to know if I was doing okay with everything, and Jasper was sending me text updates from an article he found online recapping the news about Stacy's death.

Chief Lloyd McInnis is urging residents of Central Shores to remain vigilant, as Stacy Lockner's killer is still not in police custody. Anyone with information pertinent to the case or Ms. Lockner's personal life is encouraged to come forward.

Reading his copied-and-pasted summary, I frowned into the growing darkness, and not just because Jasper was multitasking on his drive back to Dover. A murderer was out there, and it wasn't a good sign that investigators were already reaching out to the public for information. Had Stacy's family and friends not provided the police with any solid leads?

I stared out the car window into the growing night, wondering how something so awful could've transpired in my haven of a hometown. Unbidden, Stacy's crumpled, bloodied body violated my thoughts once more. I could keep telling everyone I was fine and dandy, but as much as I wanted to pretend that none of this had ever happened, I would never be able to forget the terrible scene in the break room of the Chens' store.

What on earth happened to you, Stacy?

Chapter Seven

My alarm clock started squawking all too early for the light hangover I was nursing. I wasn't a big drinker and having two Midori sours at The Pearl had put me over the edge, the wooziness not hitting me until I fell into the comforting arms of my pillows last night. Searching blindly for my phone, I silenced the ringer and pushed myself out of bed, only taking a quick moment to peer out the window at the blissful sand dunes caressed by the ocean's edge. I wasn't one to lounge around and hit the snooze button repeatedly when I had to prep for early morning meetings.

Hudson was still sound asleep by the time I emerged from the shower, my rose-gold hair blown out, sleek and shiny, like my trendy navy suit. I'd opted for a more formal ensemble today because I planned to go to the police station after my meeting with the Chens. I wanted Chief McInnis to know I meant business when it came to defending my clients' reputation.

I grabbed my phone and swiped through the horde of notifications that had come in through my Instagram account overnight. A familiar swell of satisfaction rose when I saw the reaction to the Valencia-filter enhanced photo I'd posted of my Caprese salad with capellini Bolognese at The Pearl. Despite a weird industry taboo, foodie pictures were very much still a thing and the number of likes my photo had garnered proved it. I took some time to scroll through the comments, replying here and there, hoping to make someone's day knowing that an internet celebrity had noticed them. There were a fair share of comments begging me to post a copycat recipe on *Trending Topic.* Even though I'd semi-retired food topics from the blog, I

69

occasionally sprung a surprise cooking video on my followers. I considered the post title, "A Dinner to Impress the In-Laws." Hmmm, perhaps Mom could help me whip up something in the upcoming weeks…

I was just responding with the blowing-a-kiss emoji to someone named @grantygrantee when I noticed a slew of new comments popping up.

Is that Hudson Caruthers in the background? What a dreamboat.

Does anyone know his account handle?

Why is she taking pictures of food when she has that hottie beside her?

I nearly choked on my coffee as morning social media perusers began blowing up my photo with comments about Hudson's blurry figure in the background. Seeing the geotag on my photo for The Pearl, I realized people in the surrounding area were likely seeing this pic pop up in their newsfeed, hence the recognition of Hudson. He might have been a rising star at WMTG, but he certainly was nowhere near a household name across the country, where my fanbase spanned. Still, it bothered me to see Hudson become the focus of *my* picture. I decided to leave those new comments unanswered and unnoticed, muting the post on my phone for now. After a post hit ten thousand likes, I usually silenced notifications for it anyway, so I didn't feel too guilty that my bruised ego was the real reason behind the swift setting adjustment.

I checked my Center of Attention email, pleased to see a flurry of acceptances from past remote clients whom I'd invited to a webinar on Facebook trends that I planned to host tomorrow. The goal of the CoA seminar was to outline the ideal times for businesses to post, key phrases and words that were successful at drawing attention, and types of visual media that worked best for getting users to visit a business page. This was the first time I was presenting to multiple clients at once, and I was excited to see the results. It would free up a lot of my time if I could do these types of paid trainings in a more condensed fashion, allowing more freedom in my schedule to grow Center of Attention and its services.

My final task before leaving was to pull up my calendar and map out my day. My morning had to be dedicated to the Chens, but I planned to be home by one-thirty to do a prep session for tomorrow, as well as write an outline for my next *Trending Topic* post. This week I aimed to feature budget-friendly spring redecorating tips, as well as great ways to recycle products around the house. The post would detail how a few simple items, like scented candles and wooden crates, could be repurposed into new, tasteful focal pieces to enhance a room's décor. I also planned to highlight how a feature wall, a fun DIY project, could revitalize a space without too much sweat. Thanks to Charlotte lending me the wall of her guest bedroom a few weeks ago, I knew from firsthand experience the success of this new trend. My plan was to draft the article tomorrow and take pictures of my designs to showcase on the blog and across my social media accounts. I'd then publish the piece on Saturday morning, when most people had the time to leisurely putz around the internet. I also had to account for the fact that I had Hudson's impromptu fundraiser this evening, meaning I needed to make sure I had something glamorous to wear.

Before we drove out of The Pearl's parking lot last night, Jasper had provided me with a stunningly huge amethyst necklace and matching teardrop earrings. Purple always heightened the green in my eyes and brought out the shimmery rose-gold tones in my dyed hair. If I had time, I would swing by Quincy's on the strip to find a complementary dress on my way home from the police station. *Yeesh, I never thought I'd have* that *on my to-do list.* If I couldn't find something suitable, I was sure my luxurious walk-in closet would have something fitting for the philanthropic occasion.

I placed a note on the counter that told Hudson to have a good day, kissing the Post-It to leave a print of my lipstick behind for him. It was my signature way of saying goodbye to the love of my life, as well as helping me blot my lips. I grabbed my travel mug of coffee and keys and raced down to the garage, hopping into Jolly. The clock on the center console glowed seven forty a.m., meaning I had twenty minutes to make the twelve-minute trip to Millionaires' Row, which *should* get me there in plenty of time, I assured my punctual neurosis.

Millionaires' Row, or Canopy Cove, as its residents called it, rested two miles north of the strip, off the main coastal road. Canopy Cove was a giant cul-de-sac that curved around a small inlet the residents claimed to be their own private beach. In reality, it was public property for the residents of Central Shores, but none of the locals wanted to deal with the hoity-toity attitudes of the Mill Row dwellers. With each sizeable estate boasting waterfront property, it was a very beautiful area. I drove past four-door garages, gates yawning open and sporty vehicles emerging to begin the daily commute to Milton or Dover. Although, from the looks of many closed garage doors, most folks in this neck of the woods either worked from home, or didn't have to work. Oh, to be that rich.

In recent years, as old, stately Canopy Cove homes sold to new money, historically crafted buildings were torn down in favor of modern, sleek multi-building compounds. Hardly an estate in Mill Row had anything less than a main house, a guest house, a greenhouse, and a pool house. Even though I'd lived in Central Shores for practically my whole life, it always threw me for a bit of a loop that my little hometown had grown into a haven for such polarizing socioeconomic statuses. You had your born-and-bred seaside folks who frequented the establishments along the strip, and then you had your millionaire imports who drove their Porsches and Maybachs up to Cyprus or the Crestview Country Club, which was a few towns over in - you guessed it - Crestview. When I began looking for a home in the Central Shores community, I had initially set my sights on living in Mill Row but quickly found out my meager three-million-dollar buyout would only buy me half a pool house in the swanky neighborhood and, even then, it wasn't guaranteed to be on waterfront property. So, I set my sights elsewhere and luckily found my Sunny Shores dream home.

I arrived at the entrance of the Chens' property, passing under a gorgeous brick archway on my way up the circular driveway. I parked Jolly near the front door and hopped out, marveling at the beautiful mansion until eight o'clock arrived on my phone screen.

Unlike many of their neighbors, the Chens had chosen to not remodel the house, instead keeping the beautiful colonial brick in pristine condition. I ambled up the white wooden stairs and knocked gingerly on the polished black door. Expecting their housekeeper to appear and greet me, I was surprised to see that Sean was the one who ushered me inside the grand home.

"Thank you for coming out so early, Coco. I hope it wasn't too much of an ordeal," Sean apologized, which seemed to be a perpetual state of mind for him these days.

I assessed his frumpy appearance. Usually dressed to the nines in khakis, a dress shirt, and a sweater vest, it was out of character to see him in gray sweatpants and a blue Nike T-shirt.

He must have noticed my expression because his cheeks blossomed into an even deeper shade of red. "Sorry for the rag-tag look. I just got off the treadmill. I'm running a bit behind this morning."

Regaining my professionalism, I gave him a tight smile. "It was no trouble at all, Sean. Traffic was light, so I enjoyed my coffee while I admired your home. The new hedges are stunning. You put the rest of the Cove to shame." I looked around the spacious foyer. "Where's Magda?" I referred to their portly housekeeper.

"She's been visiting her family in the Czech Republic for the past two weeks." He sighed. "She offered to fly back early and help take care of us through this whole nightmare. As much as I miss her cooking, I told her we'd survive until she comes back next weekend."

I smiled, admiring Sean's consideration toward his employees and their personal lives. His wife, on the other hand...

"Coco? Is that you?" Olivia's nasally voice walloped through the French doors at the end of the hall.

Sean winced beside me. "She's in one of her moods this morning, so I apologize upfront. Please, make yourself at home in the kitchen, Coco. I'll be there in a few minutes." He waved me down the long foyer and disappeared upstairs, taking the steps two at a time. Olivia had shown me their master suite the first time I came here. It took up the entire second floor.

Pushing one of the French doors open, I walked into the sprawling chef's kitchen, which was nearly the size of the first floor of my condo. "Hi there, Olivia. How are you holding up?" As if *she'd* been the one to walk right into a murder scene.

Small as she was, Olivia's dramatic presence filled the room. "Oh, you would not believe what a horror show this has been! I was on the phone with the insurance company for most of the day after the police left yesterday. This is going to completely ruin our grand opening."

I kept my lips pressed tight, determined not to roll my eyes. "Yes, Stacy's death has been incredibly inconvenient."

If she noticed my sarcasm, she didn't act like it. "I know. Think of all the time and energy we wasted training her." Throwing her thin, pale arms up in defeat, Olivia floated over to the granite island and sat on one of the beckoning bar stools. "I don't want to even think about hiring another assistant for the store right now."

Without waiting for an invitation, I joined her. "I think you and Sean will be able to handle inventory management without a problem. It's very likely you won't be drumming up enough business in the opening weeks to warrant having another full-time employee."

Olivia shot me a panicked look. "What do you mean we won't get enough business?"

I sighed, getting ready to give the speech I'd given Olivia nearly two dozen times since our engagement had started. "The first three months are going to be an uphill battle. Success doesn't come to local business owners overnight. We'll need to work on your image within the community after the opening to ensure we see a boost in traffic both online and in the store."

Olivia buried her face in her hands, her midnight black hair like a shroud. "I can't believe we've invested everything we have into this place. What was I thinking?" she sobbed to herself.

Sean breezed into the room, his short, dark hair still wet from the shower. "Olivia, how many times do I have to tell you this?" He put a gentle hand on her slender shoulder. "We've put enough money aside that we'll be more than fine for the next few years if things don't take off right away."

Olivia stilled under his comforting touch. "No, Sean, we won't!" she moaned, propping her elbows on the countertop with a defeated huff.

I shot Sean a questioning glance. Olivia had never been the most optimistic person in the world, but this seemed a bit defeatist, even for her.

"Come on, Liv. That's no way to think." Sean perched onto a barstool next to his wife. "We've got the money saved up. We'll be fine."

"That's just it, Sean. We don't. Not anymore." Olivia dissolved once more into blubbering whimpers. "I-I used those savings to buy a tea set belonging to the Royal Family from an auction house over in London." Her wailing confession rattled against my eardrums.

Sean's fair skin drained of all its natural color. "What?"

"I took the money we set aside and bought some high-end stock for the store last month. There, are you happy?" Olivia barked back, her dark eyes red with tears.

"When were you going to tell me this?" Sean was doing his best to keep his calm façade, but this must have been a punch to the gut for him. I'd known the Chens less than a month, and Sean had reminded his wife about their rainy-day fund on a daily basis, his enthusiasm for their pet project never dampening, because they had something to fall back on. Hearing that their money had been blown on a tea set…well, I really didn't want to be around for the conversation that followed.

"I wasn't going to." Olivia sniffled. "I figured we'd make it all back soon enough."

"Make it all back? Liv, we had two *million* set aside in that account! How much in God's name did you spend?" Sean bellowed, his composure completely obliterated by his wife's oblivious statement.

Olivia crumpled once again, her words a mumbling mess.

"How much?" Sean repeated, this time, his tone cooler and more collected.

"One point eight million!" Olivia burst out. "I spent one point eight million dollars on china that Queen Elizabeth used while dining at Sandringham. Rumor has it that it was last brought out for a welcome luncheon for Meghan Markle and her mother, Doria Ragland. How could I pass something like that up? Besides, the auction was for a good cause…I think."

She…thinks? I dropped my jaw, unable to compute the logic Olivia had used when making such an extravagant purchase.

Perhaps because he'd been married to Olivia for fifteen years, Sean put a comforting arm around his wife's heaving shoulders. "So, we have two

75

hundred thousand dollars to our name if this store fails." He wasn't asking a question; he was simply confirming that the damage had been done. "Well, Coco, I hope your services really do work," he said with humorless defeat.

I shifted in my seat, trying to figure out how to pick up the pieces of this mess. I mean, two hundred thousand dollars was surely nothing to scoff at, but the Chens were used to a certain lifestyle. If Once Used, Twice Buy failed, they'd basically be starring in their own *Schitt's Creek* spin-off. "As the saying goes, no publicity is bad publicity. We just need to approach this awful scenario with class and intelligence. I'm sure you're already planning on this, but I expect you to both be in attendance at Stacy's funeral, whenever that may be." I didn't know how long it took for murder victims to be released to their family for burial. "And I still think it's a good idea to make at least a charitable donation in Stacy's name." From the sounds of their vanquished finances, the Chens really didn't have enough extra money lying around to create a scholarship fund, so we'd have to set our sights on something a *bit* smaller.

Olivia still sobbed into her hands, tears and snot leaking between the cracks of her fingers. I reached for a paper towel and handed it to her. "I'm going to speak with the police after I leave here. I want to get a sense of the timeline we're up against." I looked between the two business partners. "Can you tell me about your conversations with the police yesterday?"

Olivia nodded, pulling herself back together. "We arrived at the front of the shop yesterday at around twelve-thirty." She had the decency to look guilty for being late. "Sean and I stopped by Brewed to Perfection for a quick cup of coffee, but the line was so long, we ended up leaving well after noon. By the time we reached the storefront, police cars were parked out front and the tight-lipped officer we spoke to wouldn't let us in. He wouldn't even tell us about Stacy until I threatened to sue him for trespassing."

I grimaced, not pleased that Olivia had already issued an unwarranted threat to the police. No wonder Officer Adrian Riley had been gobsmacked after confronting the Chens. "Did anyone question you while you were outside Once Used, Twice Buy?"

Sean shook his head. "The officer manning the front door told us to go home and wait. A detective from the county office came by around three in the afternoon and spoke with us." He reached for his wife's hand, their argument regarding the Queen's tea set seemingly forgiven for now. "She asked us how well we knew Stacy, if she was a good worker, and if she ever left the store with anyone in particular once her shifts were over."

Since I knew so little about her, I encouraged him to share more. "What did you tell them?"

"That Stacy was great. I mean, she'd been with us for several months, helping us take the store from concept to reality."

Olivia cleared her throat. "We were even paying for her to take business classes at the community college in Milton."

"So, she was more than an employee? She was a partner in this venture?" I asked for confirmation.

"No, I wouldn't go that far," Sean said with a light chuckle. "We appreciated her ideas and her enthusiasm, of course, but Stacy was just our assistant, helping us find new stock and brainstorming ways to drum up business. She never executed any business decisions. Those were our call." Sean motioned between him and his wife.

I switched topics. "Did her friends ever come by the store? Any boyfriends?"

"Not that we can remember." Olivia sighed. "Like Sean said, she was a great worker, but we knew very little about her personal life."

"Did the detective ask you anything else?"

Olivia tucked a strand of hair behind her ear. "They asked us why she was working alone that morning. I told them I was actually supposed to be there with her, but we had a doctor's appointment that we couldn't miss." She paused, and Sean reached for her hand once more. "You see, we've been trying in vitro fertilization, and yesterday was our first appointment to see if the treatment took." Despite seeing her cry mere moments ago, I thought in this moment that Olivia looked truly devastated. "It didn't work this time around."

Knowing I was encroaching on an extremely private matter, I gave the couple a minute to gather their thoughts.

"We drove home after the appointment instead of heading into the store. We figured Stacy could handle things by herself for a bit. I needed to lay down and catch my breath before our meeting." Olivia gave me the most vulnerable smile I had ever seen on her pretty face.

Sean patted the back of his wife's hand. "I spent the rest of the morning tracking inventory shipments to make sure everything would arrive before the opening. I didn't want to wake her, but Liv overslept her alarm, so once I realized how late it was, I woke her up around eleven forty-five. We had to rush out of here pretty quickly."

"On the drive over, I thought a shot of espresso would help pull me out of my stupor, which led us to take a detour through Brewed to Perfection before heading to the shop. Which reminds me, coffee?" Olivia got up and went over to the barista-quality machine glistening on the kitchen counter.

I nodded my thanks and turned back to Sean. "When you were speaking with the police, did they ask you if anything had been stolen?"

Sean shrugged. "We haven't even been inside the shop to see if anything is missing yet. Olivia gave the detective a printout of our recorded inventory for their review, along with my key to the store."

Across the kitchen, Olivia's face sagged. "You don't think we were robbed, do you? Did you notice anything out of place, Coco?"

It was my turn to look sheepish. "I really don't remember anything about it too vividly. I think I'm still coming to terms with seeing Stacy…on the floor," I choked out, reaching for the aromatic beverage she placed in front of me.

Sean put a hand on my trembling arm. "I'm so sorry about all of this, Coco. Here we are, moaning about our problems when you're dealing with something much worse."

Taking a refreshing sip of the gourmet pick-me-up, I took a second to collect myself before plastering a tight smile on my face. "It was horrible and shocking, but I'm fine. I just hope the police can get this matter wrapped up quickly. It's a little unnerving knowing the killer is still out there."

Both Olivia and Sean exchanged worried glances.

"You don't think they'll come back to the scene of the crime, do you?"

Olivia asked.

Sean's question was more sensitive. "Are the police protecting you, Coco? You being the one to discover Stacy and all. You're not in danger, are you?"

I shook my head. "Hudson had the very same reaction." I reached into my purse to pull out a small notepad. As much as I loved my phone, I was a big believer in making physical checklists. Saving my thoughts to the cloud just didn't have the same go-getter effect as seeing them outlined in front of me. "Considering I barely remember anything from the incident, I wasn't much help to the police, so I don't think I'm a credible witness. But I am being careful, just in case."

Sean breathed a sigh of relief and took a grateful sip of the coffee his wife offered him.

"As for coming back to the crime scene, I don't see why they would. From what I can tell, the police didn't find anything that the killer would come back for," I assured Olivia. "When I check in at the station after this, I'll make sure to ask them about noticing any stolen merchandise."

She waved a hand, swatting away my reassurance. "I'm not concerned about things being stolen. Everything is insured…" Her voice trailed off, taking a few beats to glance around the room. "Oh God, except the Royal Tea Set!"

Sean's face crumbled. "You mean the one you sunk our savings into?"

"Yes." Olivia's worn-out expression wilted even more. "The shipment only arrived two days ago. I was supposed to call the insurance company yesterday morning to add it to our coverage, but I got sidetracked with the doctor's appointment and then with this whole fiasco."

"Do you have a picture of the tea set? I can show it to the police and ask them to check on it." Once more, I sensed tensions flaring in the room.

"Yes, yes, I have one. It's in my office. I'll be right back." Olivia excused herself.

Sean watched her disappear down the hallway. "Normally, Livvie would never forget something so monumental as that," he said, more to himself than to me. "I worry what this is doing to her health, with the IVF and all." His sad gaze turned to me.

"Forgive me for prying, Sean, but starting a new business is incredibly stressful. Is Olivia's doctor aware of the external factors going on in her life?" I asked out of genuine concern.

"Yes, Dr. Dodan was very upfront about how difficult a process this can be and that we weren't doing it at the best time. But Liv wouldn't hear of it. She said she could handle it." Sean ran a hand through his thinning hair. "Maybe I should try to convince her to hold off on further treatment while this gets all sorted out."

I nodded silent agreement as Olivia reentered the room, holding a computer printout. She held it out to me. "I hadn't gotten around to unpacking the boxes, so the set will be in the back of the store somewhere," she explained. "I can't quite remember where I put it."

I took the paper and examined the photo cataloging the expansive tea set. Considering it was worth one point eight million dollars, I didn't know why I was so astonished it contained seventy-eight pieces. "I'll show this to the police and let you know what I learn. In the meantime," I reached for my notepad and pen, "we need to decide how to proceed with Once Used, Twice Buy."

"What are the odds we'll have our store back in time for the grand opening?" Sean pulled up his calendar on his smartphone. "It's next Saturday."

"I'll have a more concrete timeline once I speak with the police, but let's assume we can open as planned. I don't think the police hold on to crime scenes for very long, but I'll see what I can do to persuade them to move quickly." I was ever the optimist. "Before I forget," I paused, reaching into my Cole Haan bag to pull out the printed PDF that my lawyer had emailed me last night, "here's the amendment you suggested." I chewed on my lower lip as I thumbed through the document. I didn't want to insult my clients, but their personal finances were in complete shambles. "But maybe we should just toss it out the window?"

Sean sighed. "I appreciate your concern, Coco, but we need a successful store launch now more than ever, and that won't happen if Liv or I are tempted to pester the police."

CHAPTER SEVEN

He picked up a pen from the counter and etched his signature across the page, pushing it over to his wife.

Olivia rolled her eyes before signing her name below her husband's.

"Are you able to continue your inventory work remotely?" I directed my next question to Olivia as I put the document away.

Her eyes scanned the room, like she was doing phantom math right before our eyes. "I have all the merchandise photos uploaded to my cloud drive, so I'll be able to import them into the website using my home computer."

"Is all the inventory at the store, or do you have some here?" I ticked the next box on my list.

"Most of it is at Once Used, Twice Buy," Sean replied, "but we did have a few shipments sent here and several more arriving over the next few days. Why?"

I considered our options for a moment. I wasn't one hundred percent sure that the police would give us access to Once Used, Twice Buy before next Saturday, and we had the store's image to consider. The more I thought about it, it would probably seem distasteful for the Chens to open right after their employee was murdered, no matter how badly they needed to turn a personal profit. "I think we should plan a soft opening online. We can launch targeted promos for the event across your social media platforms, so there's an exclusivity vibe to it. It will make customers feel like it's 'invite-only'. You can feature the pieces that were sent here, so if someone does buy something, you'll be able to process it here at home and ship it out. If we start selling pieces that are in stock at Once Used, Twice Buy, who knows if the police will be willing to let us retrieve them for shipping."

Olivia didn't look pleased. "That's less than a quarter of our inventory! If we only advertise what's here at the house, people will think our store is a joke."

I didn't *not* agree with her but knew our options were limited. "A soft opening gets your name out there in the retail world and allows for possible cash flow." Another PR idea popped into my mind. "You could also sponsor a benefit, where you auction off pieces in your collection with the proceeds going to Stacy's family. It would be great press, but you'd have to take a hit to your bottom line."

As Olivia swelled in protest, I held up a hand to calm her down. "Let me go speak with the police before we make any concrete decisions. I'll call you once I have more details." I picked up my bag, preparing for my next assignment.

"Thank you, Coco. We really appreciate you going above and beyond on this one." Sean gave me a weary smile as he escorted me to the door.

"I hope I don't let you down." I waved goodbye and climbed into Jolly, sounding a lot more confident than I felt.

Chapter Eight

As I drove out of Mill Row, taking a right onto the main road toward the police station, I practiced my speech to Chief McInnis, trying to come up with reasonable retorts for any flack he might give me about the Chens' store. By the time I pulled into a parking spot across the Commons, I had my little soliloquy memorized, and was ready to take center stage.

"Omigod, Coco Cline? Is that you?"

I cringed as the airy voice assaulted my eardrums. Turning around with a strained smile, I waved gingerly to Amanda Highgrove as she shimmied toward me. Dressed head-to-toe in designer clothes, she practically burned holes in the ozone as the sun's glare reflected off the gold buckle accents running along her Dolce & Gabbana spring jacket and PRADA handbag.

"Hi, Amanda. Fancy seeing you here," I said through gritted teeth.

You know how, in high school, you couldn't wait to get out and show all those brats who were mean to you how amazing and awesome you grew up to be? Yeah, well, it was nothing like I'd imagined it would be.

Amanda Highgrove was the worst, and I mean, *the* worst person in high school. She made it her life's work to make every girl around her feel inferior by exposing our weaknesses and exploiting them like only a queen bee can. I still had nightmares replaying the exact moment it happened to me. The summer before freshman year, I ran into Amanda as she and her cronies were leaving the mall. I was on my way to the American Eagle fitting room, clutching a pair of size eight, stylishly ripped jeans to try on. And when I said I ran into her, I literally ran into her. Our collision caused the jeans to skid across the floor, and Amanda grabbed them before I could. Seeing their non-zero size, she branded me "Gourdy Cordy," and the fat-shaming nickname followed me all the way to graduation. I didn't have to suffer her torture alone, though. She gave every girl in our grade, including her own friends, some type of self-image complex with her cruelty. Not to mention, Amanda made us all feel like dirt when she flashed her parents' money in our faces. She was a founding child of Mill Row, back when it first became clear that a wave of new money aimed to descend on Central Shores and claim it for themselves. Amanda still lived there now, with her techie billionaire husband, just three houses down from her parents. Rumor had it they bought her the house as a wedding gift.

When I graduated high school, I had no plans of coming back to Central Shores, but after my time in the spotlight, I realized how much I missed it here, and, hence, I'd settled down into my seaside condo. Although, I couldn't help but dread running into Amanda after moving back, and I purposefully went out of my way to avoid her around town.

My luck ran out after three blissful months, and we crossed paths for the first time while I was window-shopping along the strip. I saw her strutting down the sidewalk like she owned the place, and, unable to make a graceful escape, I steeled myself for a hurricane of insults. Instead, Amanda spent our reunion gushing about LiveIt's success, and how much she adored *Trending Topic*. "I carve out time every weekend to read your words of wisdom." She'd even complimented me on how fierce and glamorous I'd looked during my *Today Show* appearance.

Me, glamorous? That was a far cry from Gourdy Cordy. I was utterly speechless at the time. Unfortunately, my silence seemed to convey that I'd forgiven Amanda for all her high school transgressions, and that now we were friends.

"Wow. I absolutely love your suit. So high-power businesswoman of you," Amanda chirped, pulling her half-a-million-dollar Chopard shades down to assess my ensemble. "Love to see you taking your own advice." She winked, likely referring to a post I'd written about fashion in the workplace two weeks ago.

"Thanks," I said flatly, not able to summon the fake enthusiasm I usually reserved for moments like these.

"Have you heard the latest? Such awful news." She didn't bother waiting for me to reply. "Stacy Lockner was found *dead* at a place on the Boardwalk."

Inwardly, I groaned at her use of the term "Boardwalk." Those living on Mill Row had readily accepted the boujee moniker that heightened the sophistication of our little town. On the outside, I plastered an expression of shock across my face. "Dead? What happened to her?" At least word hadn't gotten around that I was the one who had found Stacy's body. If anyone was bound to find out details about the murder through the gossip channels, it was Amanda.

"No one really knows much." She looked like she was practically bursting at the seams. "Arthur's speaking with the police now. Yesterday, he was flying some new drone he's been developing at the beach. He's offering to let the police examine the footage, should the drone's camera have caught something going on near the Boardwalk."

My eyebrows raised in surprise at the usefulness of this information. "Did he already look at the footage himself?"

Amanda rolled her eyes in a dramatic fashion. "No, he was a total stick in the mud about it. He insisted on bringing it straight over to the police."

I smiled, trying to mask my sarcasm. "Well, I'm sure Chief McInnis appreciated that."

She brushed imaginary dirt off her sleeve. "Yes, well, you know my husband. Always trying to be the best civil servant he can be."

I nodded. The tech company Arthur Bushman founded had helped develop innovative technologies in the criminology field. How a smart, caring man like him had ended up with the likes of Amanda...

"Mandy! Everything's all set. The police will review the film and let me know when I can come collect Bessie." Arthur's lanky, pale figure arrived at his wife's side, not seeming to notice me until Amanda had given him a peck on the cheek. "Hey, Coco! Everything well with you and Hudson?"

Much to my chagrin, Hudson and Arthur had become close friends through a biweekly Central Shores poker club. The group consisted of local guys under the age of thirty-five, and Hudson had been invited to join the minute he moved in with me. He and Arthur had quickly bonded, and it wasn't long before Arthur started showing up at our condo for Sunday football. What's more, Arthur was actually really great. It was impossible not to like him, as much as I disliked his taste in women. In an ideal world, I would have paired him up with a woman like Charlotte or someone with a heart. "Everything's great. Amanda and I were just catching up."

He cast a sidelong glance at his wife, who nodded her delighted agreement. While he never had the courage to ask about our past, I think Arthur was smart enough to figure out that I did *not* consider Amanda's bullying to be water under the bridge, even if she did. "Well, wonderful running into you, but we must get ourselves home. I have a conference call with the DOJ about a contract they'd like me to review." Since selling his company for twenty-seven billion—yes, *billion*—dollars, Arthur now spent his days doing tech consulting for intelligence and criminal justice organizations.

My eyes widened at his blasé mention of the Department of Justice...the *United States* Department of Justice. "Sounds much more thrilling than my afternoon."

"Oh, now, stop! If I remember correctly, there's a new *Trending Topic* post due out soon." Amanda gave a giggling squeal. "I can't wait to read it."

I stared at her for a moment, still not believing the horrible Queen of Conceit, who made fun of everything I ever did during high school, was now one of my devoted social media followers. In fact, I frequently saw her username on my blog's Most Valuable Commenter ticker. The title was a badge given to followers whose comments had been upvoted by other users on the site. "I hope you enjoy it," I lied. This woman neither cleaned her own home nor decorated it herself. She had "people" to handle all that for her. My "Spring for a New Vibe" article wouldn't be the most useful of reads for the likes of Amanda.

"We'll see you at the fundraiser tonight, I hope." Arthur gave a cheerful wave.

Thank Adele they had already turned around and walked away, or they would have been put off by the look of horror on my face. Amanda was going to be at the WMTG gala? I rolled my eyes to the skies. I guess I shouldn't have been surprised. Anything with charity or fundraiser attached to it would surely bring in a lot of the big spenders in the surrounding community. Considering how much Arthur was worth, even without his wife's old money, the Highgrove-Bushmans would no doubt grace us lowly peons with their presence.

Collecting myself, I smoothed back my hair and made sure my blazer was in pristine condition before I breezed through the entrance of the police department.

"Do you have an appointment, Coco?" Maude's nasal voice asked from behind the front desk.

I leaned over the counter to see her disapproving stare. "I don't—do I need one?"

As she released an exasperated sigh, I realized Maude was frazzled by her job for likely the first time in her life. The Central Shores P.D. hadn't dealt with anything like Stacy's murder in recent memory. The pressure was clearly getting to its employees.

"Who are you here to see?"

Instead of answering, I gave her a sympathetic glance. Bags sagged under her dark eyes. Her two desk phones had been taken off the hook, and a breakfast sandwich lay untouched next to a pile of papers.

"Everything all right, Maude?"

The receptionist bit her lip, her gaze darting around the room. "You wouldn't believe the three-ring circus this has all turned into." She rubbed her temples as her dark-framed glasses fell down the bridge of her slender nose. "The chief's in an uproar over County taking point on poor Stacy's death. He's under a lot of stress regarding the station's future, and he's taking it out on everyone here."

"What do you mean, the station's future?" Her words triggered a foggy memory. Hadn't I heard Chief McInnis mention something about the station being in jeopardy when he'd stopped by the crime scene yesterday?

"The mayor wants to shut us down and reallocate everything to the county level so the town can make some room in the budget," Maude divulged. "He says Central Shores doesn't warrant its own police department anymore, since crime has been virtually nonexistent."

"Doesn't that mean the police are doing their job?" I countered, to which Maude gave an eye roll.

She huffed. "You'd think, but Mayor Beaufort sees it as a waste of resources that could be used to revitalize the town and attract more tourism."

"Well," I paused, trying to be tactful, "doesn't Stacy's murder suggest otherwise?"

"Our dear mayor was in here arguing *that* very point not an hour ago. He's now changed his tune, saying our department is incapable of handling crime and wants policing transferred to County." Maude lowered her voice to a whisper. "He basically issued an ultimatum. If Central Shores cracks this case before County, then the station stays open. If not..." Maude's attention was momentarily diverted by a clatter in one of the back rooms.

I scoffed at Mayor Beaufort's audacity. He obviously didn't believe the local police could solve this case on their own, or he wouldn't have issued such a challenge. Why was the mayor so intent on shutting down the P.D.? Was it really for more tourism dollars? "The police should be working together with the crime lab, not against them."

Maude gave me a knowing look. "Makes it all the more difficult since Detective Whatshername took up residency in the conference room."

"Detective Forester is here?" I figured she'd be up at her high-tech lab, reviewing evidence.

Maude nodded. "She brought a few members of her team down here with some of their equipment. She wanted to be closer to the pulse of things."

I examined the door leading to the inner workings of the police station. I could almost feel the friction boiling behind it. Despite my disapproval of Chief McInnis's volatile personality, the Central Shores Police Department employed multiple members of our community, and I hated the thought of it being shut down purely for the mayor's political agenda. "May I speak with the chief about the Chens' store?"

"Better you than me." Maude gave a dark chuckle, buzzing open the door leading to the bowels of the station.

Hushed voices greeted my ears as I tiptoed down the hallway. I slowed my pace even more as I glided past the conference room, taking stock of its inhabitants.

"Coco?" Deacon's warm, dark eyes met my curious gaze. "Can I help you?" He stood up from the long, oval table, where he had been reviewing some documents.

"Ms. Cline." Detective Forester's voice was dry. "I don't believe you're authorized to be back here."

"Sorry," I sputtered, unnerved by their grave expressions. "I'm here to speak with Chief McInnis about the Chens' store."

Detective Forester crossed her arms and raised an eyebrow. "I am the lead investigator on this case. You can direct any questions you have regarding the active crime scene to me."

"Well," I stalled, shooting a glance down the hallway to the chief's closed office door, "I was just wondering when Once Used, Twice Buy would be released back to my clients. You see, the grand opening of their store is supposed to be next Saturday..." I withered under the detective's stern gaze.

"A woman has been killed, and you're concerned about a store being able to open on time?" The tone in her voice wasn't kind.

I flushed at her obvious disdain. "Detective Forester, of course my clients are heartbroken over Stacy's death, but they're not impervious to being concerned about their livelihood. They've put their entire savings into the store's success." I tried to contain my seething temper. Her reaction told me what I'd feared. We would absolutely need to postpone the opening to avoid any bad blood between the Chens and the community.

"What's going on out here?" Chief McInnis emerged from his office, his eyes narrowing directly on me as he marched over.

I stood firm as he reached my side. "I just came down to the station to inquire about Once Used, Twice Buy. The Chens are anxious to know when it will be released from *your* custody." I put the emphasis on "your" to hopefully convey that I believed Chief McInnis to still be in charge of the investigation, not the county team.

Growling under his breath, the chief jerked his head for me to follow him to his office. I didn't look back at Detective Forester, but I felt her gaze burning a hole in my suit coat. Obviously, she was just as happy to be here as the chief was to have her here.

Taking a seat in his worn leather desk chair, the chief pressed his hands together as I stood before him. "Now, what's this about the Chens?"

"Their grand opening is supposed to be next Saturday. With all that's happened…" I fidgeted under his frowning gaze. "Well, I wanted to check in and see what kind of timeline we're looking at."

"Timeline? You think we have a definitive timeline as to when we'll have this murder solved?" Chief McInnis asked with incredulity.

His condescending words made me shudder, as I tried not to think too hard about the term 'murder'. "No, of course not, but if I just had an idea as to when the Chens can have access back to their store—"

The chief cut me off with a slash of his hand. "I've got enough problems trying to get this thing solved. I don't need you breathing down my neck about it, missy."

I was on the fence as to whether I should feel bad about asking him an insensitive question or feel offended at being referred to as "missy" when the chief had known my name since I was a little kid. "I'm not here to breathe down your neck, Chief." I inched closer to his desk, casting a furtive glance out the small window in his door. "I just think you and I have mutual interests, that's all."

He cocked a bushy eyebrow. "Oh yeah? And what's that?"

I folded my arms across my chest, hoping I seemed calmer and more collected than I really felt. "I think we both want this case to be tidied up by the *Central Shores* Police Department, and soon."

Chief McInnis looked me up and down, his lips settling into a grim line. "Well, even if that might be true, Coco, unless you can miraculously tell us something we don't already know, I'm afraid we'll be holding onto the Chens' store for at least a couple more days while we finish processing everything."

I deflated at his candidness. "The folks from the crime lab don't have any leads?"

His brow furrowed. "They're either being incredibly tight-lipped and just sitting on their butts in that conference room for the fun of it, or they've hit a dead-end, too."

I took a seat in one of the wooden chairs across from the chief's desk, as uninviting as they looked. "Someone must have seen something. Everyone in this town knows each other's business. Do you know roughly what time Stacy was attacked?"

Looking like he was debating a moment as to whether it was appropriate to share the information with a civilian, Chief McInnis picked up a folder on his desk, skimming through the pages. "Time of death is estimated at around ten-thirty yesterday morning." He surprised me by revealing this detail.

A tight thread of stress snapped inside me. If Stacy had been killed around ten-thirty, the culprit should have been long gone before I arrived. I didn't realize I'd actually been on edge about my own safety until the chief's statement put those buried fears to ease. "Are there any security cameras on the strip that can be used?"

"We asked the surrounding businesses, but no one saw or captured anything. The Chens hadn't set up their in-store security yet, so we have no footage of the immediate area. Gavin is going over some material that Arthur Bushman provided us with just a few minutes ago to see if anything looks suspicious." The chief slapped Stacy's folder down on the desk. "The killer came in and out the back door of the store, locking the door behind him or her. Do you know anyone who would've had access to the place besides yourself and the Chens?"

Drumming my fingers on my bouncing knee, I tried to think. "No. It wouldn't make sense for anyone else to have access."

The chief rotated his chair just a bit so he could stare out the window. "We found most of the murder weapon outside the back door in the alleyway, wiped clean of prints." He met my astonished gaze. "It appears that our killer bashed Stacy's head in with a teapot."

My eyes must have looked like they were popping out of my skull. Why the chief was sharing this with me, I didn't entirely understand. "How awful," was all I could think to say.

"Olivia Chen provided a list of the store's inventory, so we could cross-reference items at the crime scene. It doesn't appear this particular teapot was a part of their collection." Chief McInnis read from another report on his desk. "Which begs the question, where did it come from?"

"Do you have a picture of it?" I sat up eagerly in my chair.

Chief McInnis seemed to weigh the merits of showing me more confidential police information. I must have struck the right chord, implying I wanted his team to take credit for this case, because he pulled out a heavy envelope. "Does this look familiar?" He expelled a sigh of resignation, handing me an enlarged photo.

I examined the intricate cherry blossom design, cringing at the smears of blood along the jagged edges of the broken teapot. "Yes, actually, it does. It turns out Olivia purchased some incredibly pricey china from England not long ago." I reached a hand into my bag and pulled out the picture of the complete Royal Tea Set. "Looks like it's this piece here." I pointed to one of seven teapots included in the collection. As Chief McInnis took the printout, I noticed Olivia had also included the value of each piece on the back of the image. "Stacy Lockner was killed with an eighty-thousand-dollar teapot."

The chief released a low whistle. "I know these people are your clients, Coco, but that's just stupid money right there."

I resisted a grim nod. "Olivia told me that this tea set arrived two days ago, which was probably why it wasn't on the in-store inventory list she gave you. She hasn't gotten around to calling the insurance company about her acquisition, either."

The chief stroked his beard thoughtfully. "Either she's as dumb as a doornail to not insure this thing ahead of time, or she wasn't the one who used a damn-near priceless teapot to kill Stacy."

I gasped. "You have her listed as a suspect?"

The chief's steely blue eyes flashed over my stunned expression. "Coco, you and the Chens are the only ones with access to the store. We'd be remiss to not pursue all lines of questioning."

I didn't think I could be more shocked, but I was. "You think *I'm* a suspect?"

The chief was silent for a moment before waving a hand aside. "You were briefly considered for a time, but your helpful little social media posts have proven you were nowhere near the strip at ten-thirty yesterday morning."

I threw a confused look his way. "What do you mean?"

Chief McInnis chuckled as he leaned back in his chair. "Of all things, a geotag cleared you." The chief picked up an iPad lying on his desk, his fingers moving across the privacy screen with surprising speed. "It appears that at ten thirty-two, you were posting about your favorite cleaning products from the confines of your own home."

He turned the tablet to face me, and I found myself on a Facebook newsfeed, staring at a sepia-filtered image featuring freshly folded laundry styled artistically next to my favorite organic laundry detergent and dryer sheets.

"Oh." I'd uploaded the image to Instagram yesterday during my morning chores and automatically shared it across all my social media accounts, including Facebook. I'd tagged Pelican Beach in the photo, since the waves of Central Shores's southernmost beach could be seen off in the distance through my condo's windows.

"We can reasonably conclude that you didn't murder Stacy, then zoom home in two minutes to 'gram about clean laundry," the chief stated gruffly, although there was a trace amount of humor in his eyes.

Unless I had scheduled the post to be shared ahead of time. But I kept that incriminating little thought to myself. I could hardly believe the police used a Facebook post to clear my name, let alone get over Chief McInnis's casual use of the term *'gram*. "The wonders of technology." I was slightly unnerved by the fact that it had even crossed his mind that I could be guilty. I could understand that from the county crime lab folks who hadn't known me since I was born, but not Chief McInnis and his team. Good grief, I'd gone to junior prom with his nephew, Gavin!

"The Chens, on the other hand..." the chief commented, "do not have as solid of an alibi."

"Olivia and Sean were at a doctor's appointment," I protested, finding it hard to believe that my clients were the main suspects in this case.

"An appointment that ended at nine forty-five, according to their doctor."

Chief McInnis gave me a knowing look. "Plenty of time for either of them to drive back into town and assault Miss Lockner."

I thought back to Sean and Olivia, huddled around their kitchen counter in each other's arms. "This store is their entire life. What motive could they have to ruin their chance of success?"

"Who knows?" The chief paced slowly around his office. "But suspects with no apparent motives are easier to investigate than no suspects at all, Coco. At this point, things aren't looking good for the Chens."

"What about old boyfriends? Have you spoken with any of Stacy's friends?" I felt a bit frantic. Not only did I have to deal with somehow promoting a business-turned-crime-scene, but now it was beginning to sound like my clients' personal lives were on the line.

The chief paused at the window. "Unfortunately, no one has shared anything useful at this point. Stacy's parents say she wasn't dating anyone seriously, and her friends didn't seem to know about any men in her life, either."

I rolled my eyes behind his back. The chief must have a few screws loose if he truly believed that. *Of course*, Stacy's friends would know about her love life. It seemed that they just didn't want anyone *else* knowing about it. Or more particularly, the police. Which likely meant that Stacy was up to something less than scrupulous. "Well, Chief, I appreciate your candid conversation." I stood up, an idea quickly taking shape in my spinning mind. "I'll let you get back to your investigation." I smiled as encouragingly as I could before ducking back into the hallway.

"Coco," his gruff voice called out behind me.

I gulped. "Yes?"

He glared at me. "This information stays between you and me. If I hear it around town, I'll know who I'm arresting for obstruction of justice."

Chapter Nine

I opened my mouth to protest, but the chief's door slammed shut in my face. A pit of dread grew in my stomach. Whoever said knowledge was power must have never been tangled up in a murder investigation.

As I passed the conference room on my way out, I noticed Deacon was the only member of his team left. "Fancy seeing you here." I tossed him a friendly wave from the doorway.

He looked up from his laptop, his eyes crinkling. "Hey, there, Coco. Sorry about the chilly reception earlier. Harriet is a little territorial about this case, now that the mayor has called in a favor to make sure this ordeal is wrapped up quickly."

"Mayor Beaufort?" I asked, curious about the Central Shores elected official and his continued meddling in the case.

Deacon nodded. "Yeah, I guess he and the crime lab director are old golfing buddies. He put in a call to make sure this case is given top priority by our team."

I cast a sidelong look at the chief's closed office door. "Wouldn't it be in the best interest for both sides to work together on this one? There *is* a killer on the loose, after all."

"That's what Harriet had originally planned to do. But yesterday she got a call from Director Morrison telling her that she was to take point on the Lockner case, and that there was no need for the Central Shores police to be kept in the loop."

"Why on earth would he ask Detective Forester to do that? Doesn't Chief McInnis have jurisdiction or something?"

Deacon got up from his seat at the table and poked his head out into the hall, surveying the abandoned area. He then motioned me inside the conference room, lowering his voice. "It's been brought to our attention that Stacy was renting an apartment in Crestview."

"Stacy lived in Crestview?" This was news to me. "I always thought she lived at home with her parents?"

Deacon shook his head. "She signed a lease about a month and a half ago, and, due to her main residence being outside the town lines, Mayor Beaufort wants it handled at the county level."

I could guess the mayor's motivations from there. "So he can spin it publicly that Stacy's killer followed her from big, bad Crestview and not from our safe little haven of Central Shores."

Deacon nodded, his strong jaw set with disapproval. "Director Morrison is looking to run for state senate next year, and I can only imagine that Mayor Beaufort was willing to contribute some campaign funds in exchange for this little favor."

My mouth dropped open at the blatant act of corruption.

"Not that any of us can prove it," he quickly amended his statement, "which is why Harriet is following marching orders."

I exhaled my frustration. While I wasn't too well acquainted with Mayor Beaufort, his brother and his sister-in-law ran one of the most exclusive French restaurants in the area. Hudson and I frequented Beaufort's when we weren't up to cooking at home, and Fred and Natalia always welcomed us with open arms. It was hard for me to picture anyone related to kind-hearted Fred as corrupt, even if he was a politician.

"Where is everyone?" I changed the subject, looking at the empty room.

"They went back to Once Used, Twice Buy in the hopes of finding something we may have missed. Even at the county level, we don't come across many murders, so we want to make sure the whole team was thorough with their work." Deacon leaned against the windowsill.

"I guess I better start figuring out how the Chens can clear their name *and* launch their business while the physical location is still in police custody," I muttered, adding the burdening item to my to-do list.

"Unless your plan involves you solving this whole mess, I suggest the Chens postpone their grand opening until this is all wrapped up," Deacon offered with a joking chuckle.

Hmm, that might help move things along. Not only was my reputation as a successful PR consultant on the line, but so were the Chens' entire fortune and freedom. Maybe I *could* do a little digging on their behalf. The police didn't seem to know much about Stacy's private life, so who better than a glorified gossip blogger to uncover the juicy details about what was really going on in her world? Stacy never mentioned moving out of Central Shores whenever I asked how her folks were doing during moments of idle chitchat, and I knew for a fact that her hourly paycheck from Once Used, Twice Buy wasn't enough to cover even a studio apartment in upper-crust Crestview. There was definitely more going on in Stacy's life than the police or the county lab had uncovered.

Deacon must have seen the wheels turning in my head. "That was a joke, Coco. This is a police matter, despite our own petty jurisdiction battle. I think both Chief McInnis and I have been talking way out of line about this case." His face became a hardened mask of determination, and I could see the justice warrior within him. "Now, it's probably best that you leave us to do our jobs."

"Of course." I feigned meekness, following his hand as he motioned me out the door. "I hope to see you and Charlotte soon." Despite his gruff dismissal just now, I really admired Deacon, and thought he was a good fit for Charlotte. He also had a knack for decoding what women were thinking, considering his clear reprimand at my idea of solving this case on my own.

Out of the corner of my eye, I saw him lean against the doorframe, watching me slink through the lobby, no doubt ensuring I made it out of the building without gathering any more intel concerning Stacy's death.

Maude waved as I headed out the front door. I mouthed "good luck" to her before stepping outside. I took a deep breath, relieved to have that awkward visit behind me. The warm spring air was a refreshing welcome after the sterile smell of the police station.

I glanced at my phone, astonished it was already past noon. My morning had really gotten away from me. I also had three missed calls from Olivia and immediately punched the Redial button.

"How did it go, Coco?" she asked without any greeting.

I bit my lip. "Not as well as I had hoped. For the foreseeable future, we're going to plan to launch your store remotely, as we discussed this morning. We'll brand it as a soft online open, with the hopes of doing a big, in-store event in a few weeks."

"A few weeks?" Olivia's shriek caused me to fumble my phone, almost sending it crashing to the sidewalk as I hustled toward Jolly.

"Neither the chief nor the crime lab have a definitive timeline as to when the store will be released, and I think it's too risky to assume we can have it professionally cleaned and ready in ten days. I guess they're back there now doing another sweep of the place as we speak," I explained as I sank into the warm leather of the driver's seat.

I heard a rustling at the end of the line, and Sean's voice filled the car's Bluetooth speakers. "I'm sure you did everything you could, Coco. I'll begin updating the inventory to reflect only what we have stockpiled in the pool house."

I smiled, feeling the calm reassurance in Sean's voice work its magic on me. "Great, and I'll work on posting some new promos to highlight the soft opening. This way, it will seem more exclusive to potential clients, which will hopefully boost online traffic." I paused a moment before saying what was really on my mind. "But, Sean, even if we do get the physical store back within the week, I don't think it's a good idea to open until there's some closure regarding Stacy's death. You'll come off as callous and coldhearted if you and Olivia are seen blazing on ahead like nothing has happened. Press like that would do incredible damage to the store's success in the long run."

"I agree with you one hundred percent." Sean lowered his voice. I pictured him seeking refuge from his wife's hysterics. "Thanks for making the best of a terrible situation."

My cheeks warmed at his praise. "Of course. I didn't get a chance to tell Olivia this either, and I'm not sure I want to get her hopes up, but my chat with Chief McInnis got me thinking. If the police had more information about Stacy's personal life, it might help them find a viable suspect for who did this to her." I didn't want to break the news that currently, he and his wife occupied the top slots. "I'm going to see if I can dig up some deets that might help."

"If anyone can get the 'deets,' it's you." Sean chuckled. "Didn't *Trending Topic* start off as sort of a celebrity gossip column?"

I grinned, remembering those early days at LiveIt when I was buried up to my eyeballs in tabloids and DMs from tipsters. "You got it. I'm hoping to put some of that savviness to work. I'll check in with you guys later regarding the social media overhaul."

After signing off, I debated my next move. I still had to outline my blog post for tomorrow's writing session, as well as contend with the WMTG fundraiser this evening. My growling stomach made the final decision, and I hung a left at the traffic light, heading toward the strip. I'd grab a smoothie at Squeezed—the juice bar—and pop into Quincy's Finds to see if the shop had a dress that caught my eye for tonight.

I voice-dialed Charlotte's cell and waited for her to answer.

She picked up after the second ring. "Hey, girl, what's up?"

Her singsong voice made me grin. "Got a few minutes to spare? I'm on my way over to Quincy's to see if I can find a dress for Hudson's work event."

Charlotte hemmed and hawed on the other end of the line. But as much as she hated leaving her coffee shop solely in the hands of her high school-aged barista, her desire to shop won out. "Give me twenty minutes for the lunch rush to die down, then I'll be over."

I pumped a fist in triumph as she hung up. Charlotte had been one of the last business owners to sign on for the community's work-study program, all because she didn't trust teenagers to handle her baby with care. "I know how irresponsible I was when I was seventeen," she complained at the time. "I don't want little versions of me ruining my coffee shop." Luckily for her, and for my impromptu afternoon shopping trips, her part-time employee, Bethany, was an honors student who'd been accepted to Brown early admission and had proven herself completely trustworthy in the three months she'd been working for Charlotte.

Five minutes later, I slipped Jolly into a space in the rather empty residential parking lot and made my way to Squeezed for a late lunch. I hadn't been a fan of the place at first because everything was laced with either spinach or kale, but Lacie had recently incorporated fruit smoothies into her menu. The one I loved in particular was less heavy on the fruit and more on the peanut butter and chocolate.

"Hey, Coco! Haven't seen you in a while. How are things?" Lacie greeted me with a bright smile as I entered the green and white juice bar.

"Hi there." I grinned back at her. Lacie Burbank was a few years older than me, but I'd known her my whole life. Her parents lived down the street from mine, and Lacie had been my parents' go-to babysitter for me and Thea when we were little. She'd opened Squeezed last summer with the inheritance left by her grandmother, and the juice bar flourished within the community. "Life is good." *If you don't count the fact that I'm involved in a murder investigation.* "I can't complain. What about you? How's the shop doing?"

"Great!" Lacie adjusted her Squeezed cap with pride. Ever since she'd ordered hats branded with her store logo, it was rare to see her without one. She wore it, not only for advertisement purposes, but to keep her thick, black hair out of her face. "Business is starting to pick up for the season, although today has been kinda quiet. I haven't seen many folks out and about."

I kept my snarky commentary to myself. *Having a murderer on the loose isn't exactly great for business.*

With a final wipe of her butcher block countertop, Lacie tossed her cleaning rag aside and surveyed her domain. "I keep meaning to ask if you'll be available in the upcoming weeks to help me with a little ad campaign. I've got some new summer flavors coming soon, and I want to drum up some hype for tourists planning their beach getaways."

I waved a hand aside. "For you, I'll make time whenever you need my help."

"You're the best, Coco. I can always count on you. Now, what can I get you? A banana peanut butter smoothie?" Lacie tightened her apron strings around her curvy waistline and grabbed a fresh pair of disposable gloves.

"With chocolate." I didn't feel the least bit of shame at the overindulgence. The fundraiser tonight would no doubt be dripping with fresh-caught Delaware seafood, so I needed to satiate myself ahead of time or I'd starve through the evening. I'd yet to figure out why it was assumed that everyone who lived in a coastal town loved guzzling crab, lobster, and shrimp. I'd been to enough parties over the years to realize it was a common misconception, and my unfed stomach had suffered for it.

"Coming right up." Lacie went to work, tossing the fresh ingredients into a high-powered blender. She poured a liberal amount of homemade chocolate syrup into the mix. "Did you hear about what happened yesterday?"

I decided to take a more covert route in the hopes to get some fresh intel from Lacie. "What do you mean?"

"Stacy Lockner was found dead in the back of the Chens' new store, right next door." Lacie said with an incredulous whisper, even though we were alone in her shop. Her warm brown eyes nearly popped out of their sockets with the extreme gossip.

I put on my best surprised face, relieved that my involvement was still unknown. "Dead? Oh my God! What happened to her?"

Lacie poured a generous helping of the smoothie goodness into a large plastic cup. "Seriously? This didn't make your fancy newsfeed? It was all over the TV last night. Didn't Hudson mention it? Someone found her body yesterday around lunchtime. The police think it's murder." She shivered as she placed my drink on the countertop. "Can you believe that? Murder, in our little town?"

I had to agree with her on that. Never had I thought something this tragic would befall the community. Considering I'd been the one to find Stacy, I was shocked by the brutal violence behind the crime. "Who on earth could have done something so awful?" I leaned in, my elbows on the counter, ready for potentially helpful gossip.

Lacie removed her gloves and tossed them into a nearby trash bin. "I have no idea. I can't imagine who. The Central Shores PD was in here yesterday, along with some county detective, asking if I'd heard or seen anything. I can't believe it happened on the other side of our shared alley. I didn't hear a thing." She shook her head sadly.

I frowned, not impressed with her information, or lack thereof. "Poor Stacy. I wasn't too close with her, but it's still so horrible."

"No kidding. I always thought she was a bit of a bimbo, if you get my drift." She clapped a hand over her mouth. "Omigosh, forget I said that. What am I thinking, speaking ill of the dead?" Her brown skin darkened with embarrassment.

I wasn't about to drop that little tidbit. "Did she date a lot of guys or something?" I was curious about the label Lacie had smacked across the victim. Stacy never seemed boy-crazy to me.

Lacie shrugged. "She and her gaggle of girls often popped in here either on their way to or from Quincy's. Always yammering on about needing a dress for the new man she was dating. But," she paused, biting her lower lip, "Stacy hadn't been coming in with the girls as much as she used to, now that I think about it."

"Maybe one of her suitors decided to stick around," I guessed aloud, becoming more intrigued with Stacy's dating life by the minute. "Did you recognize the girls she was with?"

Lacie shook her head. "Not enough to know them by name."

Changing topics before Lacie could ask why I was so full of questions, I asked, "What do I owe you for this delightful beverage?" I motioned to the cup in my hand, which was already half empty.

She waved a hand aside. "Consider it as part of your retainer for my eventual need for your social media services."

"Thanks, Lace. I'll email you later, and we can find some time to sit down and talk shop."

"Perfect. See you soon, Coco." Lacie beamed as she went back to work behind the counter. "And be careful out there!"

Her words left me feeling unsettled as I emerged back out onto the sun-drenched sidewalk. Never before had I been uneasy in my hometown. Yet, looking down the sidewalk at the crime scene tape stretched across the storefront of Once Used, Twice Buy, I couldn't suppress a tingle of fear that jolted down my spine. The peace and tranquility I'd been searching for when I left my life in the big city behind suddenly seemed naively unattainable.

Chapter Ten

"Hey, you!" Charlotte's melodic voice brought my thoughts back from the grim darkness. Waving, she hastened past the bleak china shop, her lustrous waves of amber hair shimmering in the afternoon light. "Are the Chens already back inside?" She pointed her thumb over her shoulder to the store's window once she reached my side.

I shook my head. "The county crime lab is there right now, revisiting the scene."

"Deacon mentioned they'd been assigned to the case as a priority one. Do you know when the Chens will get their store back?" Charlotte asked, concern written all over her stunning features.

I shrugged, not bothering to hide my annoyance from her at the whole fiasco. "I spoke with both Chief McInnis and Deacon this morning. Deacon says they'll likely hold onto the place for a few more days, if there isn't some other break in the case."

"That must throw a wrench in your CoA plans." Charlotte patted my shoulder.

"We're readjusting the Chens' grand opening." I smiled in reassurance. "It doesn't sit well with me to push onward like nothing has happened. We'll give the town some time to grieve and come to terms with everything, then regroup. Luckily, Sean Chen agrees with me," I paused, not able to contain a scowl, "but his wife, not so much. It's going to be an uphill battle to get her on board."

"Well, sounds like some retail therapy is definitely in order." Tugging me the remaining length of the sidewalk, Charlotte led the way to Quincy's

Finds' front door.

Inside, we were assailed by the strong scent of lavender and peppermint from the oil diffusers stationed every few feet or so. Quincy Novak was a big believer in aromatherapy, although my protesting lungs wondered if she'd overdone it a little.

"Hello? May I help you?" A trilling voice called from the back of the store, and seconds later, Quincy emerged from behind the pink curtain of her inventory room. "Coco! Charlotte! What a lovely surprise to see you girls." Even though she was only in her mid-forties, the woman's eccentric style and personality often made her seem more like a kindly grandmother.

I appraised her vivid ensemble, consisting of a bright purple muumuu, a pink headscarf, and white leather boots. She sure didn't shop in her own designer-label store.

"Hi, Quincy, so good to see you!" I kissed her on the cheek in greeting. "How have you been?"

"Well, I'd be doing much better if there wasn't a murderer on the loose." Quincy gave Charlotte a quick hug before turning her worried gaze back to me. "I'm trying to ward away all the bad vibes, if you can't tell." She motioned to the myriad of essential oil diffusers peppered around the store. "Lavender and peppermint were Stacy's favorite scents." Her eyes grew wet around the rims.

I put a comforting hand on her sagging shoulder. "I'm sorry. I didn't know you were close with her."

Quincy moved out from under my hand, straightening a display of bright floral-print shorts. "She was a good customer. She liked her dresses short and skimpy. I didn't really know the poor thing beyond that." She stared off for a moment before shaking her head, her graying hair springing from its clasp. "To think something so horrible could happen in our little town."

"It's all anyone could talk about at the coffee shop today." Charlotte began looking through a rack of cocktail dresses. "I can't believe the police don't know more."

"Lacie Burbank mentioned that Stacy used to come in here with her friends a lot," I stated nonchalantly, looking to Quincy for more information.

"As I said, she liked her dresses short and skimpy," Quincy retorted, becoming a little disgruntled, if I wasn't mistaken. "She liked to impress her 'flavors of the week.' Can you believe that's what she called her beaus?"

I hid a smirk at her matronly disdain. "The police said neither her parents nor her friends knew if she was dating someone."

"Ha! That girl was never *not* dating someone." Quincy scoffed. "I find it hard to believe her little squad didn't know who she was into this week."

"Who did she normally swing by the shop with?" I received a curious look from Charlotte. My slew of probing statements must have clued her in that I was fishing for something.

Quincy was silent a moment. "Let's see…" She tapped her chin. "Her usual crew was Rochelle Frost, Liz Clarke, and Claudia Harris."

The surnames Quincy mentioned sounded familiar, but I wasn't personally acquainted with any of the women. I definitely didn't remember going to school with them.

"Don't the Frosts have a home on Mill Row?" Charlotte's forehead wrinkled.

I snapped my fingers. "They bought the Kessler estate a few years back, didn't they? I didn't realize they had a daughter."

"She lives in Crestview, along with the other two girls," Quincy explained.

"That's why I've heard those names before. The Harrises and the Clarkes bought the Crestview Country Club back in twenty-ten." I crossed my arms in triumph, although my enthusiasm left Charlotte and Quincy exchanging odd looks with one another. Little did they know, this intel narrowed down the places I'd have to scope out in order to locate Stacy's inner circle. I'd be willing to bet my next paycheck from the Chens that I'd find these ladies wining and dining at the posh country club their parents owned.

"Anyway," I quickly changed the subject, "I'm looking for a last-minute dress to wear to the WMTG fundraiser tonight. Any recommendations, Quincy?" I threw a helpless look her way, knowing I needed to focus on the task at hand.

She pursed her lips. "Well, I just got this cute little number in this morning. With your hair and eyes, it would look splendid." Disappearing back into

106

her storeroom, she emerged moments later with a dress box. "I haven't even had time to hang it up."

I took the box from her outstretched hands and lifted the lid.

"Oh, Coco, you have to get it," Charlotte cooed from my side.

Even folded up, the dress looked amazing. The fabric was a shimmery teal satin that looked like mermaid scales in the sunlight streaming in from the storefront window. Pulling it out of the box and holding it against me, I watched with delight as the dress cascaded down, resting just above my knees. The sleeves were three-quarter length, which contrasted nicely with the plunging neckline down the front and back of the dress. "This is perfect. Hudson won't know what hit him."

"I grabbed your size. Go try it on!" Quincy hurried me into one of the mirrored dressing rooms, pulling the curtain closed so I could change in private.

The material felt like buttery heaven as I slipped it over my head, reveling in the feel of designer clothing.

"How do I look?" I stepped out, striking a model pose for Charlotte and Quincy.

Both clapped in approval, and Charlotte released a teasing wolf-whistle as I sashayed around the cozy store.

I stopped in front of one of the full-length mirrors, admiring how sensual my curves looked in the gown. "Jasper loaned me some fabulous jewelry that will go perfectly with this. A simple pair of nude pumps, and I'm good to go." I squealed with delight, racing back to the dressing room. It was only then that I spotted the price on the side of the box. "Four hundred dollars?" I balked at the numbers glaring back at me. Even though I made good money for myself, the thought of paying anything over fifty dollars for any article of clothing always left me feeling slightly ill. What could I say? I was a sucker for clearance-rack shopping. But sizing up my reflection once more, I decided I would ditch my bargain-savvy ways for tonight and treat myself.

"I'll take it," I declared a few moments later, emerging from the dressing room with the box tucked securely under my arm.

"You'll be the belle of the ball, Coco," Quincy gushed as she quickly rang me up, swiping my credit card with flair. "Don't forget to tag the store in pictures." She winked, knowing full well I could drum up business for her at the drop of an Instagram post.

Waving goodbye to Quincy, Charlotte and I left the store.

As soon as the door closed behind us, Charlotte rounded on me. "Let's head to the café for a pick-me-up. I want to know why you were asking all those questions about Stacy and her friends." She arched an eyebrow, clearly intrigued.

Glancing at my phone, I figured that with the successful shopping trip completed ahead of schedule, I had a few minutes to spare for my best girlfriend. "All right, I'm down for a coffee, but let's find someplace private. I can't have anyone overhearing us."

Charlotte's silvery gray eyes brightened. "It's usually pretty quiet in the café until three, or we can always talk out on the benches." She referred to the small beach-side park nestled right across the street from the strip. "Depending on how top-secret you need to be, and all."

Within ten minutes, we were situated on the most remote bench we could find, iced macchiatos in hand.

Charlotte took a long, savory sip from her cup. "Why all the sudden interest in Stacy? I thought you didn't know her very well?"

My face burned with guilt. "Well, I can't say my interest comes purely out of the goodness of my heart." I stared at my feet nestled in the sand. "You have to promise not to say anything to anyone about this…"

"On my honor," Charlotte pledged, holding up her right hand in a solemn vow.

Taking a deep breath, I took the plunge and relayed all the deets I'd gathered about our small-town murder.

To Charlotte's credit, she kept quiet until the very end, reserving judgment until she had all the facts. "When did you get the insane idea that you're the only one who can figure out what happened to Stacy?" Her eyes were wide with incredulity.

"When I realized that none of Stacy's friends are telling the truth about what they know. And while they may not want to share anything with the police, I'd be willing to bet they'd love to dish to a celebrity influencer." Determined pride crept into my voice.

"And her trusted sidekick," Charlotte pointed out.

I gave her a look. "What do you mean?"

"If you think you're going to go talk to those women without backup, you're sorely mistaken." Charlotte rolled her eyes. "I mean, has it crossed your mind that any one of them could be the murderer?"

Frowning, I had to concede that, no, it hadn't crossed my mind. "But, in all seriousness, I can't imagine why they would?"

"That's because you've been investigating this murder for all of, what, an hour?" Charlotte squeezed my free hand. "I'm not going to try to persuade you *not* to do this. I'll leave that to Hudson, but geez, Cokes, you've got to be smart about this. You can't just go rushing headfirst into danger."

I lowered my gaze with a sigh. "I guess you're right. I wasn't thinking about it like that." I silently cursed my naiveté.

"Of course, I'm right. Which is why I'll go with you to the country club, and we can scope out things together. Even better, let's have Jasper meet us there. It would be good to have someone who at least *looks* like he could protect us."

I chuckled at the idea of Jasper wrestling a gang of homicidal socialites. "Pick you up tomorrow night?"

Charlotte pulled out her smartphone from her hemp tote and checked her calendar. "I'll close the coffee shop at four so we can go up early and case the joint."

"Why, we're beginning to sound like real detectives." I grinned.

Charlotte looked skyward. "Heaven help us all."

Chapter Eleven

"What?"

I scowled at Jasper's flat response. "I said, I need you to meet Charlotte and me at the Crestview Country Club tomorrow night to help us weed out the deets from Stacy's friends about who she may have been dating," I repeated into the phone, tapping my fingernails impatiently on the kitchen countertop.

"Oh no, I heard you. I'm just questioning your sanity."

My eyes did gymnastics into the back of my head. "Spare me the dramatics. I really need your help with this."

"And how are you going to convince these women to actually talk with you?" Jasper countered.

I pictured his snarky expression as he, no doubt, lounged back in his posh desk chair.

"*Trending Topic* used to be all about blogging gossip—"

"The key words here are *used to*, sweetness. Those women aren't going to dish to a has-been."

I opened my mouth to protest, but Jasper's blasé monologue continued. "If you really want to get them to talk, you'll need to entice them with something that gives them instant celebrity status around here. You and your blog might be popular on the interwebs, but, around here, you don't have as much street cred as, say, *Divulge* does."

His comment about being a has-been still stung. Blogging might not be as popular as it once was, but I'd transitioned very successfully into the realm of social media influencers and *Trending Topic*'s enduring popularity proved it. However, as much as I wanted to refute Jasper's assault on my ego, I figured that in the minds of the Crestview elite, who frequented the country club, he was probably right. "What are you suggesting then?"

"That *I* interview them for...let me think...an exposé on Stacy and her tragic life?"

"We can't print any of this! Chief McInnis will lock me up if he finds out I told you and Charlotte what I know."

"It's called a *ruse*, Cokes. I'm not actually running an article about a little no-name shopkeeper."

Cringing at the blatant disrespect Jasper showed the dead, I had to admit his plan would likely get Stacy's socialite friends talking. "If that's the story, then what's my reason for being there?"

His smartphone speaker picked up what sounded like Jasper tapping his chin in thought. "How about I introduce you as my guest editor for the piece, since you knew and worked with Stacy?"

Gazing out at the sand dunes lining my view from the kitchen window, I nodded. "Sounds like a plan. I'll fill Charlotte in on the charade when I pick her up tomorrow."

"Girl, take a cab. We're heading to the bar after we finish playing Veronica Mars," Jasper ordered with a scoff, disconnecting the call before I could object.

I tossed my iPhone onto the coffee table as I threw myself across the couch, relishing a moment of downtime to bask in my accomplishments.

After I'd said goodbye to Charlotte at Brewed to Perfection, I'd returned home to outline my spring décor post for *Trending Topic*, design some promo materials for the Chens' "exclusive" online launch, and put the final touches on my PowerPoint for tomorrow's client seminar. Once I'd completed my Center of Attention tasks, I'd phoned Jasper to fill him in on our plan for questioning Stacy's friends. It had only taken a little begging on my part to get him to agree to join our sleuthing adventure.

Now, I had a few hours to spare before meeting Hudson at the Milton Botanical Gardens for the fundraising event. Grabbing my iPad, I took some time to check in on my blog, commenting and liking numerous fan posts here and there.

When I'd parted ways with LiveIt after the Facebook buyout, I developed a special forum where *Trending Topic* subscribers could connect with one another through my website, rather than interfacing my blog with some third-party application. Mostly, my followers shared their own recreations of outfits I'd blogged about or hairstyles I'd posted. While many showcased their successes, some pictures made me die laughing at the dreadful outcomes of their earnest attempts. Because failure *always* trends online, I expanded the scope of my #FlawlessFails hashtag beyond baking, and encouraged my fans to share their epic DIY disasters. The fun hashtag allowed us all to easily connect on social media and scope out the trouble other followers had gotten themselves into. The worst to date had been a poor girl who'd melted her hair off right before prom trying to replicate an updo I'd featured. Fortunately for *Trending Topic's* reputation, her post earned her fifteen minutes of fame when it was picked up from my site by both *People* and *Glamour* magazine. Rather than blame me and my beauty advice for causing her new pixie cut, my adoring fan gushed about how *Trending Topic* had changed her life "by forcing her to go a new direction" during her *People Live* interview. She was the epitome of the age-old adage: people would say anything to get their face in front of a camera. Okay, maybe not an age-old adage, but certainly a Hollywood one.

After several "Looks amazing!" and "Way to go!" comments, paired with thumbs-up emojis, I decided I'd appeased my fanbase enough with my afternoon online presence. I moved onto my Instagram and Twitter DMs, filtering out spam messages while narrowing down potential collab opportunities. I did my best to partner online with upstart beauty and fashion brands with body-positive messages, as well as businesses with diverse leadership, much like LiveIt had been. Only a few DMs passed my initial vetting, so I flagged their products for further research. Collaborations were all a part of the social media influencer game, but I tried not to overwhelm my followers with product sponsorship. Instead, I chose to promote companies and products that could really make a difference in the world with a bigger platform.

With my social media work done for the day, I tossed my iPad aside and grabbed my phone before shuffling into the bedroom to throw on my bathing suit. While the Delaware Atlantic was too chilly for a swim, I could relax on the Sunny Shores private beach and grab some sun before styling preparations for the evening began.

There was nothing like having a beach all to yourself, and today was no exception. The hot sun glittered across the sand, my feet warming with each step toward the water as my tote bag bounced across my back. The Sunny Shores condo association maintained a small shed near the dunes for residents to store chairs, umbrellas, and other beach necessities. Using my communal key, I undid the lock for the first time this year and dragged my lounging contraption closer to the water. Through the wonders of targeted online marketing, this high-end lounger had appeared on my Facebook feed one day, and I couldn't scroll past it. The specialty chair was complete with a detachable footrest, two cup holders, a magazine/iPad holder, and an expandable arm that served as a towel rack. Not to mention it was nearly weightless for lugging to the beach and super comfy.

Settling down into the chair, I skimmed through a handful of mystery novels I'd grabbed from my office bookcase. I hadn't brought them down to read for pleasure, but rather to analyze the questions the characters asked their suspects, and the covert behavior they exhibited when fishing for information. I took mental notes as I planned out how to approach Stacy's friends tomorrow evening. If women who ran bakeries and bookstores could solve crimes, why couldn't I?

I let the sun caress my SPF-laden skin for nearly two hours before packing up my things and heading back to the house. After reading about one character's glamorous adventures attending a New Year's Eve bash while stalking an art thief, I decided I would really go all out for tonight's fundraiser. Which, for me, meant attempting to do something with my hair.

As beautiful as the strawberry-champagne color was, my lifeless hair proved to be a nightmare when it came to styling, something a lot of my *Trending Topic* followers identified with. I'd been known to use cans of hairspray to maintain a single curl, and I prayed as I walked into the master bathroom that I had plenty on hand. The heroine in one of the novels I'd been skimming described her luscious curls in intricate detail, and it made me crave soft ringlets of my own. So, after a quick shower to wash the chalky residue of SPF off me, I went to work blow-drying and molding my hair into something wavy and chic.

My second can of Drybar hairspray sputtered its dying breaths after nearly an hour of work, and my grumpy reflection showcased the success I'd been having. I stayed away from blogging about curls for this very reason: I was bad at them. Give me a lattice braid or a tendril twist any day. "I give up." I threw my hands up in defeat. Mousse, gel, powders, curlers, and a curling iron had done nothing but put a little flip on the lower strands of my hair and given me a bump that looked like I'd been wearing it up in a ponytail all day. So much for emulating the stylish heroines of my afternoon research.

In the end, I opted for a sleek ponytail, focusing more on my makeup, since my skin was a more cooperative canvas than my hair. I fished out some turquoise eye shadow and paired it with gold eyeliner on my lower lids, along with sweeping midnight eyeliner on the uppers. The colors intensified my sea-foam green eyes to the max, and, after a few swipes of highlighter, bronzer, and mascara, I slipped into my new dress.

The shimmery fabric looked better than I'd remembered, and I practically had to sit on my hands to prevent myself from posting a picture on Instagram. I didn't want to risk Hudson seeing a photo of me online and ruining the surprise before I glided through the gates of the botanical gardens, where the event was being held.

My phone buzzed from my nightstand, and I dragged myself away from the floor-length mirror to scoop it up.

Just wrapped at the station. Heading over now if u want 2 meet me there early so we can scope out the food sitch.

I smiled at Hudson's text message. He knew me too well. A party was only ever worth attending if they had good food.

Sliding on my prized pair of L.K. Bennett nude pumps, which happened to be the very same ones that Catherine, the Duchess of Cambridge swore by, I grabbed the small gold clutch containing my life for the evening. Besides my cell phone, credit card, driver's license, and keys, I made sure my favorite Buxom lip gloss and Tarte mascara were on hand. Heading for the door, I did a quick check to make sure the lights were off before dashing out to Jolly. The botanical gardens were thirty minutes away, so I jacked up my favorite playlist and sang at operatic levels as I drove toward the waning sunset.

"Wow." Hudson's eyes darkened with desire as I zigzagged my way toward him through the gathering crowd. Handing me a champagne flute, he leaned in and kissed my cheek, lingering a moment like he wanted more. "You look amazing, babes. Why don't we just head home now?" He nuzzled my neck with a suggestive grin.

"You need to show me off a bit more before that." I gave him a coy smile that hinted he would get what he wanted by the end of the night. "I hardly know any of your new coworkers." I tore my gaze away from his, knowing I would be tempted to up-and-leave if he kept undressing me with his eyes like that.

Growling under his breath, Hudson placed a hand on the small of my back and guided me through the well-dressed crowd. Even though we'd arrived early for the food, it seemed everyone else had arrived early for the open bar. As we wove our way through folks dripping in head-to-toe designer wear, a vaguely familiar-looking brunette clacked her way toward us in four-inch heels.

"Hey, stranger," she cooed, locking gazes with Hudson before giving him a tight squeeze.

Envying her cascading ringlets of long, silky hair, it clicked into place how I knew her. Or at least, knew of her. Tori Beals was Hudson's co-anchor on the evening news, and I'd seen her perky reports several times.

As my boyfriend pulled away from Tori's embrace, her fingertips lingered on his shoulder blades a bit too long to be considered appropriate, and a barb of jealousy vaulted from my heart to my head. With my left hand, I reached for Hudson's arm and tugged him to my side, while simultaneously stepping forward with my right hand outstretched in greeting. "Hi, there.

I'm Coco Cline, Hudson's girlfriend."

As if seeing me for the first time, Tori's bubbly expression soured. She took my hand reluctantly, her grasp as cold as her hazel-eyed stare. "Oh, hey. Hudson's mentioned you once or twice."

My prepared reply of "It's so nice to meet you" died in my throat.

"I assume you know who I am. Hudson and I seem to be everywhere on TV these days." Tori threaded her slender, well-toned arm through Hudson's, and she let out a tittering giggle that oozed with condescension.

I could have told her that hardly anyone born after 1980 watched the news on TV anymore, but I didn't want to insult Hudson.

He wiggled away from Tori's grip once more and planted himself at my side. Whether or not my boyfriend sensed the chill coating the air around us, I couldn't tell. "Tori started with the evening news team a few months before I did. She was with a Baltimore morning show before that."

I nodded with feigned interest. Tori's flirtatious attitude hadn't gained her any brownie points with me, and I was more than ready to move past her.

"I could have stayed in Baltimore for a few more years and made the evening anchor team there," Tori twirled a silky ringlet around her finger, dragging the conversation on, "but I wanted to live near a sandy beach. See, I grew up in California." She flashed a dazzling smile at Hudson, and he shifted on his feet beside me. "Living in the city, I missed the sand and the surf. When I heard about the WMTG position, I jumped at the chance to relocate."

I tried to summon a smile. "How nice."

"I'm so glad I did. The critics have been raving how Hudson and I have such great on-air chemistry," she gushed. "Anyway, I got this beautiful place on the water over in Crestview. I keep telling Hudson he needs to move there. There's so much more going on there than in...where did you say you lived again, Hud?"

I wanted to vomit at her choice of nickname, and judging by the look on his face, so did Hudson.

"Coco and I live in Central Shores," he responded tersely.

"Oh, I thought you mentioned this morning that you had an apartment in

Milton?" Her expression was the picture of innocence.

And I thought you couldn't remember where he lived? Steam curled from my ears. Was this woman really trying to drive a wedge between Hudson and me at this party? Did she think Hudson kept his apartment a secret from me, and its revelation would cause a scene? Her desperation almost made me feel sorry for her.

"I keep the apartment in case I need a place to crash after a late night's work." Hudson's explanation was old news to me by now.

Tori laughed, apparently unfazed by his frosty response. "Oh, I'm sure we'll have plenty of late nights coming our way."

Me smacking her across the face would have been in the realm of possibility if Hudson hadn't reached for my hand and held me close to his side. "Enjoy the party, Tori." While he managed a polite smile, it didn't reach his brown eyes.

Imagining giant pustules erupting all over her face, I noticed the hopeful light extinguish in Tori's doe eyes. "Okay, I'll see you around, Hud." She waved and bounced away without a word of goodbye to me.

"Well," I cleared my throat, "if *that* isn't throwing down the gauntlet, I don't know what is."

Hudson whirled me around to face him, planting his hands on both my shoulders. "What the hell was that?"

At first, I thought he was chastising *me* for *my* behavior, but his next words silenced my offended remarks.

"Like, seriously, what the hell? I'm sorry, babes. I don't know what just happened. Tori's never, *ever*, been like that before."

"Oh, that performance wasn't for your benefit. It was for me." I scowled. "I bet she's the sweet, girl-next-door type when you two are alone."

Hudson ran a hand through his dark hair. "I can't believe this. She practically threw herself at me."

"Well, you certainly didn't say anything to discourage her," I muttered.

"What do you mean? I told her you and I lived together!" Hudson's defensive words took on a hardening tone. "I ended the conversation when she crossed the line."

"And you think she understood those cues? Geez, even I had a hard time figuring out what you were thinking, '*Hud*.'" All right, I knew him well enough to recognize he'd been uncomfortable with her actions, but my possessive anger fueled the white lie.

He flinched at the corny nickname. "Look, I know that was awkward, but I promise you it's the first time she's ever behaved that way. She's very professional when we're taping together. Maybe she's had a bit too much to drink already."

I didn't buy into his reasoning for a second, but Hudson was visibly devastated by the encounter, so it was hard to stay mad at him. Tori, on the other hand, had played the scene with expert calculation. The fact that she'd thrown Hudson's apartment into the mix proved it. No doubt, she had planned on it being a source of tension between the two of us, even if Hudson hadn't been keeping it a secret from me. It could be seen as a weakness in our relationship that less scrupulous women, such as Tori, could try to exploit. A relative stranger pointing out my boyfriend's hesitation to fully commit certainly stung. She might have been forced to retreat tonight, but I wasn't naive enough to think she'd backed off for good. I vowed to keep my eye on her.

Chapter Twelve

"You don't need to worry." As if sensing the turmoil churning in my head, Hudson took my hands and pressed them each to his lips. The tender kisses melted my heart. "You're the only one for me, babes."

"Can you blame me for being jealous?" I nudged his arm. "Come on. If a guy spoke to me like that, how would you feel?"

A storm brewed in his dark eyes. "I would have throttled the dude to the ground." He circled his arms around me and pulled me up against his chest. "I'm sorry our evening started off like this."

"It's going to take some time to get used to this new effect you have on women."

Hudson had always been an attractive guy, but the aura of star power around him seemed to intensify his magnetic attraction. I let loose a dramatic sigh, tossing an arm across my forehead. "Oh, woe is me."

He shut me up with a steamy kiss, and for a moment, I forgot we were in the middle of a bustling party.

"All better?" he asked as he pulled away.

Breathlessly, I gave him a light peck on the cheek. "All better." And for the most part, I was telling the truth. Tori's jabs still looped around my brain, but I buried my insecurities and focused on the evening ahead.

Hudson's shoulders relaxed, and the strain faded from his expression. "Millie wanted me to make sure she saw you this evening, so why don't we get that over with," he said rather laboriously, referring to his producer and boss, Millicent Stabler.

I grinned with anticipation. I absolutely adored Millie. Contrary to what her nickname might suggest, she was assertive and domineering and rarely cracked a smile, but for some reason, she loved me. When Hudson had first introduced me to her nearly three years ago when he was just a junior sportscaster, I'd been scared straight to meet her after all the horrible stories he'd brought home from the station. But, to my surprise and Hudson's relief, Millie was a huge fan of *Trending Topic,* and thus, we got on splendidly. I often ribbed Hudson that his meteoric rise to success at the station was all due to Millie having a girl crush on me, knowing full well Hudson was a leading anchor because he was truly talented.

"Coco! My God, you are a vision!" Millie's throaty voice went to an octave I didn't know she was capable of reaching as we glided toward her.

I wrapped my arms around her imposing frame, greeting her warmly. One thing Millie loved about *Trending Topic* was my emphasis on all body types in fashion posts. Standing over six feet tall, Millie had told me she'd spent her whole life wondering what would best suit her athletically toned, yet broad figure, and my website had helped her see the light. "Millie, it's been ages since I've seen you. You cut your hair!" I fawned over her sleek black bob, normally used to seeing her raven hair wrapped in a tight bun at the peak of her head.

Millie flipped her locks with a girlish giggle. "I got it on a whim. Do you like?"

I nodded, rarely seeing the drastic look worn so well off the runway.

"I kid you not, the words 'What would Coco do?' went through my mind when my stylist asked what I wanted."

Before I could thank her for her unnecessary flattery, Millie bulldozed onward. "Darling, you must schedule an interview with us soon. It's been *ages* since you did the news circuit. People want to know what Coco Cline has been up to. I see the chatter on your blog. You need to come out of hiding and give the world what it wants."

I giggled. "I've hardly been hiding, Mil."

"I know. It's just…well, you were so confident and gorgeous when Hoda and Savannah were peppering you with questions. Few people can be at such ease on live TV. You would have made for a lovely TV personality…" Millie released a heavy sigh, as if reflecting on a huge loss.

My cheeks burned under my bronzer as Hudson chuckled at his boss's antics. "Oh, goodness. You're making me blush." I patted her arm. "Maybe sometime down the road, but I'm really loving the challenge of my consulting business right now." *Challenge* was certainly one word for what I was dealing with at the moment.

Her sharp features dissolved into a mask of concern. "Such dreadful news coming out of Central Shores about that poor dead girl. Hudson tells me you worked with her." Millie dove right into what I assumed would be a hot topic for the night.

"Yes. I'm doing some PR consulting for the business she works…worked… at."

Hudson's arm wrapped around me, lending me his silent support.

"Stacy's death has been a complete shock, but I'm managing as well as can be." My smile felt forced. I had to be careful and not let slip to Millie that I had been the one to find Stacy's body, or she'd drag me in front of the cameras bound in a straitjacket if she had to.

"How tragic." Millie crossed her arms, leaning her sharp body closer. "But I will say it's doing wonders for our ratings. We had a forty percent boost in viewership when we ran the story last night." Ever the businesswoman, she almost looked happy, shooting Hudson a conspiratorial wink.

I cringed at her media mogul attitude. "Something this awful hasn't happened so close to home in a long time, that's for sure."

"Our contacts at the police department have been less than forthcoming." Millie frowned. "It almost sounds as if they have nothing to go on. Certainly, it makes me wonder how competent they are. It's not like there's a criminal mastermind living in Central Shores who's planned the perfect crime."

"I'm sure the police are doing their best." I sent a sidelong glance to Hudson, a bit wary of continuing this conversation. If word got around that I was overheard badmouthing Chief McInnis and his team, who knew when the police would decide to release the Chens' store?

"Well, be that as it may, I need to figure out a way to keep this story going.

If I can keep WMTG at the top through network news awards season..."
Millie's starry-eyed gaze trailed away with her voice. "Oh, there are the
Wellingtons. I need to thank them for their generous donation." With a
quick air kiss, she darted into the crowd.

I threw a troubled look Hudson's way. "What did she mean by needing to
figure out a way to keep this story going?"

Hudson dug his hands into his pockets, suddenly looking uncomfortable
with my undivided attention. "Well, we *did* have a meeting today with the
full team to discuss coverage of this nightmare. Millie wants us to run hard
with it since stuff like this is ratings gold."

"Stuff like *this*? A young woman is dead, Hudson. A young woman I
knew." I folded my arms. "What does running hard with it entail, exactly?"
My eyes narrowed dangerously, practically smelling the nervousness
radiating from my boyfriend.

"Millie wants us to railroad the Chens. Claim that their poor security for
their unopened store led to Stacy's death. Something along the lines of..."
Hudson paused, miming a punchy headline, "Business Owners Fail to Keep
Employee Safe."

A snort at the absurdity of the story escaped me, followed by a burst of
rage. "Oh, please. Dragging the Chens and their store down will hardly
maintain ratings. All it will do is dampen their chances for success when
Once Used, Twice Buy actually opens."

Hudson eyed me warily. "Millie is pretty determined to pursue it."

I looked across the room in search of the networking producer. "Maybe
she just needs a better idea to fall into her lap. One that keeps my clients'
character untarnished through this whole debacle." I needed to sell Millie
on a tasteful, in-depth tribute piece about a beautiful young woman gone
too soon.

Hudson grinned at me, his eyes twinkling. "Well, now's your chance to
make a pitch for that segment you floated by me yesterday." He motioned to
Millie's re-approaching figure through the swelling crowd.

Seizing my chance, I reached out to touch her pointy elbow, soliciting her
attention. "Millie, I mentioned I've been working directly with Sean and

Olivia Chen, right? The owners of Once Used, Twice Buy?"

"The place where the dead girl was found? What about them?" Millie's eye twitched with trained suspicion.

"Wouldn't your viewers love a behind-the-scenes look at Stacy Lockner's life before it was so cruelly cut short?" I dangled the proverbial carrot in front of Millie. "I'm sure my clients would be more than willing to chat about their time working alongside Stacy and the bright future she had ahead of her. Why, you could even include interviews featuring Stacy's family and friends, highlighting for viewers what a charming young woman she was and what a devastating loss her death is to the Central Shores community. And of course, you could end the segment by rallying the public to assist the police in any way they can? Something so personal and poignant would be ratings gold."

In less than five minutes, I had Millie agreeing to an exclusive interview with Sean and Olivia for a Stacy Lockner tribute piece, scheduled to air Sunday night. Millie's assistant would call me later with the details to set up a time to speak with the Chens.

"It's a little scary how you can take something as gruesome as murder and turn it into a glorified media opportunity." Hudson gave a cautious chuckle as Millie triumphantly floated away to gush about her upcoming news segment.

I failed to resist a major eye roll. "If *that* isn't the pot calling the kettle black."

Chapter Thirteen

Laughing with more gusto, Hudson tossed back the rest of his drink and went in search of a refill, leaving me alone in the middle of a room full of strangers. I searched the crowd, keeping an eye out for Tori Beals and her scene-stealing ringlets. I wouldn't put it past her to ambush Hudson once he was alone. Thankfully, I spotted her cozying up to a group of slick-haired guys in matching gray suits, looking very much at home.

A little ashamed by the blatant relief washing over me, I turned my focus back to Hudson's handsome figure. I didn't want to be one of those women who second-guessed the strength of their relationship. We had been together for four years. I trusted him. But between the flirty waitresses at The Pearl and Tori, well…I struggled somewhat to maintain my confidence.

From across the room, Hudson and I locked gazes with one another, and those nagging doubts drifted away. He loved me. That much was clear. I swelled with pride as he was met with handshakes and pats on the back along his route to the bar. I was happy to give him the chance to shine amongst his coworkers without me tagging along as the third wheel to every conversation. I didn't mind being left to my own devices. That's what cell phones and Instagram Reels were made for.

"Coco!"

Hearing my name called by a familiar, cringe-inducing voice, I suddenly wished I'd followed my boyfriend.

"Oh my! You look stunning." Amanda Highgrove arrived at the small table I'd laid claim to. "Love that dress."

I chided myself for the amount of time it took for me to make eye contact. Even in the face of adversity, I wasn't normally this rude. There was just something about Amanda that made the phrase "treat others the way you want to be treated" fly out the window.

"Amanda," I managed with a strained smile. "You look nice as well."

In fact, she looked more than nice. Wearing a strapless, pearl-encrusted pink gown with a slit running nearly the full length of her toned legs, she looked like a million bucks. Which was probably what her ensemble cost.

Forcing myself to stand, we exchanged air-kisses before she took a seat at the small table. "Arthur is on his way over with a platter of brie and apples. If I recall, that's one of your favorite party snacks, right?"

Amazed and somewhat touched that she remembered such a mundane detail about me, I bobbed my head. Hudson and I had been invited to the Highgrove-Bushman holiday party by Arthur last Christmas, and the only enjoyment I'd found at the hoity-toity gathering was the catered food.

Amanda beamed and, may God strike me now, it seemed genuine. "I keep meaning to try some of those recipes you posted last month. Especially the sparkling wine pear-infused sangria."

"Be careful with that one," I said, allowing myself to relax a little in her overbearing company. "It's too easy to drink the whole pitcher by yourself."

"You came up with such a cute name. 'Party Pear Sangria.' We'll have you and Hudson over once we open the pool for the season. Then, we can try the drink out in style." Amanda's giggle was friendly. "Which should be any day now. I can't believe how hot it's gotten out already. Global warming, am I right? This might be the first year we've opened the pool in April."

"Yeah, I got some color at the beach today." I held out my arm for her to examine. "The sun was fierce." Was I really chatting about the weather with Amanda Highgrove?

Before she could reply, our attention was diverted to her approaching husband, and I shook my head at the whole scene. If someone in high school had told me one day Amanda would be my saving grace from loneliness at a party, I would have called an institution to come collect them.

"Is this where the most glamorous girls in the room are sitting?" Arthur announced his arrival by kissing Amanda on the cheek and placing a small platter of brie, crostini, and apples in front of me.

"Considering Coco is the only woman here who can remotely hold a candle to me, I figured it would be best for us to be on display together," Amanda said with teasing warmth.

I shuddered. Had she had a lobotomy and erased "Gourdy Cordy" from her memory? This was getting weird.

Pushing aside flashbacks of high school torture, I turned to Arthur, activating my Nancy Drew prowess to do some digging. "Amanda mentioned earlier you captured some video of the Boardwalk yesterday. Have the police given you your drone back yet?"

Shaking his head, he took a long sip from his crystal tumbler. "I got a call just as we were leaving that I can pick up Bessie tomorrow morning. Apparently, they didn't find anything of use on her."

I smiled at his term of endearment for his piece of tech, but inwardly, my hopes sank. "That's too bad."

Amanda took Arthur's hand and stroked it gently. "I can't believe there's a killer on the loose in Central Shores and the police have practically nothing to go on. How does something like that happen right under their noses without them having a clue?" Her old, critical self started to ooze through her gritted teeth.

"The police aren't the only ones who don't seem to know anything," I ventured lightly, going off a budding hunch. "I heard Stacy's friends weren't able to shed any light on her life to further the investigation."

Amanda snorted, her perfectly sloped nose scrunching uncharacteristically. "As if. Those girls are so tight-knit, they practically share a brain."

Bingo. "Do you know them?"

Examining her nails, Amanda sighed. "Only peripherally. We're all executive members at the Crestview Country Club. I usually run into them at the VIP spa. Just because they're a few years younger than me, they think they're so hot and all that." I was surprised by the veiled insecurity trembling in her throat. "Not that I want to be a part of their stupid little squad, anyway."

I bit into an apple slice smothered with gooey cheese. If Stacy's friends were so close, why weren't they being more helpful in finding her killer? Didn't they want justice for their friend?

"A few businesses along the Boardwalk have reached out to me requesting that I review their security setups." Arthur's strong brow furrowed as he changed the direction of the subject. "There's not a lot of confidence right now that our police department will find the killer before they strike again."

Strike again? I hadn't even contemplated the chance of more attacks until now.

"The Chamber of Commerce has even asked Arthur to appraise the security measures in place for the annual ball." Amanda beamed with pride.

With everything else going on, the Chamber of Commerce Gala had totally slipped my mind, which was saying something since I was one of the honorees this year. The phone call had come two weeks ago telling me that I'd won the Influential Business award. Another event which I had yet to buy an outfit for.

I scooted my chair closer to the elegant couple. "Do people really think there's a serial killer on the loose?"

Amanda flashed me a spooked look. "Nobody knows what to think at this point. Barely any details about Stacy's death have been released. We don't even know who found her. God, they must be traumatized."

I nodded my agreement, trying not to look too guilty.

She waved the topic aside. "You must be relieved to hear that Arthur is consulting the Chamber of Commerce in preparation for the gala. Daddy told me you're one of this year's award recipients."

I smirked at the cringe-y way she said "Daddy." Her father, Thurston Highgrove, was the president of the Board of Directors for the Chamber, a position widely considered to be "just a hobby" of his in his retirement. "Well, to be honest, I wasn't all that worried to begin with."

Amanda sighed, shooting an expectant look at her husband. "I told you, Artie. Coco has always been fearless, even in high school. I've always admired her confidence so much."

My mouth dropped open before I could catch myself. There were a million things I wanted to say to her in that moment, all bubbling down to her having a funny way of showing it, but Arthur patted his wife fondly on the arm.

"I've heard the stories, my dear. Coco Cline is indeed a force to be reckoned with." He sent a wink in my direction, leaving me completely baffled by this conversation.

"I asked Daddy to make sure that you and Hudson are seated at our table at the gala." The way she said it, you would have thought it was the highest honor in the world.

I deflated in my seat. I had been hoping to share a table with Lacie, Charlotte, and the Chens. "How nice of you," I managed through gritted teeth.

Amanda must have mistaken my grimace as a genuine smile. "It will be such fun."

Arthur's face brightened as Hudson appeared at my side. "Looking good, Boss." He raised his tumbler in Hudson's direction.

With a tender squeeze of my hand, Hudson sat down and clinked glasses with his buddy. "Hey, man, glad you made it. My producer has been itching to meet you all night. She wants a story at some point about your rise to greatness in the technology world." With an exaggerated sigh, he protectively draped an arm around my shoulders. "As a consolation prize, of course. Coco won't give Millie the scoop she *really* wants."

Arthur chuckled. "That's Millie talking to the Wellingtons, right?" He pointed across the room to a stylish young couple. "We play tennis with them at the club. Honey, why don't we go say hello to Diane and Philip and introduce ourselves to Hudson's boss?"

Amanda pouted momentarily—I guess she'd really been enjoying my company—before pushing back her chair and giving Hudson and me a charming wave. "We'll see you two later." She linked arms with her husband and strode over to where Millie was engaged in animated conversation.

I mouthed a silent "Thank you," to Hudson, taking a long sip of the drink he'd brought back for me.

He gave me an amused frown. "She's not really that bad, is she? Every time we're together, Amanda seems quite besotted with you."

I shook my head in wonder. "It's as if she's had a brain transplant or something. How can she not remember how cruel she was to me in high school?"

Hudson kissed my hand. "Well, she's gone for now, so let's enjoy some alone time while we can." He winked. "Tell me about your day."

I grimaced, knowing he wasn't going to be happy with my detective exploits.

His eyebrows drew together. "Uh oh. That can't be good."

Keeping my tone low, I launched into a detailed rundown of the day's events. "So, Jasper, Charlotte, and I are driving up to the Crestview Country Club tomorrow to see if we can ferret out any information from Stacy's friends that the police couldn't."

To his credit, Hudson sat in silence for a moment, probably processing everything I'd just told him, from my meeting with the Chens to the rivalry between the Central Shores Police and the Sussex County Crime Lab. "Let me get this straight. You think Stacy's friends would rather let her murderer go free than report what they know to the police?"

I flinched under his skeptical stare. "Well, yeah, I guess."

He ran a hand through his dark hair, only to begin rapping his knuckles anxiously on the table. "May I remind you that you have a communications degree, not one in criminal justice? What are you going to do if you find out that her friends have been lying? Tell the police?"

I decided it was best not to make direct eye contact. "Of course I'll tell them...eventually." My words came rushing out as I thwarted Hudson's retort. "I'll tell them when I have all the facts."

"All the facts? You can't possibly think it's a good idea to keep investigating this on your own if you learn something valuable." Hudson looked at me like I'd lost all sanity.

"I won't be on my own." I stuck my chin out. "Charlotte and Jasper have agreed to help me."

Hudson rubbed at his temples. "I know you want to save the Chens' business, but this is a bit over the top, even for you, Coco."

"Well, I'm worried that if I only give the police half the picture, Chief

129

McInnis and his team will mess things up and the crime lab will run them out of town. Good people work at the station. They need those jobs!" I ended my protest on a confident note.

Hudson's eyes narrowed, examining every inch of my innocent expression. "I'm sure your concern for town employment opportunities is the *real* reason behind all this." His words dripped with sarcasm. "I just don't want the love of my life getting herself into trouble fulfilling a weird childhood fantasy about being Nancy Drew or something."

My heart melted a little at his uncharacteristic affirmation of affection. Hudson wasn't one to be verbose with his feelings. "I'm not going to get into any trouble, I promise." I took his hand. "All I'm doing is asking Stacy's friends a few questions, that's it. It probably won't lead to anything. And like I said, Jasper and Charlotte will be there to back me up."

"Well, I'm going with you, too. When you three are together, all common sense gets tossed out the window."

"Aw…" I lightly pinched Hudson's cheek. "You just want the chance to live out a deep-seated Hardy Boys fantasy, don't you? Which one was it, Frank or Joe?"

He batted my hand away but couldn't suppress a grin at my silliness. "I'm more of an Encyclopedia Brown, I'll have you know." He looked around the room. "Shall we go on food patrol?"

Ten minutes later, we returned to our table with plates piled high with various delicacies. Hudson's wrist struggled to balance a heaping dish of shrimp, olives, and lobster claws, while I used two hands to carry pulled pork and riblets. For round two, I had my eye on the truffle mac 'n' cheese station.

Over the next three hours or so, we ate our way through the fundraiser, mingling with big wigs from the station along the way. Our tense encounter with Tori long forgotten, I relaxed and enjoyed meeting the interesting, affluent people that supported WMTG. Hudson even introduced me to the president of the network, who, to my surprise, was also a fan of *Trending Topic*, his favorite part being the movie reviews I occasionally wrote.

"I'd love to add a critic's review segment to our Friday morning show…

at some point," Mr. Lane drawled. "If you would consider it, Ms. Cline, I'd love to have you on the panel. It would bring the millennial and Gen Z crowd we quite desperately need to attract."

It wasn't every day I was offered my own local programming gig, and I responded in kind. "What a flattering opportunity, sir. I'd love to speak with you more about it in the near future." Center of Attention was still too much in its infancy right now, but I wasn't opposed to the idea of being a TV personality at *some* point in my life.

"Imagine you, a television host." Hudson gave an exaggerated eye roll as we walked toward the parking lot after finally saying our goodbyes to everyone. "The size of your head is never going to stop growing, is it?"

I pushed his arm away gently, giving him a feigned scowl. "I'm a star on the rise. You knew that when you met me, so don't pretend you didn't know what you were getting yourself into."

"That I did." He sealed his confession with a deep kiss. "Meet you back home?"

I reached for Jolly's door, giving him my best "come hither" look. "I'll be waiting." I giggled at the power of my feminine allure as I watched him race between cars toward his Beamer.

Chapter Fourteen

The next morning, the sound of my alarm forced my eyes open with a snap. Despite not falling asleep until after two a.m., adrenaline surged through my veins, propelling me into the shower. My nerves for my big Facebook marketing seminar this afternoon churned with fierce determination. I had a habit of dwelling on things, so I planned to keep myself preoccupied until one in the hopes of preventing any needless obsessing. As soon as the coffee was poured, I began to prep for my upcoming décor blog post in my office. I took several rustic wooden crates purchased from HomeGoods and repurposed them into a towering, chic bookcase. Adding fake plants and picture frames to the shelves to serve as bright accents, I snapped some photos to accompany the online feature.

Hudson slept soundly throughout my early morning routine. At ten, he emerged, sleepy-eyed, from the bedroom, just as I was polishing my final draft for tomorrow's *Trending Topic* post.

"Good morning, sunshine," I said with too much enthusiasm for his sleep-addled brain.

He grumbled a greeting in return, punching the Keurig until it began to spout his brew of choice. We didn't speak as he scrolled through his phone, the coffee dripping to completion.

"Damn it, Millie wants me in the studio to help with this tribute segment for Stacy." Hudson gave me a pointed look. "Apparently, her parents can only come by this afternoon for an interview. Maybe I can meet you in Crestview later?" he asked after downing a big gulp of caffeine.

"That's fine, babe. Your being there wasn't a part of *my* plan to begin with."

I stuck my tongue out at him like the little brat I could be.

"Just promise me you'll be careful." Hudson's eyes failed to crinkle with any trace of amusement.

I popped up from my seat at the counter and kissed him on the cheek. "I promise."

"So, how about I take you out for an early lunch before your big presentation?" He turned me around so he could massage my shoulders. "To help loosen you up before the big show?"

I glanced nervously at the clock over my six-range oven. "I need to be back here by twelve-thirty..."

It was Hudson's turn to kiss me reassuringly. "I'll shower, and we'll be at Pock Knock by eleven. Plenty of time to enjoy each other's company."

My stomach rumbled at the prospect of eating at Pock Knock. Stationed on the northern outskirts of town a little way up the coast, the eatery was well-known for having the best fried chicken in the greater Delaware area. It also happened to be one of my favorite places to eat, although, for the sake of my waistline, I tried to limit my visits to once a month. "Then get your butt moving!" I squealed, playfully smacking his booty into action.

I was reviewing my seminar notes for what felt like the billionth time when Hudson emerged from the bedroom wearing jeans and a polo, his hair still glistening from the shower.

"Ready?" His grin was teasing as he wrenched the notecards out of my white-knuckled grip. He kissed me lightly on the forehead. "You're going to knock this out of the park," he whispered supportively.

We were seated in our favorite corner booth, side-by-side, thirteen minutes later, skimming Pock Knock's menu to put on the appearance that we both didn't already know what we wanted. Without fail, I always ordered the honey mustard chicken tender basket, while Hudson opted for fried shrimp and grits. Our college-age waitress, who must have been new since we didn't recognize her, took our order efficiently and left us to sip on our soft drinks.

"Millie sent me the questions she wants to ask the Lockners this afternoon." Hudson pulled out his phone, eyeing me to see if my interest was piqued.

Which, of course, it was. "And?"

He scrolled through the email, a grimace marring his handsome face. "They are totally engineered to make the Lockners fall apart on screen. This business is so slimy sometimes."

"Sometimes?"

He threw his wadded straw wrapper at my forehead. "At least it looks like we're going to end the segment by asking for information about Stacy's life and for donations toward a scholarship in her name."

I stirred my Diet Pepsi in thought. "Do you think anyone will call in with a credible tip?"

"Maybe if we were offering a reward, but Millie doesn't want to expense that *and* a scholarship donation."

I could tell from the darkness in his eyes that Hudson wasn't pleased with the decisions made by the station. Sometimes his jaded attitude made me wonder if his kind and noble heart was really cut out for the cruel and often vile world of network journalism. Not that I would ever try and steer him away from what he considered to be his dream job. Rubbing his arm, I searched for a different topic. "So, the Chamber of Commerce gala is next week."

He chuckled. "I've only had your invite on my calendar since Thurston Highgrove made the call about your award." He put his arm around me, a perk of sitting on the same side of the vinyl booth. "I'm so proud of you, you know that? You've been hustling nonstop ever since you've moved back here, building your business from the ground up. You deserve the recognition for what you've done with CoA, and I can't wait to celebrate that with you. I've made sure I'm off Wednesday night. I just need to get my suit dry cleaned."

Beaming at his warm praise, I happily dug into my crunchy chicken tenders as soon as our waitress delivered the goods. "Best idea you've ever had," I said through a mouthful of juicy meat and sauce.

Hudson nodded agreement, his mouth preoccupied with a spoonful of cheesy grits. "I've been told I'm a genius."

"By anyone other than your mother?" I knew just how high the pedestal was that Irene Caruthers kept her son on.

Hudson's lack of reply told me what I needed to know. I wasn't surprised. Given how successful Drs. Irene and Winston Caruthers were, they expected the same greatness from their offspring. I got along well with my almost in-laws, mostly because I'd had a relationship with them before ever meeting their son...or knowing he existed. Irene was the first black woman to head a department at Bayside University. I'd taken several of her anthropology courses and long admired her. I'd like to think I'd earn her respect by achieving A's in her notoriously tough classes. Irene had met her husband of thirty-seven years while Winston had been traveling the world after graduating from King's College London. A descendent of founding father John Dickinson, Winston had been visiting the man's historic Dover home and museum the same day Irene had. It was love at first sight, with Winston eventually upending his life in London to move to the states. He, too, now taught at Bayside University. Dr. W was one of the most popular professors in the history department.

Fifteen minutes later, Hudson and I were back in his black Beamer, him driving toward home while I watched the clock nervously. I'd make it with plenty of time to spare for the seminar, but my anxiety over being on time won out over common sense, nonetheless.

"Good luck, babes." Hudson kissed my cheek after he'd pulled the car up in front of the condo. "I'm heading into the station to prep for my interview with the Lockners. I'll text you when I'm on my way over to Crestview later tonight."

"See if you can get anything out of Stacy's parents that might help me clear the Chens while you're at it, please." I chirped with all the innocence I could muster, hopping out and slamming the door before he could protest. In a town as small as Central Shores, it seemed impossible that parents wouldn't know what their child was up to, even if they were living a few towns up the coast.

Hurrying inside and putting my mind to the task at hand, I did a quick touch-up of my hair and makeup before firing up my iMac and making sure my webcam was all set up. I'd placed a large professional photo panel behind the chair in my office, obscuring the bookcase and picture frames behind me, so that my clients wouldn't be distracted by the vivid décor during the presentation. An ornamental partition set my computer desk apart from the small amateur studio I had cobbled together in the opposite corner, where I filmed any *Trending Topic* video content.

Checking the clock, I discovered I had twenty minutes until showtime, so I dashed to the kitchen and flicked on the electric kettle. I'd read that pausing to drink during a presentation was a good way to buy yourself some time if you became flustered or needed to construct the answer to a question. As much as I tried to remind myself that public speaking was one of my favorite things to do, I was always a cluster of nerves until I opened my mouth.

With a white tea-filled mug in hand, I settled down in front of my computer and opened Zoom, my web conferencing software of choice. I watched with churning giddiness as names began to pop up in the Attendees section, smiling as I saw the familiar ones. I'd encouraged my clients to share their invite with colleagues and friends, as referrals were a good way to drum up business for CoA. Pleased to see a lot of unfamiliar names, I prayed my webinar proved useful and secured some new engagements. My existing clients had definitely taken advantage of the twenty percent discount I'd offered for referring this seminar to someone in their network, as I had a good-sized audience.

At one o'clock on the dot, I turned on my webcam, a big smile plastered on my face as it filled my computer screen. Welcoming the seventy-three attendees, I displayed my PowerPoint and launched into the presentation on Facebook trends and developing the perfect ad to boost.

An hour and a half later, I logged off of the webinar, my white tea untouched. I took a greedy sip—my throat was parched from the marathon of talking—and relaxed in my chair. "That could not have gone any better," I praised myself aloud, delighted to see raving responses from the post-seminar survey Zoom allowed me to send out to garner feedback. Along with rating the helpfulness of the content and the presenter's ability to answer questions, I'd also configured the online survey to request topic ideas for future sessions. From the looks of it, folks wanted to better understand the Twitter Analytics platform and how to best promote their tweets. That I could do in my sleep. With the renowned LiveIt acquisition and *Trending Topic*'s popularity, I had amassed over nine hundred thousand Twitter followers on my personal profile. I was *quite* familiar with the advertising nuances of the platform. I flipped through the computer calendar synced to my iPhone and added an event placeholder to host another Zoom in four weeks.

Deciding to reward my stellar performance, I shut down my iMac and muted notifications on all my work-related accounts for the day. I was going to kick the weekend off a bit early. Heading to my closet to find a change of clothes suitable for the high-end country club, I grinned as I heard Hudson's signature video-game-themed text tone beeping from my pocket.

How'd it go?????

His overuse of question marks had me laughing. Texting him a quick play-by-play, I signed off with a few kiss emojis before diving into my closet. While the Crestview Country Club wasn't as trendy as Cyprus in Cherry Springs, it still required a cocktail attire dress code in the evening. Feeling fierce from my kick-butt webinar, I slipped into a slinky silver dress with a hem that landed just above my knees. Since it was sleeveless, I grabbed a black, three-quarter-length jacket and boot socks. I'd rock my knee-high leather boots this evening to keep my legs somewhat covered in case it got chilly.

I'd told Charlotte I would swing by Brewed to Perfection to pick her up at four, so I decided some retail therapy was in order to pass the time. While I took pride in my patronage of the strip's boutique shops, sometimes a girl just needed to hit up the T.J. Maxx a few towns over for a good, old-fashioned shopping spree.

At four, I beeped Jolly's shrill little horn, straining to see if Charlotte was making moves to vacate the counter of Brewed to Perfection. Within moments, she glided out the front door, looking absolutely stunning in a white cocktail dress laced with printed cherry blossoms.

"How did you wear that all day without getting coffee stains on it?" I gasped as she slid into the passenger's seat with enough grace to shame

Gisele Bündchen.

Charlotte shrugged as she clipped her seatbelt. "I changed in the back when I saw you arrive."

"I can't stand that it takes you two minutes to look ready for a runway. It's a real pain to have you as a friend, you know?" I said with somewhat feigned annoyance.

"Please. You're a smoke show, too."

"Because I stopped by Sephora and got a makeover."

She gave me a touché look. Another one of the many reasons why I loved her so much. She recognized she was beautiful, and she wasn't going to argue with it, but she always did her best to make others feel good about themselves, too.

As I passed the last building on the strip on our drive along the coastal road, Charlotte interrupted our comfortable silence. "Okay, I can't take it anymore. What did you think of Deacon? I never got a full assessment from you."

I shot her a quick look. "Oh no. Please don't tell me Jasper did."

"Via email this morning. Fourteen bullet points."

I laughed. As insane as it sounded, it was definitely in Jasper's wheelhouse to draft up a formal report about a potential new member of our friend group. I was also oddly touched by how deeply he cared for Charlotte and valued her friendship. When I first introduced the two of them, I had been worried Jasper would think Charlotte was a threat to his best friend status, but he had welcomed her with open arms. "How did Deacon rate on the Hastings scale of 'meh to okay'?"

"You haven't answered my question." Charlotte's face fell. "You didn't like him, did you?"

I reached over and squeezed her hand. "Of course, I liked him. What's not to like? He's funny, smart, incredibly attractive, and, not to mention, he has a cool job. In this economy, that's the whole package, sweetie."

Charlotte sank into her seat, toying with the strap of her purse. "You don't think dealing with dead bodies is a turn-off?"

I kept my gaze focused on the road while doing my best to reassure her. "It doesn't matter what I think. It sounds like you might not be all that jazzed about it."

"It *is* kind of weird."

"I get it. But I'm sure Deacon washes his hands before he comes a-knockin' on your door."

"Gross. You're disgusting." Charlotte failed to contain a preemptive snort before dissolving into a full-on fit of giggles. Wiping her eyes after the laughter subsided, she sighed. "You're right, though. He's doing important work, even if it's a tad morbid. Definitely something I can live with."

"So, you like him?"

Her beaming smile almost made me cry with joy. "Yeah, I really do."

"I'm so happy for you, Char. If anyone deserves the perfect guy, it's you."

Charlotte rolled her eyes. "I think Hudson already has the perfect guy thing on lockdown."

I hesitated a millisecond, Tori's enviable curls flashing in my mind's eye, before starting to agree, but Charlotte cut me off. "Uh oh. Did something happen between you two?"

I cursed how well she knew me. "Not exactly." I sighed. "We just had a really awkward run-in with his co-anchor last night at the WMTG fundraiser."

I rehashed our encounter with Tori, feeling somewhat vindicated as Charlotte's disbelief at the woman's audacity grew and grew throughout the story.

"You're making this up, Cokes. Please tell me you're making this up."

I shrugged. "I wish I was."

"What a hag." Charlotte folded her arms. "I'm sorry, but I think you're totally within your right to be pissed at Hudson for his reaction. Or lack of one."

"Confrontation isn't his thing. You've seen how he lets my jabs about his apartment roll off his shoulders." I shot her a knowing look.

"Yeah, I suppose so." Charlotte still didn't seem convinced.

"I trust him." In that declaration, I felt confident. "It's Tori I'm worried about. I mean, who acts like that in front of someone else's girlfriend?"

"Someone who thrives off drama and attention. She sounds like the East Coast version of Christine Quinn on *Selling Sunset*." Charlotte shuddered at the comparison, even though *Selling Sunset* was one of our favorite reality TV shows to binge. "After what she said to your face, you have a right to be concerned."

"You think so? You don't think I'm blowing things out of proportion?"

Charlotte patted my arm. "Definitely not. This woman has made her intentions quite clear. I'd watch out for her."

I shivered at her warning. "I told you this hoping you'd make me feel better, not more on edge about her."

"Sorry." Charlotte's expression was genuinely pained. "I love you and Hudson to death, and you're right. He would never do anything to jeopardize your relationship intentionally. But this Tori nightmare sounds like she's looking to stir the pot."

Despite my renewed worries, a rush of warmth swept over me as I listened to Charlotte come to my defense. I had the absolute best friends.

"So, what's the plan for our covert operation this evening?" She changed the subject, likely understanding that I'd had enough of dwelling on Hudson's flirty coworker.

Happy to focus on something else, I told her about Jasper's idea and how we were going to pretend to interview Stacy's friends for *Divulge*. "Maybe while we're doing that, you can use your feminine wiles on the male bartenders to see if they'll dish on anything about Stacy. She could have been a club regular if her friends are always there."

"I can't believe your insider source is *Amanda* of all people." Charlotte shook her head of long, amber hair. She knew all about our intense rivalry in high school.

"Me neither. And I could tell she's not a fan of Stacy's friends."

"Yikes. If Regina George 2.0 thinks they're awful, they should be a friggin' delight to talk to. Better you than me." Charlotte's eyebrows wriggled with irony at her *Mean Girls* reference, a favorite teen movie we had each grown up with. We both knew it was impossible for Charlotte not to be able to make friendly conversation. Her warmth and kindness were just two of the reasons why her coffee shop was always bustling.

"No kidding. If Amanda thinks they're bratty, I can only imagine the horror shows they'll be." I contemplated my everchanging assumptions about the Chens' assistant. "It's hard to believe Stacy would be in their inner circle. I mean, she was a retail clerk, not an heiress." Knowing her parents lived in the same neighborhood as my folks, the Lockner family was well off, but nowhere near the level of the Harrises, the Frosts, or the Clarkes.

"Maybe they'll surprise us and be totally down to earth," Charlotte replied with true optimism.

My side-eye glance told her I highly doubted that would be the case.

Chapter Fifteen

"I thought I told you to take a cab," Jasper complained the moment we breezed through the entryway of the country club. He must have seen me hand Jolly over to the valet.

I laughed at his childish disappointment. "I can't get my drink on tonight. I need a clear head to get to the bottom of what's going on. Besides, I have to get up early tomorrow morning to post my article."

"Sometimes, I wish you weren't completely neurotic and just scheduled your posts like a normal blogger." Jasper sighed.

I sniffed at his barb. "What can I say? I like to be in control." I also had a secret, irrational fear that my uploaded content would mysteriously disappear, never to be found again, if I relinquished the reins and set my posts to be published through the website's scheduling application.

Charlotte ignored my lame excuse and met Jasper's icy blue gaze with a wink. "Coco's my ride home, so I'm definitely not driving tonight."

His face melted into a devilish grin. "Let me open my tab."

Our early arrival at the Crestview Country Club meant we had plenty of time to scope out the best people-watching seats in the house. With the influence both Jasper and I carried due to our notable reputations, the maître d' let us pick a table of our choosing. We positioned ourselves at a round booth halfway between the swanky bar and the elegant entryway. From here, there'd be no way for Stacy's friends to arrive and mingle around the club without us noticing them.

While Jasper and Charlotte retrieved their first round of drinks at the bar, I assessed the new changes to the club with a critical eye. The place had been open for almost one hundred years and had changed owners many times throughout the decades, each leaving their mark on the club's interior design. In the sixties, the owners had ripped up the lounge floor and put in an inground swimming pool, which the Clarkes and Harrises later covered and converted into a fountain surrounded by a Zen Garden after they bought the place. No doubt competing with the posh and popular Cyprus, Crestview Country Club had recently morphed into something more sleek and modern, rather than the old-money sophistication it was known for. It had been a few months since I'd been here, and I had to admit, I missed the vintage charm that had been bulldozed and redesigned.

"I think we're going to look a little out-of-place." Jasper frowned as he sauntered back from the bar, swirling his espresso martini as he slid into the booth. "There's a theme tonight. Egyptian Paradise."

I grimaced, knowing that, by the time the Friday-night crowd descended on this place, we'd be surrounded by Cleopatras and Marc Antonys. "How original."

At least now the video I'd seen earlier on Claudia Harris's TikTok profile made sense. I'd taken the initiative of swiping through Claudia's, Liz's, and Rochelle's social media while I'd been waiting in line at T.J. Maxx. Since I had no clue what Stacy's friends even looked like, I'd memorized their faces to make sure I'd be able to recognize them in a packed room. On TikTok, Claudia had been very thorough in documenting her over-the-top cat's eye application. For a Cleopatra costume though, it made total sense.

My gaze flashed to Charlotte, who looked to be in deep conversation with one of the hunky bartenders. "What's she up to?"

"Getting a preliminary report on Stacy and her friends. She told him she was an old friend of Stacy's from college and wanted to share her condolences with people who knew her."

Charlotte's ingenuity impressed me, but I couldn't resist a cringing glance her way. "I'm not sure Stacy even went to college."

Jasper tossed a shoulder. "I don't think the bartender has heard a word that's come out of Charlotte's mouth since she leaned in with her boobs pressed up against the counter."

Trying not to choke on my water, I waited for my laughter to pass before taking another long sip.

"How did your little online thingy go today?" Jasper asked conversationally.

"My *business seminar* went quite well, thank you very much." Giving him a pointed look, I dared Jasper to belittle the importance of what I did for my livelihood. He'd voiced, on more than one occasion, that I was wasting my talents on CoA and that I should come work for him at *Divulge*. "I'm already scheduled to host another one."

His drink rapidly depleted. "That's nice." His blue eyes searched for a roving waiter, and Jasper motioned to his empty glass. "I thought Dad was joining us this evening?" His teasing comment referred to Hudson.

"He's interviewing Stacy's parents for a tribute segment WMTG is running. He'll be here when it wraps up."

"I hope Hudson gets some deets from them. How could they not know anything about their daughter? Didn't Stacy live with them?"

"Actually, Deacon told me that Stacy moved into an apartment here in Crestview a few weeks ago." I filled him in on what I'd learned from the police yesterday at the station.

Jasper looked at me disapprovingly. "You didn't tell me this when you called."

"Sorry! It's hard to keep everything straight." I shrugged, not feeling all that sorry. If Jasper ever found himself at the center of a murder investigation, he'd understand the pressure.

"How could a retail assistant afford an apartment in this town? I mean, real estate here is top-notch." Jasper asked the very same question that had been wandering through my mind.

"I don't know. I hope her friends can help shed some light on it." I scanned the room as more people began trickling in, dressed in modern-day versions of—surprise, surprise—Cleopatra and Marc Antony.

Jasper pulled out his phone, swiping around to open a note-taking app. "Well, let's brainstorm some ideas about how she scraped up enough cash to live here. If these friends of hers refuse to talk about it, maybe we can force them into sharing if we make the right guess."

I propped my elbows on the table, pressing my balled fists under my chin. "Well, the first thing that comes to mind is that she stole the money for it."

"Ooo, from zero to catty in two point three seconds," Jasper said with a sassy snap. "I was going to propose that she asked her parents for a loan." He chuckled at his uncharacteristically angelic response.

I blushed with immediate guilt. "I guess it's kinda harsh to assume she'd steal."

Jasper stroked his chin. "Yes, but you could be right. What if she was stealing from the Chens..." he trailed off while I processed his theory.

Picturing my clients, I grew alarmed by how easy it was to imagine an incensed Olivia flying off the handle if she found out a trusted employee had been stealing from her. "I hate to admit it, but Olivia might have it in her to kill someone if she found out she was being swindled."

"What about her husband?"

I remembered how Sean had kept his cool when his wife told him that she'd drained their savings on royal china. "I have a tough time picturing Sean getting angry over anything, but I guess no one is above suspicion when it comes to financial pains."

"Do you think you could probe into the Chens' finances? See if they're missing any money?" Jasper looked mildly uncomfortable asking me to dig into people's private affairs.

"If I need to. I'll figure out a way to do it diplomatically." I hoped it wouldn't come to that, though.

"Okay, where else could Stacy have gotten the cashola?"

Quincy and Lacie's words about Stacy's revolving door of a dating life suddenly echoed in my mind. "Apparently, she had quite the abundance of suitors..."

Jasper's eyes widened. "If you tell me you think she was being paid to sleep with them, I might faint from the scandal of it all."

I shrugged with a wry smirk. "Your words, not mine."

My bestie typed furiously on his phone. "So, we have: one, a loan from her parents, two, stolen money, and three..." He snickered as his fingers danced across the screen. "...profits from prostitution."

"Please tell me you didn't actually write that down!"

"You said she had a lot of men in her life. I'm just telling it like it is."

I glanced at the ceiling, praying for forgiveness for thinking so poorly of a dead woman in the prime of her life.

"You two look like you're having fun." Charlotte sat down next to me, drinking a gin and tonic.

"We're just making a list of ways Stacy could afford a pricy Crestview apartment," Jasper summarized matter-of-factly, "concluding with Coco accusing her of hooking."

Charlotte's jaw dropped open as she smacked me in the arm. "Cokes! That's horrible."

I sank low in my seat at her admonishment. "We're just trying to cover all possible angles here."

Charlotte pressed her lips together. "Well, while you two were speaking ill of the dead, I was doing some serious investigating."

"Yeah, that's what it looked like from here." Jasper wiggled his eyebrows.

She sputtered in her defense. "I'll have you know that I am a happily taken woman."

"Hey, we're glad things are going well with you and Deacon," I said with a deadpan stare, "but get to the good stuff."

Sighing, Charlotte leaned in to avoid being overheard. "Well, Samuel the bartender was able to fill me in on Stacy's evolution here at the club."

"Evolution?" Jasper and I both parroted. It was an odd choice of word.

Charlotte responded with a reprimanding eye roll at our impatience. "Yes, apparently, she started out working here as an assistant on the event planning team."

"It took a team of people to come up with *this*?" Jasper signaled unenthusiastically to the underwhelming decorations highlighting the lackluster theme.

Ignoring his quip, Charlotte continued, "Samuel says Stacy was a huge asset to the club. I guess he's in the same boat as Jasper about how the committee's been managing since her departure last November."

If Stacy had left her job here at the club in November, she must have been hired by the Chens shortly afterward. "Did Samuel know why she left?" I scooted to the edge of my seat, thoroughly intrigued.

"He wasn't entirely sure how it came about. One moment Stacy was running a Vegas-themed cocktail party, the next she's chilling at a VIP table with Claudia, Liz, and Rochelle."

"The plot thickens. How'd the help make it into the club's inner circle?" Jasper pondered aloud.

"I guess there were all types of rumors flying around when it happened," Charlotte lowered her voice even more, "even some as vicious as labeling Stacy a drug dealer for the Crestview elite."

Chapter Sixteen

A startled guffaw burst from my mouth. "That sounds absolutely absurd. This is Crestview we're talking about. Not L.A. or Miami." "Drugs could be the reason she was killed." Jasper gave me a look that said I shouldn't brush rumors aside. After all, the two of us began our careers finding the truth buried beneath gossip.

I held up my hand. "Detective Forester assured me that Stacy was in good health. You can't tell me that doing drugs wouldn't have affected her system in some way."

"I didn't say she was *doing* drugs," Jasper retorted, "just that she *could* have been dealing them. That would definitely explain where she got her money."

I shook my head in disbelief, my gaze flicking toward the club's entrance. "Well, whatever the case, it looks like our targets just walked in." I spotted three designer-clad bombshells sauntering through the front doors like royalty.

"Damn, they are fierce." Jasper whistled under his breath.

Watching the trio glide across the room like they owned it, which I guess two of them did, I had a hard time picturing quiet, hardworking Stacy hanging out with these women.

Charlotte shot an encouraging look our way and smiled. "Good luck grilling those ice queens. I'll head back to the bar and see if I can learn anything else from the other two bartenders."

Parting ways, Jasper and I strolled over to the lavish couch the ladies had claimed for themselves.

"Ms. Clarke, Ms. Harris, Ms. Frost?"

I almost balked at the suave tone Jasper managed to greet them with.

Claudia Harris narrowed her dark gaze at us. The crystal chandelier overhead dripped shimmering prismatic light across her brown skin. "Yes?"

"I'm Jasper Hastings, Editor-In-Chief of *Divulge*. I'm sure three sophisticated women such as yourselves have heard of it?" He winked—yes, winked—at them.

Liz Clarke gave him a demure smile as she flipped her sleek blond hair over her tanned shoulder. "Mr. Hastings. It's a pleasure to meet you."

Petite and bubbly Rochelle Frost showed less restraint. "Omigosh. Yes, we've heard of *Divulge*. I loved that explosive piece you did about the Duvallie siblings," she gushed, referring to an exposé Jasper had personally written about an infamous, millionaire-turned-bankrupt Dover family.

"Ah, a mess, weren't they? Certainly put Enron to shame." Jasper smiled once more, his arm stretching out in my direction. "Let me introduce my dear friend, Coco Cline. The brains and beauty behind the lifestyle blog, *Trending Topic*."

Claudia tilted her head in my direction. "I've heard of you. You're the girl dating that new WMTG hottie, right?"

"Yes, Hudson Caruthers is my boyfriend." My heart clenched at her remark, irked that I hadn't been recognized for my own deeds as a social media entrepreneur. I hadn't expected Hudson's rising star power to affect my professional image this way.

"Boyfriend?" Rochelle interrupted whatever Claudia had been planning to say in response. "Honey, he needs to be locked down now before he's scooped up by CNN or something."

I forced a tight smile, doing my best to bite my tongue. *Maybe I should have gone with Charlotte to the bar.*

Sensing my simmering frustration, Jasper gallantly jumped back into the fray. "We're hoping to ask you a few questions for a piece Coco is guest editing for the May issue." He slid down between Rochelle and Liz, looking right at home on the couch. "You see, I'd like to do an in-depth feature on Stacy Lockner, and we hear you were friends."

At the mention of Stacy's name, the three heiresses crumbled before my very eyes.

"Oh God, Stacy," Rochelle wailed, burying her face into her perfectly manicured hands.

Liz wiped away the emotion filling her sapphire eyes, while Claudia managed to choke out, "Talking to the police about her was completely surreal. It's so hard to believe she's gone." Claudia looked between her two friends, who nodded in agreement.

"You four were close?" I perched on the arm of a plush chair adjacent to the couch.

"Like sisters, practically," Rochelle cried. "We'd gotten to know her so well over the past few months."

"How did you meet?" Jasper began his questioning, brow determined.

Liz cleared her throat before answering. "Right here, at the club."

"Was she a member?" I asked in follow-up.

"No, actually." Liz examined her French manicure. "She'd been working on the events team for a few years, so we knew of her but we never hung out with her. She threw such amazing parties. It was a huge bummer when she left because club events went downhill really quickly."

Jasper and I shared a hopeful look. "Why did Stacy leave?"

Liz lowered her voice. "She didn't quit. She was fired, right after the club's annual Halloween party."

Jasper scooted to the edge of his seat. "Do you know why she was let go?"

"Her boss was insanely jealous. She was afraid Stacy was going to replace her one of these days, so she preemptively fired her." Liz took the lead, as Claudia struggled to console a weeping Rochelle.

"Am I correct in stating that your family is part owner of this club?" Jasper prodded.

"Yes, but I didn't find out about all this until after Stacy'd been sacked. Claudia didn't either. By that time, Stacy had already found a new job and didn't want her old one back."

Since the three women were focused entirely on Jasper, I didn't bother hiding my confusion. Why on earth would Stacy pursue a job as a retail assistant at a dishware shop over being the event planner of a high-end club?

Scribbling down a few more notes on his phone, Jasper changed the subject. "How did you reconnect with Stacy, after she left the club?"

"We bumped into her at a morning yoga class down at a studio near the beach." Claudia dug through her Fendi purse. "I recognized her from the club and told her the place hadn't been the same since she'd left. God, the Thanksgiving benefit was a disaster." She handed a tissue to a flushed Rochelle.

"We got to talking after class and, by the time we left, we'd invited her to join us for brunch that same day," Liz finished.

"That's very charitable of you." I feigned a high-and-mighty smirk.

"If you're referring to the fact Stacy didn't come from money," Rochelle finally looked up from her damp hands, somewhat composed, "I'll have you know that we're not *that* shallow. Stacy was a blast to hang out with, and her roller coaster love life was always entertaining to hear about."

Becoming the good cop to my bad cop, Jasper leaned closer to the girls. "Love life? My informants at the police department," he disregarded the heat from my scolding look, "tell me she wasn't dating anyone."

Rochelle rolled her eyes. "I mean, who *wasn't* that girl dating? We didn't even try to keep track of her boy toys." She received a silencing look of daggers from Liz.

"Did you mention this to the police when you spoke with them?" Jasper pressed Rochelle further, as it was becoming increasingly obvious that she was the weak link.

Rochelle shook her head, and shame filled her eyes. I could have sworn I also detected something else, something like fear. What or who could these women be afraid of?

I summoned my best sympathetic expression. "Is there a reason why you didn't tell the police about Stacy's dating history?"

"I think we're done here," Liz said coolly, making moves to stand up.

My gut instinct forced the next questions out of my mouth. "Are you ladies afraid of one of Stacy's exes? That he'll come after you if you talk?"

Claudia and Rochelle both stilled at my suggestion, and even Liz's calm, beautiful façade faltered.

"Ladies," Jasper cooed, taking the lead, "we can help you if you trust us."

My shoulders grew heavy at the weight of his promise. Could we, though? A young woman was dead, after all. Just what had I gotten my friends into?

"Stacy had a lot of boyfriends," Claudia finally broke the strained silence. "It's silly to call them boyfriends because, well, a lot of them were older men. *Married*, older men."

Jasper and I shared a startled look. His earlier disparaging remark about prostitution hadn't been *that* far off the mark. Who would have guessed quiet, unassuming Stacy Lockner was a femme fatale?

"Stacy was having affairs with married men?" Jasper's brow furrowed in question.

"Stacy Lockner?" I repeated, just to make sure we were all still talking about the same person. Apparently, I was having a harder time than Jasper accepting this new development.

Rochelle nodded with the eagerness of a hungry puppy. "Stacy met a lot of men while she worked here and took advantage of their offers."

"Was that the real reason she was fired?" I couldn't restrain myself enough to let Jasper ask the question first. "Because she was sleeping with club members?"

Rochelle shook her head, her luscious blond hair swirling around her pretty face. "No, I don't think so. We were totally stunned when she eventually told us, and we know everything that goes on here. And I mean *everything*. She wasn't even that upset when she got fired, because she had accumulated some, ahem, financial stability all on her own."

Another knowing look bounced between Jasper and me.

Liz must have seen the suspicion on our faces, as she quickly jumped in to clarify. "They weren't paying her to sleep with them, but they did give her nice gifts. Big presents. Like clothes, jewelry, a car...even her new apartment."

Yikes. Guys with enough expendable dough to buy their mistress a car? My mind immediately went to the slew of older gentlemen who inhabited Mill Row.

Before I could unpack my speculation further, Claudia reached out and took my hand. "This is completely off the record, but once, Stacy implied she'd even been with the Central Shores *mayor* for a time."

"May—Mayor Beaufort?" I stuttered through my shock.

Nodding vigorously, Claudia suddenly looked like she wanted to disappear under the intense scrutiny coming from her two friends.

"Do you three have any idea who her other gentlemen callers were?" Somehow, Jasper was able to play this wild situation way cooler than I was.

Rochelle flipped her hair back. "I mean, there was always someone in her life, but she rarely gave us any specifics. She only told us the weird, kinky stuff they asked her to do."

"She was really tightlipped about who they were, for the most part," Liz said with a shrug. "That's why they valued her companionship so much. Besides the mayor, the only other time she slipped up was when she mentioned a steamy tryst with some big-wig tech guy. Stacy told us he made her cosplay as some anime character." Liz shuddered at the notion.

I stifled a little giggle at her squeamish reaction. Anime cosplaying was relativity tame when it came to bedroom fantasies.

"But that was someone she dated last summer," Claudia interrupted, "back before we started hanging out with her. She didn't give us a name when she dished about him, just what he did for a living. She never, ever mentioned names."

Hmm, a big-wig tech guy? Arthur Bushman couldn't possibly have been cheating on Amanda, could he? I racked my brain for another married man in the area with a tech background but couldn't find one. "Do you have any idea who this tech guy could have been? Any guesses?"

All three shook their heads in rhythm.

"Was Stacy afraid of any of her suitors?" Jasper asked.

Liz seemed to consider his words briefly before answering. "No. When Stacy's affairs ended, it was always amicable. Probably because the sleaze bags' wives never found out about her."

"Had she been seeing anyone recently?" I pressed further, dying to understand Stacy's whirlwind dating life that she so expertly kept hidden from me and the Chens.

Rochelle bit her ruby red lip. "Well, to be honest, in the last few months, Stacy hadn't exactly been forthcoming with her dating life. Last she told us, she'd started seeing someone new back in February. He even spent Valentine's Day with *her*, and not his wife. But every time we asked how things were progressing, she clammed up and changed the subject." She paused, looking innocently between Jasper and me. "That's why we didn't tell the police about her romantic past. We didn't want to tarnish her name when all her affairs ended so peacefully."

Naiveté was written all over the young woman's face.

"Are you sure they *all* ended amicably?" I challenged.

Liz didn't meet my gaze as I turned to face her, seeing as she'd taken the lead for much of our little interview. "I mean, she told us they were all fine with parting ways."

"Did Stacy ever mention if any of them bothered her after a breakup?"

"Well…" Liz looked like she was desperately trying to remember. "There was a guy she complained about who'd been somewhat controlling and possessive while they were together. That's why he'd bought her the car as a gift in the first place. He had some tracking software installed on it."

I shivered. "How did that relationship end?"

"The guy decided he wanted to fix his marriage or something, so he broke it off only a couple weeks after he bought her the car. Stacy kept it, but had a mechanic remove all its GPS tracking features."

Jasper tented his fingertips together. "How long ago did that happen?"

"Not sure. They dated before we started hanging out with her," Rochelle replied. "She only ever griped about him when she was having car troubles."

I swiped a strand of loose, strawberry hair back behind my ear. "Do you remember what kind of car she had?"

"No, I don't—" Rochelle looked at her girlfriends and they also shook their heads. "If it's not a Jag or a Bentley, I'm afraid I wouldn't recognize it."

Even without the model of the vehicle, this was incredibly useful information, and from the spark in Jasper's eyes, he knew we'd hit the payload. If we could find out what kind of car Stacy drove, we just might be able to track down the dealership where it came from and find out who bought it for her. Any man who wanted to keep tabs on his mistress that closely definitely warranted further investigation. Not to mention their tip about Mayor Beaufort...

"Well, ladies, you've been very helpful. If you think of anything else, please don't hesitate to reach out to me." Jasper, with renewed suaveness, slid his business card into each of their hands.

"Please, I know you're doing an article about Stacy, but could you refrain from publishing what we've told you tonight?" Liz looked uncharacteristically chastened by our revealing conversation. "Just quote us saying she was the life of the party, and we miss her dearly."

We nodded in solemn promise, seeing as how we weren't really writing an article to begin with, before backing away from the dazzling trio.

"Wow," Jasper bellowed as we plopped down at our table on the far side of the room.

I stared at my hands, my mind spinning with all the information we'd just unearthed. I tried reconciling the Stacy I knew with the picture Liz and her friends had painted. I just couldn't make the two versions add up.

"Hey, guys, I found Charlotte at the bar." The arrival of Hudson pulled my attention upward as he and Charlotte took their seats at the table. "I texted you I was on my way, but you didn't answer." His eyes were chocolate pools of concern.

Guilt trickled through my thoughts. Hudson had made it clear after our dinner date with Deacon that he was worried about me being involved with a murder investigation. I hadn't exactly been taking those fears into account, and I could see from the shadows under his eyes that it was wearing him down. "Sorry, babe." Drained from the tsunami of information we'd just been hit with, I managed to summon an apologetic smile.

"Did you guys get the deets?" Charlotte propped her elbows on the table, looking at us expectantly.

Jasper released a low whistle, tension deflating his larger-than-life presence. "Girl, we got the scoop of the year."

Chapter Seventeen

Hudson ordered a round of drinks and a charcuterie board for the table before Jasper and I launched into explaining what Stacy's friends had shared with us. Munching away on cured meats and gourmet cheeses with no grace at all, we took turns divulging the news that Stacy had actively pursued married men in the community and financially benefited from them.

"Stacy Lockner? The quiet little thing that worked at the Chens' store?" Charlotte had a hard time wrapping her head around the concept. "She always ordered chocolate sprinkles on her latte."

"I can't believe she was involved with the mayor." Hudson stirred his whiskey ginger. "Beaufort is like sixty-something years old. Didn't he throw some big fundraiser last year to celebrate his fortieth wedding anniversary?"

I nodded, chewing prosciutto and goat cheese with vigor. "Yeah, he invited everyone in Central Shores, remember? I went to it while you were out of town at a conference." I shuddered as the memory of the rotund mayor pawing his equally wrinkly wife in front of the attendees tortured my mind. "Isn't it wild?"

"My journalistic integrity is telling me we can't assume these rumors are true," Jasper lectured us before draining his third espresso martini. "The question is, what do we do with this new intel?"

"Well, obviously, you share it with the police. This opens up a whole new pool of suspects." Hudson's tone didn't leave room for any argument.

Or so he thought. "We promised Stacy's friends we wouldn't air her dirty laundry without good reason."

A scowl began to brew on my boyfriend's handsome face.

"Besides, Jasper's right. These are just rumors. We can't go sullying people's names without evidence to back it up. We'd get sued for slander!"

"Then what do we do next?" Charlotte asked.

I looked at Jasper for his input. "I know where I would start. The car. If we could track down who bought it for Stacy, that would be solid proof she was having an affair with a married man."

"A married man who was so paranoid, he tracked her every move while they were together," Jasper confirmed. "Sounds like the type of guy who might go after her if she did something to upset him."

Hudson's grip tightened around my hand.

"We won't confront him, of course," I said to quickly reassure his fears. "We'll share our findings with the police once we have proof."

"What about her apartment? Is there a way to figure out which dude paid for that?" Charlotte popped the cherry from her fruity drink into her mouth. "That's also an extravagant gift for a mistress."

I bit my lip. "Based on what Deacon told me about Stacy having a place in Crestview, her name must be the only one on the lease. I'm guessing someone gave her the money for the apartment."

"I'll see if I can coax more out of him, just to be sure," Charlotte mused, smiling as she likely plotted the ways to get her new beau to talk. "Her out-of-town apartment is what's giving County a leg up on the case, after all."

"I think the most telling thing about this whole saga is that Stacy inexplicably stopped sharing her love life with her friends," Jasper said with quiet intensity.

I arched my eyebrows. "You think that Mr. Valentine's Day became more than a fling, don't you?" His nod confirmed my suspicions. Turning to Hudson and Charlotte, I explained a theory I'd been sitting on. "Rochelle told us Stacy started seeing someone new at the start of the year, around Valentine's Day. Unlike her other dates, Stacy didn't share any deets about this guy, so much so, her friends weren't even sure she was dating anyone anymore. Every time they asked about how things were going, she changed the subject."

Hudson frowned at this news. "When did you say Stacy moved to Crestview?"

I was surprised by his question. "Around a month and a half ago. It would've been early March."

"So, it's possible Mr. Valentine's Day footed the bill for her apartment. Maybe to keep their affair under wraps as it got more intense," he puzzled aloud.

"That does make sense," Jasper admitted. "Clothes and jewelry, and, hell, even a car are all trinkets to people with obscene wealth. A place to live, however, that's something more intimate to bestow someone."

I contemplated our next move. "I want to find out where Stacy lived. See what kind of rent we're talking about."

"I actually have that answer for you already." Hudson's chest swelled with pride. "My interview with the Lockners revealed a few interesting tidbits of information."

Jasper threw a wadded napkin at him with dramatic flair. "Spit it out, then!"

"They mentioned Stacy had recently moved to the Villas, right on the water." Hudson folded his arms, sizing up our reactions.

"The Villas?" Charlotte's nose wrinkled.

"Back when I was house-hunting, I looked into renting an apartment at the Villas to see if I liked the area." I took a deep breath. "A one-bedroom apartment was going for three thousand a month, and that was over three years ago."

"I was just there last week," Jasper added, "looking at their condo selection with my realtor. They were advertising one-bedroom rentals for *five* grand."

Charlotte's eyes widened. "Yeesh. With a deposit and first and last months' rent, that's going to be around fifteen thousand upfront for someone to throw down."

Hudson cleared his throat. "Her parents said she moved into a spacious *two*-bedroom apartment."

It was my turn to be shocked. "If she was committing to a yearlong lease, this mystery man must have provided Stacy with nearly a hundred grand."

"That's some serious cash to shell out," Jasper said with a scoff. "Let alone commitment."

His comment struck a chord with me. Why would a guy put so much money into an affair?

As if the cosmic energy of the universe read my thoughts, our phones all bleeped around the table with an alert.

Jasper, of course, had his phone in hand the fastest, his other hand covering his mouth to stifle a gasp. I couldn't wait for him to share, and instead grabbed my iPhone to swipe past the lock screen.

"Oh my God," I murmured in horror as I read the local news alert notification. "Stacy Lockner was pregnant!"

The buzz of the Crestview Country Club fell away as my friends and I all disappeared into our newsfeeds. Hudson received a flurry of texts from Millie, who was furious she hadn't been the one to break the story. Apparently, someone leaked Stacy's private medical history to the *Central Shores Gazette*, and the paper had immediately blasted the news online through their mobile app.

Charlotte's voice trembled. "Things just got really bad, didn't they?"

None of us answered her, too consumed by what the briefing contained. The clickbait headline had been intentionally deceiving to amass interest in the short article. The *Gazette* report stated an unnamed source had spotted Stacy visiting an OBGYN a few times before her death, and questionably obtained medical records revealed she'd suffered a miscarriage in recent weeks.

I chewed on my lower lip, and Hudson's leg nudged mine.

"What are you thinking, babes?" he asked quietly under his breath.

I took a moment to collect my thoughts, troubled by these intimate, heartbreaking details being splashed across the grubby internet. "I'm guessing that whoever paid for her apartment was also the father of Stacy's child. Maybe when he found out she lost the baby, he lost his cool on her."

Hudson shuddered at the brutal scenario I had painted. "How horrible. Poor kid."

From across the room, a pained cry shattered the humming chatter. The crowd parted around the couch, where Rochelle, Liz, and Claudia all sat with tears in their eyes, their dismayed faces illuminated by the glow of their phones. They had obviously received the same news blast we did.

"This seems backward." Jasper tossed his phone onto the table with a scowl. "Dude finds out his mistress is pregnant, buys her a place to live. When she loses the baby, he kills her? Isn't it usually the other way around? A woman is killed *because* she's pregnant with a married man's baby?"

"I'm going to sneak outside to call Deacon and make sure things are okay at the station." Charlotte disappeared before we could respond, worry written all over her face.

"Who would leak such sensitive info?" I asked my remaining companions. Private health records were heavily protected information, even on the internet.

"If the paper got the tip about Stacy visiting an OB, they could have underhandedly gotten ahold of her medical records." Hudson's expression grew hard. "You'd be amazed at what some people will do for a story."

Jasper's eyebrow arched. "Sounds like you know from personal experience?"

"It was an example used in a journalism ethics course I took as an undergrad," Hudson explained. "A reporter manufactured a medical records request form using his primary care physician's letterhead. Whenever he wanted a subject's medical history, he faxed the sheet to their doctor and the records were returned within a day."

My mouth hit the floor. "Well, now I'm never going to the doctor again."

He gave me a wry grin, "Luckily, with the advent of electronic medical records, faxed requests are becoming a thing of the past, so scams like that don't happen as often."

Jasper shot a doubtful look at the two of us. "I have a hard time picturing the less-than-brilliant staff at the floundering *Central Shores Gazette* pulling off a scheme like that."

The criticism dripping in his voice made me chuckle. Jasper harbored a bit of a grudge with our hometown paper because they'd rejected his job application the summer he turned sixteen. "I think you're probably right. I can't picture anyone at the *Gazette* doing something so diabolical."

Hudson stroked his chin. "Maybe the police planted it themselves, hoping to encourage people to come forward with information? You know, since there's so little for them to go on."

I had to agree that this would certainly add fuel to the fire. If the people of Central Shores hadn't been interested in seeing Stacy's killer brought to justice, they would be now they knew she'd been expecting. Her miscarriage added a whole new dimension to the story. Who was the father? How had she lost the baby? It would certainly blaze through the local gossip circles like wildfire. "Investigators really don't have much to go on without someone volunteering additional information. From what it says here," I paused, scrolling through the article to double-check, "the father wasn't named in her health record. There's no DNA for them to cross-reference regarding the baby's paternity, either." At least I assumed there wasn't. After all, I'd majored in communications, not forensic medicine.

Charlotte returned to our table, looking a little miffed. "Deacon told me to not concern myself with *his* investigation. They've apparently got things *completely* under control." She folded her arms close around her chest.

Hudson, Jasper, and I all shared wary looks.

She chucked her phone back into her purse. "Guess he doesn't need our help figuring out that Stacy's baby daddy paid for her seaside apartment." It sounded like Charlotte was talking more to herself as she motioned for a nearby waiter to bring her another drink.

"Chief McInnis might be interested in knowing," I ventured carefully, and Hudson visibly relaxed.

"Does this clear Car Tracker Guy?" Jasper asked pointedly.

I twirled my straw in my fingers, thinking hard. "Maybe, if he and Stacy *really* ended things when Stacy told her friends they did. But there's also the chance they hooked up more recently, and Stacy just didn't mention it to her friends."

Hudson's brow furrowed. "Right. Any one of Stacy's former flames could have found out she was pregnant. They might have thought they were the father and killed her to protect themselves. Thus, your age-old tale proves true, Jasper."

"Indeed," he replied with a tip of an imaginary hat. "What's our next move?"

Everyone leaned in closer to discuss, pushing our drinks aside. Except for Charlotte, who downed the remainder of her vodka lime in one gulp.

"The car," I whispered for dramatic effect. "We need to find out what kind of car Stacy owned. That could help us tie her to at least one married man. Any ideas?" Once we knew the make and model, we could track down where it was purchased and, if we were really lucky, who had bought it for her.

"I can do that," Hudson volunteered. "Millie wants the production crew to replicate the scene outside Once Used, Twice Buy the morning Stacy died. She thought footage of Stacy's car in an empty parking lot would create a 'haunting atmosphere.'" He rolled his eyes along with the air quotes. "I'll reach out to Stacy's parents and ask them what kind of car she had, instead of one of the PAs scrounging up the info." I could tell from his pinched expression he wasn't entirely thrilled to bother the grieving parents more than he already had, but Hudson was the best one of us to track down the information without raising too many questions.

"Great. I'll orchestrate a run-in with Gavin tomorrow and tell him what we learned about Stacy's turbulent dating history. He should be more receptive to what we've uncovered than his uncle would be." I opened my calendar app on my iPhone and confirmed that all I had on the books for Saturday was a reminder to post my *Trending Topic* article in the morning. "I won't mention that Liz, Claudia, and Rochelle withheld the information themselves. I don't want to get them in trouble. I'll figure out a way to make it sound like gossip, while still providing Gavin with enough deets to take back to his uncle for further consideration. If the intel comes from his nephew, Chief McInnis might pursue it."

Charlotte's bottomless gray eyes glassed over as she accepted another vodka lime from a passing waiter. "Should we go to the Villas and ask around if anyone ever saw Stacy with a guy? Maybe we can figure out who Mr. Valentine's Day is." Her slurred words were surprisingly brilliant.

"Road trip!" Jasper held his hand in the air for a high-five, which I happily returned.

Hudson's sour expression dampened our celebration. "Whoa, guys. Slow down. You're putting yourselves in a potentially dangerous situation. What's to say her killer isn't someone living in the same complex? Maybe that's why Stacy moved to the Villas in the first place, so they could be close to each other. He might be keeping an eye on her apartment, too. Who knows what evidence he thinks might be there?"

"I didn't think of that." I bit my lower lip.

"We'll be fine. We can use the whole *Divulge* article as a cover again." Jasper flippantly waved aside Hudson's very valid concerns. "No one will suspect why we're really there."

Hudson's jaw tightened. I knew he wasn't happy with this plan, but at least he wasn't stopping us, either.

"Well, if we're doing that tomorrow, I need bed now." Charlotte pouted, looking at me somewhat helplessly. "Can you still be my ride?"

"You mean I have to drive you to your home all the way up the block from me? Fine, I guess I can do you this *one* favor." My feigned exasperation made the whole table laugh, lightening the tense mood.

Ensuring Jasper's Lyft driver arrived and collected him, Hudson and I escorted Charlotte to my car, gently lowering her into the passenger's seat. The poor, drunk thing was nearly asleep.

"I'll help you get her inside once we get back," Hudson promised, kissing my cheek.

His headlights tailed me the whole way home, and before long, we parked outside Charlotte's one-story Sunny Shores condo. Luckily, my drunken bestie had dozed in the car and snapped to attention as soon as Jolly's engine shut off.

"We're at my house?" she asked with inebriated confusion.

Laughing, I patted her back. "Oh, honey, please make sure to drink a gallon of water, will you?" I looked at the dashboard clock and winced. Although it was only ten, Charlotte had less than seven hours to sober up and squelch a hangover before she had to open Brewed to Perfection for the early Saturday morning crowds.

She must have seen the time, too. "Oh God. Why did you let me drink so much?" she moaned into her hands.

"You can berate me tomorrow. Let's get you inside so you can get some beauty rest." Not that she really needed it. Even drunk and whining, she was still a goddess.

With the help of Hudson's solid arms, we dragged Charlotte through the doorway of her charming home, decorated to look like a picturesque seaside escape using numerous style tips from *Trending Topic*, and coaxed her through two glasses of water.

"You can leave me to my misery, guys. I'll be fine." She groaned and swallowed two ibuprofens. "Thank you for seeing me home safely."

Hudson and I knew we were being kicked out for the night.

"'Night, sweetie," I called one last time from her lawn as she shut her front door.

We drove our cars a heartbeat down the road, tucking them into the two-door garage.

"What a night, am I right?" I tried to downplay the whirlwind evening.

Hudson slipped his arm around my waist, guiding me through the front door. "I guess I shouldn't have expected any less from my wannabe detective."

"Wannabe? I'll have you know we uncovered some seriously twisted stuff tonight," I exclaimed, mildly offended.

He nuzzled my hair, the feel of his lips sending a tingle pleasure down my spine. "I won't ruin the mood by reprimanding you for diving into your little investigation before I even got to the club."

"Those ladies were harmless. Jasper and I could have knocked them over with a big sigh." I snorted at the thought of either Rochelle, Liz, or Claudia lashing out at us. "Besides, what reason would they have for hurting Stacy?"

"Did you think to ask whether any of them are married?" His kisses peppered my shoulder. "Stacy might have fooled around with their husbands behind their backs. Or maybe, her so-called friends were jealous of all the men in Stacy's life and took it out on her."

I couldn't ignore the slight condescension lacing Hudson's words, as if I'd overlooked the obvious, and it quickly killed the sensual mood he'd been creating. But the more I thought about it, the more I realized he *could* be right. Any one of those women could have played Jasper and me like a well-tuned fiddle with their grief over Stacy's demise.

Chapter Eighteen

"Hey, what's wrong?" Hudson finally picked up that I had tensed in his arms.

Shimmying away from him, I plopped down on the couch. "Despite your attempt to belittle my intelligence, you do have a point. I need to do a little more digging to see if any of Stacy's friends are married." The dim light of the club had made it so I couldn't quite recall if I'd seen wedding rings on any of their fingers.

"Coco, I wasn't belittling your intelligence," Hudson replied with his cool, logical demeanor.

It certainly felt like you were. While I loved Hudson more than anything, he had yet to realize in all the time we'd been together that he had absolutely no control over how what *he* said made *me* feel. Reason and logic couldn't explain away the sting that came from innocent miscommunications.

Choosing silence as the least volatile option, I turned my attention to my phone and began scrolling through Instagram. Hudson huffed and sulked around the condo, making me ironically question who the real drama queen was in our relationship.

"Ah-ha!" I jumped up from the couch fifteen minutes later. Racing into the bedroom, where Hudson was already under the covers, I plopped down on top of him. "Don't pout, you goofball. You gave me a good idea and look!" I pushed the phone in front of his face. "Rochelle Frost *was* married."

Even though I still sat on top of him, Hudson propped himself up against the pillow and begrudgingly eyed me with caution, likely afraid I was going to flip my happy switch and erupt on him. "Go on, Enola Holmes. Tell me more."

I pulled up a series of images that had been posted online over the years. "If you weren't specifically looking for proof, you'd never know. She must have deleted anything pertaining to her ex-husband but look here." I curled up beside him with my hard-sought evidence. "In her college graduation pictures, Rochelle is wearing an engagement ring. Then fast forward a few years, she's got a wedding band on, too. Until," I paused for effect, taking back the title of resident drama queen, "about six months ago, when both rings disappear from her finger."

"Not bad." Hudson was clearly impressed with my observation skills.

"Believe me, I've become *very* attuned to noticing engagement rings." I wondered if he understood my inflection. I felt no shame in cultivating a secret Pinterest board dedicated to the different ring styles I liked.

"You think Stacy had an affair with Rochelle's husband, she found out, and they divorced?" Hudson asked.

"No way." I shook my head. "I don't think a woman like Rochelle would ever become friends with her ex-husband's mistress. *If* she knew who she was."

"How does your theory play out then?" Hudson rolled over on his side, his strong body curled around mine.

"It's possible that maybe Stacy *did* have an affair with Rochelle's husband before they ever became friends." The scenario gradually took shape in my mind. "Maybe her husband took his affair as a sign his marriage was falling apart and broke it off, with Rochelle being none the wiser that he cheated."

Hudson's fingers stroked the bare skin of my arm. His attempt to distract me didn't work.

"Maybe it wasn't until after Rochelle had befriended Stacy that she started growing suspicious about the reason her own marriage ended. Perhaps Stacy said something about one of her previous affairs that reminded Rochelle of her ex. Then she confronted Stacy at the store and killed her in a fit of rage."

"Wow," he said, with a tickling chuckle against my neck. "That sounds almost plausible. Have you ever thought about becoming a mystery writer?" Hudson pulled me closer and began kissing the special spot just below my ear, but my mind spun too wildly to focus on his advances.

Popping out of bed, I ran out of the room, leaving a confused Hudson gaping in my wake. Sitting down in front of my computer, I fired it up and impatiently waited while the home screen loaded. My fingers flew over the keyboard as I dove into all aspects of Rochelle's social media presence. I felt a bit like a hacker as I pulled up website after website, searching for the results I desperately needed. I scoured her followers and comments on Twitter, TikTok, Instagram, and Tumblr, all to no avail. Despite her lax attitude toward privacy settings, Rochelle had somehow managed to delete all things related to her failed marriage. I couldn't even find her marriage announcement in the online archives of local newspapers. Knowing how intensely people chronicled their lives online these days, it wouldn't have been an easy task to wipe her slate clean. But then again, she had the financial power to do it.

Over an hour later, after digging six years back into her Facebook timeline, I hit the payload. In her social media purge, Rochelle had overlooked a college friend's Check-In post tagging "the lovebirds" at a winery in upstate New York during their senior year. The guy mentioned had to be Rochelle's boyfriend-turned-fiancé-turned-husband-turned-ex.

Plugging "Jack Donahue" into LinkedIn's premium search feature, I whooped in triumph as my results loaded across the screen.

"Hey, it's me."

Jasper sighed into his phone. "I know, Coco. You've heard of caller ID? It's all the rage this century."

His deadpan tone made me grin.

"Why are you interrupting my beauty sleep?" He yawned.

"I think Rochelle Frost had motive to kill Stacy."

This caught his attention. "What in the name of Beyoncé are you talking about?"

"Something Hudson mentioned when we got home gave me an idea. I did some digging and found out Rochelle used to be married." My face glowed with the light of the LinkedIn profile beaming from my computer. "I think

I've found her ex-husband, and guess what? He's a managing partner at an IT software company."

It took a beat for Jasper to follow my train of thought, but he got there. "Liz Clarke told us Stacy had been involved with some big-wig tech guy!"

I hadn't FaceTimed with him, so he couldn't see me nodding with satisfaction. "Yep. So, here's my theory. What if Rochelle figured out Stacy was the reason her marriage ended? That might make someone livid enough to clobber her over the head with a teapot."

"Classy." Jasper snorted. The line went silent for a moment. "I don't know, I have a hard time picturing Rochelle being violent. I mean, she was practically sobbing the entire time we spoke with her."

"Because she was wracked with guilt!" I studied the professional headshot Jack Donahue used as his LinkedIn profile picture. He was a handsome guy, in a Connecticut-yachting-bro way. I could see why Rochelle might have been a sore loser if he broke up with her. "Or maybe she thought if she cried through the whole thing, she wouldn't say anything incriminating." I silently begged that Jasper would see my point of view. I rocked back and forth in my chair, adrenaline pumping through my veins as I waited with bated breath for his response.

"Hmmm," he mused from the other end of the line, "I guess we could swing by the club tomorrow to see if she's there, since we'll be in Crestview questioning Stacy's neighbors at the Villas. Rochelle might be a little more forthcoming if we corner her without Liz and Claudia in tow."

"A little faith is all I ask." I clicked the disconnect button in victory.

Hudson had given up and was asleep by the time I padded back into the bedroom, so I quietly changed into my PJs and washed my face free from the day's wear and tear. I slipped into bed, but I was too wired from my findings to fall right to sleep. To pass the time, I lowered the brightness of my phone and began examining the small footprint Stacy Lockner had left behind online.

I quickly found that our victim had set her Facebook profile to the highest level of the site's privacy settings. This meant that, since I'd never invited her to connect, I couldn't look through any pictures or posts she'd been tagged in or posted herself. It did at least allow me to see that she only had thirty-two friends, a small number for the popular platform. Her Twitter page was even less helpful. She hadn't tweeted in over three years. Her last tweet read: **Clouds should taste like mashed potatoes**. Very enlightening stuff.

Her Instagram, though, revealed slightly more. She'd shared a lot of pictures of her wearing lacy, barely-there dresses, posing in front of a full-length mirror. The photos definitely showcased her sexy curves, and I wondered briefly if she'd designed these posts to tease her suitors with what was in store for them. Digging through her list of followers, I discovered that many of the twenty-nine people tracking her had private accounts, meaning I couldn't see any of their posts or details without requesting access to see their profiles. Suspicion bloomed in the back of my mind. Based on the number of people these accounts were following on Instagram, most of which I could count on one hand, they were more than likely shell accounts, not regular Instagram profiles. The budding idea pushed me onward. It was only after checking the account of a @HeyMrRobinson and seeing the user had only one approved follower on their profile that I felt confident in my deduction. These shell accounts were likely created so Stacy and her lovers—ugh, gross—could communicate online through Instagram's direct messaging feature without their prying wives knowing. A DM was a little more secretive than texting, although I wasn't sure discretion was the top priority for some of these sleaze bags following her page. With a handle like @HeyMrRobinson, you were practically shouting to the world that you were an older man on the prowl.

Tapping my way back to Stacy's profile, I continued to scroll through her Instagram photos. It seemed only recently that she had started uploading pictures away from her mirror. They ranged from her bundled up in front of the tiger cage at the zoo, to sipping coffee at a beachside café, to replicating a statue's pose at an art museum. As I scanned through a handful of on-location posts, seeing her relaxed and happy body language, I wondered who had captured these moments for her. I swiped through a myriad of adventures. Had these photos been souvenirs of dates with her latest secret lover? Was he the man behind the camera?

The last picture she'd posted was uploaded April third. Warm, dark tones enhanced with orange candles made it hard to see anything but the image of an inviting cream couch with an embroidered pillow that said, "Home is Where the Heart Is."

Gag. I stuck my tongue out at the stitching of two campy stick figures holding hands inside a simple little house. It was an incredibly basic pillow, so I wasn't sure what had prompted Stacy to post it. Maybe it was her way of showing off her new apartment? If that was her end goal, she'd failed miserably, as the background was so dark, you could hardly see a thing. Her audience had obviously felt the same way. The photo had only garnered five likes. Even then, none of them were from accounts that actually followed her. They must have been drawn to the post through her blatant overuse of hashtags about home décor. Ah, the wonders of social media.

I stared at the image for another minute or two, until my eyes finally felt like they were going cross, but my intense scrutiny had done the trick. In an instant, a hidden message revealed itself. Whether it was intentional or not, the picture had been zoomed out just enough so you couldn't see the two stick figures all that clearly. But after examining the pillow for a few minutes, I noticed that while their hands appeared linked, one of the embroidered figures was holding something in the nook of their other arm.

Even with the ability to use Instagram's features to zoom in on the pillow, I couldn't quite make out what the stick figure was holding. Whatever filter Stacy used had left the image dark and grainy. So, I resorted to a method I had devised long ago out of necessity, way before Instagram let you pinch-and-zoom on your phone screen to see things up close. Back in the social media dark ages, when Instagram was just starting to catch on, users couldn't zoom in on images within the application, and it had been a source of frustration for years. Necessity bred invention. Hence my nifty workaround.

Taking a screenshot of my entire phone to capture the post, along with its handful of likes, I minimized the app and tapped my Photos icon. I'd used this method countless times on celebrity posts, storing a copy in my iCloud for safekeeping, just in case the original was hastily removed from an account due to public outrage or personal embarrassment. First rule of Blogging Celebrity Gossip 101: gotta get those receipts.

Once I'd located the screenshot in my camera roll, I zoomed in with ease. Using Apple's Photos program, I dragged the editing slider to brighten the image, eliminating the artistic shadows stretching across the couch from some unseen lamp or window. After tweaking the brightness and contrast, my keen eyes were certain of what they saw. The female stick figure on the pillow was holding a baby!

Not wanting to wake Hudson, I resisted a low whistle at the serious shade Stacy dared to post. By sharing an image of that pillow, she had basically proclaimed to the online world that she was expecting a baby. Not only that, but that the baby's father was planning on being a part of their little family. My heart ached for her as I double-checked the date. She must have posted this just days before she suffered her miscarriage.

I wondered if her baby daddy had come across this subtle announcement weeks later and gone ballistic on her in the back of the Chens' shop, not even giving Stacy time to tell him she'd lost the child. My thoughts traveled back to the club and what Jasper had said about it being possible one of Stacy's former suitors presumed the baby was his, freaked out, and killed her. Finding out your mistress was pregnant would be motive enough for some affluent men in our small community who were afraid to lose their standing.

I shuddered, sorrow racking my bones. Gosh, Stacy must have been so afraid, at the utter mercy of her attacker. Did she know her life was about to end? Did she fight back? Had she spent her final moments in pain?

Up until now, I'd been mainly—and selfishly—concerned with saving Once Used, Twice Buy and the Chens' reputation. But the more I got tangled up in Stacy's life, the more determined I felt to make whoever did this to her pay.

I lay there for a while, staring up at the ceiling. As sleep tugged at my welcoming eyelids, I prayed I would be able to ferret out some information from my "friends" at the Central Shores Police Department that would set me on the right path to finding Stacy's killer.

Chapter Nineteen

"What time did you finally come to bed last night?" Hudson stumbled into the kitchen a little after seven Saturday morning. Rarely did he ever make an appearance before nine a.m., so seeing him up this early was a pleasant surprise.

I pushed a steaming cup of joe his way. "A little after one, but it took me forever to fall asleep, and then I tossed and turned for hours. I decided to say screw it, and I got up for a sunrise beach run."

He looked at me like I'd sprouted ten heads. "A run? You don't run."

"I know. And I didn't really. It was more of a beach walk," I admitted with caffeine-infused cheeriness. "Sit down and let me catch you up on everything you missed while getting your beauty sleep."

I walked Hudson through my discovery that Rochelle's ex could possibly be the "big-wig tech guy" Stacy had had an affair with last summer, as well as my thoughts on her revealing recent Instagram posts that alluded to her growing family.

Given the fact he may have still been too tired to process everything I threw at him, Hudson showed no enthusiasm for all my late-night finds. "You've got yourself way too many suspects, babes."

I grinned, wagging a finger in his face. "That's the point. I have at least three potential people for the police to investigate: Rochelle, her ex-husband, and Stacy's baby daddy. Considering they only had the Chens on their witch-hunt list, I'm well on my way to clearing Sean and Olivia's names."

"You look deranged," Hudson deadpanned in such a way that he left me speechless. "Coco, you can't go down to the police station ranting and raving in the shape you're in. Why don't you try to take a nap or something before you head out to meet Jasper?"

I sputtered in protest, wanting to defend how I'd cracked the case wide open, but my brain was suddenly too tired to come up with words. I hadn't been sleeping well since this whole ordeal started, and it seemed to be affecting my usual wit.

Hudson put his strong arms around me, enveloping me in his reliable warmth. "I say this in the most loving of ways, but you're a hot mess right now." For effect, he held the stainless-steel electric kettle up to my face as a mirror. "Go get some rest."

I winced, assessing my reflection. The bags under my eyes were bigger than last season's PRADA satchels, not to mention the redness pooling along my eyelids. "If you insist," I finally conceded, stopping briefly in the bathroom to grab a cucumber facemask.

I emerged from my cocoon at ten, feeling a million times better and much more clearheaded.

"There she is." Hudson smiled in greeting, jumping up from the couch to give me a bear hug and a tender kiss on the forehead. He smelled like burnt toast, meaning he'd likely tried to fend for himself and make breakfast. Hudson wasn't the most resourceful person when it came to navigating a kitchen. "I was worried you'd gone off the deep end."

"As if." I fumbled with my phone.

"What's that you got there?" He hovered over my shoulder to check out my screen.

I shuffled toward the Keurig machine. "I downloaded all the incriminating evidence I could find online to support my Rochelle-killed-Stacy-because-she-ruined-her-marriage theory and made a photo album for reference, in case Gavin wants to see everything laid out in one place. The more I think about my list of suspects, the more she stands out."

Hudson folded his arms. "I can see that a solid few hours of sleep still hasn't swayed you from barging into the police station and declaring Rochelle Frost a murderer." He arched an eyebrow. "What happened to your concern about being sued for slander?"

"Well, since I don't know for certain Rochelle and Jack were married, I'm not going to declare anything to the police just yet. My theory about their marriage all hinges on a six-year-old Facebook post." I held up a hand as Hudson opened his mouth to protest. "I *am* planning to share with Gavin what we've learned about Stacy's sketchy dating history, though."

His broad shoulders relaxed only slightly.

Taking his face in my hands, I forced him to meet my gaze. "The whole reason I started poking into Stacy's death was due to the fact that the Chens were the only suspects the police had on their radar. I figured if I could dig up other options, they'd leave my clients alone so we could focus on launching their business."

"How philanthropic of you, dearest," Hudson grunted with resignation.

"But now," I held up a finger, "I really just want to bring Stacy's killer to justice. A young woman is dead. Killed. And *I'm* the one who found her, Hudson. I can't just sit on the sidelines and let potential murderers drink mimosas by the club pool without letting the police know what we've uncovered. Especially when we know they're floundering for information."

Hudson stroked his chin. "I can't argue against that, I guess." His worried gaze met mine. "Be careful, though, babes. If word spreads that you're feeding the police information, the killer might get nervous and... *do* something to you." His pained words caught in his throat, and I was reminded once more how deeply Hudson cared for me.

"I'm always careful. Believe me, I would never do anything that would take me away from coming home to you each and every night." I pulled him in for a deep, spine-tingling kiss. "Now, don't you have some intel to dig up?" I playfully reminded him of his task to find out what type of car Stacy had owned.

"Already did that, Sleeping Beauty," Hudson mimicked. "According to Mr. Lockner, toward the end of August last year, Stacy upgraded from a two thousand eight Ford Focus to a brand-new, silver Mercedes-Benz CLS Coupe."

I swore fireworks of excitement flashed before my eyes. "Good job, babe."

Pleased that I already had my answer this early in the day, I gave him a beaming smile.

He had the sense to look nervous. "Why do you look so happy?"

I didn't even need to look at the photographic evidence I'd assembled on my phone. "Guess what happened on October thirty-first, a mere two months later?" I didn't give him the chance to answer as I waved my iPhone in front of him. "Rochelle Frost changed her profile picture for the first time in seven months…to a picture where she wasn't wearing her wedding ring. Her marriage was on the rocks, if not already over."

Hudson's eyes danced with investigative intrigue. "You think the timing of all this means Stacy's car was a gift from Rochelle's ex-husband? Car Tracker Guy and Big-Wig Techie are one in the same?"

"That's what I intend to find out. The closest Benz dealership is…" I paused as I did a quick Google search on my phone, "forty minutes south of here."

Hudson headed for the door, grabbing his phone and keys. "I take it I have my marching orders?"

My heart warmed, surprised by his willingness to assist in a potential wild goose chase.

"I'd rather be the one interrogating a slimy car salesman, not you," he answered my wordless question. "Besides, I think I left behind one of my Xbox controllers at my apartment. Two birds with one stone."

The corner of my mouth twitched, and the words zipped past my lips before I could stop them. "When are you ever going to let go of that place? Is it so bad to imagine having all your things here, with me?"

Hudson's expression contorted into the exasperated look he'd given me a thousand times. "It has nothing to do with us, babes. I just like the idea of not having to drive back from the station if it's really late." He crossed his arms. "You were the one who bought a place so far away from where I worked."

"Oh, so it's my fault?"

"I didn't say that."

"It sure sounded like it. And since when is a thirty-minute drive *sooo* far?" My temper snapped. "You used to make that drive all the time when I was living in Dover, and you never complained about it."

"That's because we weren't living together, and it didn't feel so permanent at the time."

My fingers trembled around the ceramic handle of my coffee mug. "Well, with the way things are, we're not really living together now, are we?"

"How can you say that? Of course, we are." He scoffed. "I don't understand why this is such a big deal to you."

Tears threatened to rim my eyes as I struggled to sort through my emotions. "It feels like you're only pretending to commit to me and our life together. With your own apartment waiting in the wings, you could abandon me at any time." I hated admitting it out loud, but my biggest fear in life was losing Hudson.

He crossed the kitchen in three steps and had me in his arms. "When are you going to realize that you're stuck with me for life?" he murmured into my hair. "I'm not going anywhere."

I wiped away a few stray tears on his shoulder before pulling away to meet his gaze. "I want to believe that. I really do. I just get caught up in things other people say, and I get scared." I rarely was this vulnerable about my own insecurities. With Hudson, with anyone. Even myself.

"What are other people saying?"

I bit my tongue. I didn't want to add the gossip about our lack of an engagement into the mix. I *really* didn't want to bring up Tori Beals and her snide comments. This wasn't about what other people said or thought about us. It was about my own, deep-seated anxieties about our relationship. "It's not what people say that's the issue." I tugged at the ends of my hair. "It just makes me worry that something is wrong."

Hudson's brow furrowed. "If people are saying things that upset you, I wish you'd tell me. Because I'd tell you what I'm telling you now. Our lives shouldn't be dictated by what other people think. You and I are happy, right?"

I nodded, my lip still quivering. "Right."

"You know I love you."

"Yes." I glanced at the floor, momentarily ashamed I was making him feel like I didn't already know that.

"And I know you love me. We're in this together. Who cares what anyone else says or thinks?" He looked me over. "Is there anything else bothering you?"

The tension broke inside me, and I snorted at the weight of the question. "Regarding our relationship? No." I leaned into his chest once more.

He pressed his lips to the top of my forehead, and we took a moment to enjoy the silence. "All better?" he asked.

"All better." I smiled back at him.

He pulled away and headed for the door. "I'll let you know what I find out at the Mercedes dealership." He stopped as he reached for the doorknob. "Should I hit Whole Foods on my way home and pick us up something taco-related for dinner?"

I grinned as I held the screen door open for him. The way to this woman's heart was definitely through her stomach. "Sounds perfect. Thank you, babe," I whispered into his ear, giving his booty a tight squeeze as he sauntered over the threshold.

At least he left chuckling. I watched him stroll toward the garage and disappear from view. I hated fighting with Hudson. We did it so rarely that I always felt a bit dazed after a blowout. But as I replayed the conversation in my mind, the apartment's existence still remained a sore spot for me. I reminded myself that Hudson was committed to me and opted to put my anxieties on the back burner to focus on the day ahead.

I turned my attention back to my phone. Seeing the myriad of awaiting notifications, I was glad I'd had the sense to post my new *Trending Topic* article after my sunrise stroll, allowing me to catch the Saturday morning crowd. Despite a universal longing to sleep in, people were usually up and checking their newsfeeds by eight on the weekends, and I'd beat that deadline by at least two hours. Clicking on my blog icon, I scrolled through a slew of reader comments. Most thanked me for my budget-friendly decorating insight. I quickly noticed a trend in their follow-up questions. Readers wanted to know my favorite aromatherapy scents and whether I preferred soy, coconut, or paraffin wax candles better. I'd take the time to respond to them tomorrow. I felt guilty for bumping my followers off my priority list, considering they were the reason for my success, but I had bigger issues to worry about that were much closer to home.

Chapter Twenty

I backed out of my blog app, clicking on the green iMessage icon. The angry red notification badge told me I had sixteen awaiting texts. It turned out, they were all from the group chat between Charlotte, Jasper, and me.

C: If I said I was going to go to the Villas last night, I have to bail.

J: Betch, why?

As I read, I snorted at Jasper's sassy use of our could-be-considered-offensive pet name for one another.

C: Don't have café coverage.

J: Ur just bailing because ur hungover.

C: No! Woke up feeling gr8, thx for asking. Srsly, have no coverage.

J: Summon ur minion then.

C: No can do. Already promised her the weekend off.

J: Heaven forbid u man up and break ur promises.

C: I'm not a man, thank God.

J: Who's going to keep Coco on a leash? I'm certainly not.

C: She doesn't need to be kept on a leash.

J: She went batty last night. Betch called me at 12:30 ranting Rochelle Frost was our killer.

C: What? Coco, what gives?

J: Cokes? R u alive? Did Hudson finally snap and kill u?

C: Did he propose and you're in a state of shock?

J: COCO?

I debated letting their pleas go unanswered a little while longer, but I knew if we were going to scope out Stacy's life at the Villas, we needed to make waves to head there soon.

Good morning, peasants. I'd hate to see what you text each other behind my back...

Within seconds, their replies popped onto my screen.

C: Yikes. We thought something was really wrong.

J: Yeah, I was joking about Hudson and all, but I was honestly starting to wonder...

After a few rounds of witty banter, we finally decided on a plan for the day. Charlotte would sit this one out—**C: I helped u questioned Quincy. It's Jasper's turn to play sidekick**—since she had no one to cover her shift at Brewed to Perfection. Jasper and I would meet in Crestview at two, poke around the Villas to see if Stacy's neighbors knew Mr. Valentine's Day's identity, then head to the country club in hopes of running into Rochelle to ask her about her ex.

With a plan in place, I showered and threw on a navy sundress, as it was another beautiful, warm April day. I grabbed my purse and a granola bar, promising myself a more filling lunch after I'd taken care of my personal mission. Fifteen minutes later, I sat on a park bench in the Commons with my eyes locked on the police station. It was common knowledge that Gavin and the rest of the Central Shores Police Department had standing lunch orders at Zaddick's deli. I figured I'd wait for Gavin to either leave the station to pick up his lunch order or catch him as he returned. I had no desire to go inside and risk Chief McInnis or Detective Forester getting wind of my visit.

I spotted the lieutenant's sandy hair the moment he stepped into my line of sight. "Hey, Gavin!" I waved, cheerfully calling out his name across the park.

I obviously startled him, as he dropped his Zaddick's takeout bag on the sidewalk.

"Well, hey there, Coco." Gavin gave me a harried smile as he picked up his lunch. "Nice to see you outside of a crime scene."

He had meant it as a joke, but with his bumbling delivery, it fell a bit flat.

Luckily, it was the perfect opening for me. "How's everything going? Last time I spoke with your uncle, you guys were a little hard-pressed for leads."

Gavin scratched the back of his neck as he shifted on his feet. "Well, despite all the tensions flying around the station, we're doing just fine."

"Gavin, come on, it's me." I inched closer, giving him my best innocent, doe-eyed expression. Even though we'd gone to prom as friends, it was no secret he'd had a huge crush on me all through high school. I batted my eyelashes to ignite that torch once more.

Gavin's cheeks blossomed like a red rose bush, and he held his hands up in surrender. "Oh, no you don't. If you're fishing for gossip, you won't get it from me."

I pushed out my lower lip in a sultry pout—at least, I hoped it looked like that. "I guess I'll just have to share my suspicions with the county team, then."

His hazel eyes narrowed. "Suspicions? What suspicions?"

"Well…" I tucked a loose strand of hair behind my ear. "Since I told your uncle I wanted to make sure the Central Shores Police Department received credit where credit is due on this case, I figured I'd put an ear to the ground and see if I could drum up any useful information to help you guys find Stacy's killer."

"Good grief. What have you been up to, Coco?"

Although he was a uniformed officer, and an irritated one to boot, Gavin McInnis didn't ruffle me. "Nothing. Well, other than trying to clear my clients' names." I puffed out my chest, satisfied when Gavin's gaze flicked in that direction. "I saw the news blast from the *Gazette.* There's a good chance the father of Stacy's baby paid for her apartment in Crestview. According to a source, Stacy started dating someone seriously around Valentine's Day. Someone wealthy. I doubt it's a coincidence that a few weeks later she moved into an upscale apartment." I strolled around his athletic figure, building the suspense. "I also believe Stacy may have been sleeping with one of her friend's ex-husbands. I don't have proof, yet, but I will soon."

"Hold it right there." Gavin spoke with more authority than I'd ever heard him muster. "What in God's name are you spouting off about?"

"Trust me, Gav. You should look into these tips." I hoped my expression conveyed my sincerity.

"What tips? This all sounds like a bunch of gossip to me." He crossed his arms. "Are you going to give me any names at least?"

Rochelle Frost's name skated across the tip of my tongue just as my phone rang, blasting Hudson's signature *The Witcher*-theme ringtone. "Give me just a sec." I held up a finger and took a few steps back for a modicum of privacy. "Hey, babe. Did you find anything out at the Mercedes dealership?"

"I can't believe I'm about to say this, but you might be on to something, Coco." Hudson's voice was weary and disgruntled. "After an hour of getting the runaround about client confidentiality, one of the sales guys finally caved when I introduced him to my pal, Ben Franklin."

My pulse quickened. "And? Did he spill the tea?"

"He did, indeed. Turns out, he sold a silver Mercedes-Benz Coupe to a guy named Jack Donahue last August. He remembered the name because the dude paid in cash. I got him to check the dealership's records, too. From the documents on file, it looks like Jack opted to register the car himself, so unfortunately, Stacy's name wasn't on any of the paperwork."

I chewed nervously on my lower lip. Without confirmation that Jack and Stacy knew each other, my theory was dead in the water. "I suppose Jack could have bought the car for himself." Hudson's prolonged silence on the other end of the line had me wondering if he was holding out on some other vital piece of information. "This might be a stretch, given how long ago this happened, but any chance your informant remembers Stacy being with Jack when he purchased the car?" I asked.

Hudson's throaty chuckle echoed across my phone speaker. "Give me a little credit, babes. I went to school to be an investigative journalist." He lowered his voice. "I showed him a picture of Stacy from Instagram."

"Spill it, will you?" I hissed as quietly as I could. Gavin's watchful gaze analyzed my every move.

I could practically hear the smirk on Hudson's face dripping through the phone waves. He was enjoying dragging all this out. "The sales guy said he'd never forget a blond with legs like hers. You won't believe how glad I am that you weren't the one who came here."

I punched the air in victory. Even though I had yet to confirm that Rochelle and Jack had actually been married, it all seemed too big of a coincidence for it not to be true. "So, I was right about Jack and Stacy having a relationship. I told you so!" I taunted my boyfriend for only a moment. "But seriously, you're the best. Gotta go, bye!" I disconnected the call and met Gavin's confused gaze.

"What was that all about?" He looked tired.

"*That* was confirmation of a name I think you and the chief should vet," I replied matter-of-factly. "Have you ever heard of a guy by the name of Jack Donahue?"

"Can't say as I have." I could tell from his sigh that Gavin was getting tired of me stringing him along. But this was a lot more fun than I expected.

"Well, I have a source—"

"You don't have to pretend." Gavin cut me off, his patience waning from my theatrics. "I know you were talking with Hudson just now."

My shoulders flinched at his irritable retort, and I decided to shelve the dramatics for the moment. "Fine. During an interview with Stacy's parents," I shaded the truth a little, "Hudson found out that Stacy got a new car back in August. It wasn't a sports car or anything, but it was definitely way above her paygrade. Anyway," I was cautious of Gavin's scowl, "we did a little investigating of our own. A guy named Jack Donahue bought the car for her and paid for it in cash. That's a pretty big gift, don't you think?"

Gavin paused, clearly surprised by my reveal. "We knew about her car, as it's registered in her name," he chastised me a little, "but, I'll be honest. We had no idea it was a gift."

"Purchased in cash. No one buys a car with straight-up cash these days." I rubbed my hands together nervously because I realized I'd actually bought Jolly the same way with my LiveIt money, but that was beside the point. "People use cash for things they don't want traced back to their credit cards."

"I'm capable of following your train of thought," Gavin said coolly.

Boy, I was really offending his intelligence on this glorious Saturday afternoon.

I held my tongue about Rochelle's possible involvement. I didn't have solid proof she'd been married to Jack, and I didn't want to send the police after her without being one-hundred-percent certain. I was humble enough to admit the results of my online sleuthing could be wildly off base. I decided it was best to keep my mouth shut while Gavin processed all this new information.

After a minute or two, he concluded by taking some notes in a tiny notepad he'd pulled from his back pocket and offered me a tight smile. "I'll share this with my unc—I mean, Chief McInnis. We'll be in touch if we have any further questions, Coco." With a tip of his hat, Gavin turned around and headed inside the police department.

Chapter Twenty-One

I decided to congratulate myself with a caramel macchiato, swinging by Brewed to Perfection to check on Charlotte. Of course, she looked amazing. Her dewy skin was luminous, the remnants of her hangover long gone.

"How'd your meeting with Gavin go?" she whispered once she'd handed me my order.

I glanced around the busy coffee shop and figured all the other patrons were too wrapped up in their own lives to be eavesdropping on mine. "He didn't brush me off, at least. I can't tell if he'll do anything with the information I shared." I took a sip of sweet caffeine and savored it before brightening with more news. "Hudson called halfway through, though. He tracked down the sales guy who sold Stacy's Mercedes to Jack Donahue. In cash."

Charlotte's perfectly groomed eyebrows rose with intrigue. "Jack Donahue? The guy you think is Rochelle's ex-husband?"

"I'm like ninety-nine percent sure of it. But I need to be a hundred percent certain before I sic the police on her." I brimmed with rekindled confidence. "Hopefully, Jasper and I can track Rochelle down at the club later today."

"Be careful," Charlotte warned. "If she did learn of her husband's infidelity, there's a very real chance Rochelle could have taken her anger out on Stacy."

I frowned. "Do you think she'd still be holding onto enough anger to warrant killing Stacy after all this time?"

"If it was a nasty divorce, sure. People can harbor ill feelings for years in those cases. Besides," Charlotte lowered her voice even more as she began to wipe down the coffee counter, "Rochelle comes from a very wealthy family. You can't tell me there wouldn't have been some type of prenup agreement."

My eyes lit up at Charlotte's genius. "With an infidelity clause. If Jack decided to cut ties with Rochelle before his affair was uncovered, he may have gotten more money in the settlement than was rightfully his."

My bestie nodded with sage wisdom. "If she found out she'd been swindled, that definitely would have made Rochelle livid."

Yet another explanation popped into my head. "I guess there's also the fact that Rochelle would have felt betrayed by Stacy. Based on what we've gathered, the affair happened before they became friends, but even then, that would still sting."

"How did Stacy live with the fact she'd secretly ruined her friend's marriage?" Charlotte wondered.

I didn't have an answer for her.

Since I wasn't supposed to meet Jasper in Crestview for at least another forty-five minutes, I decided to sip my coffee and stroll down the beach path for some fresh air and sun on my way to Zaddick's to grab a salad. My mind swirled like a hurricane, and I needed a few minutes to sort things out.

My main goal in looking into this case had been to find other credible suspects for Chief McInnis to focus on, besides Olivia and Sean Chen. Instead, I'd gotten completely swept up in playing detective and hardly given a second thought as to how my clients were doing amidst all this drama. I needed to carve out some time today to check in on the Chens. They were paying me to promote Once Used, Twice Buy, after all. But rather than focusing on boosting their business and being at their side through this crisis, I'd been spending my energy diving headlong into Stacy's messy love life to bring her killer to justice. But after yesterday's jaw-dropping developments, it was nearly impossible to focus on my CoA clients at the moment. To know Stacy had been pregnant and was planning on raising a family made me incredibly sad. The young woman I'd interacted with on a daily basis seemed so spacey and carefree. Who knew she was hiding all these secrets? It must have taken its toll on her.

"Coco? Is that you?"

Deacon's swoon-worthy voice pulled me from my reverie as he walked along the beach path in my direction.

"Hey there. What brings you to the dunes on this fine afternoon?"

He squinted at me with his dark eyes, trying to shade his brow from the blinding sun with a hand. "I needed some fresh air to clear my head. I've been stuck inside all morning, doing some final processing work on the crime scene. Between you and me, I think we'll be able to release the place back to the Chens by the end of the day."

The messy details of this case had really taken their toll on my priorities. I had completely forgotten that I had been worried the police would hang onto Once Used, Twice Buy for weeks on end. "Oh, wow, that's great news." I felt like a neglectful consultant.

"Yeah, maybe for the Chens, but not so much for us." Deacon glanced at his feet with a frown.

"No new breaks in the case?" Based on the scowl etched into his face, it seemed Chief McInnis and Gavin were keeping my tip about Jack Donahue to themselves for now. Although, I cursed the strong possibility they had dismissed the information as gossip altogether, considering Gavin's reaction to my coy delivery.

"Nothing solid enough for us to go on." Deacon pushed his hands into his khaki pockets. "Want to sit down and join me for a moment?"

I was surprised by his invitation and followed him to a nearby bench, temporarily abandoning my plan to head to Zaddick's for a salad. Sweeping the bench clear of sand that had blown up from the beach, I turned to face him. I studied his worn expression from behind my Tom Ford sunglasses. "What's up?"

"I need to puzzle out a few things with someone other than Harriet. The pressure from the mayor and Director Morrison is getting to her, I think. She's becoming harder to work with." Deacon met my gaze. "Can I trust you to keep this between the two of us?"

I was flattered he thought I'd be helpful. "Of course."

"I want to go over the crime scene with you. Since you're familiar with the store, you might be able to help me understand some things."

"Such as?"

"How Stacy's killer got in and out of the building."

This overlooked detail put a huge damper on all my budding theories. "Do you know for certain they came in through the back door?" The front door had been locked when I arrived.

Deacon nodded. "Yes, but to make matters more confusing, the back door was locked when police first arrived at the scene. In Gavin's report, he noted Adrian Riley used *your* key to unlock it." He examined me intently. "Did you forget to mention during your formal statement that you locked the back door after finding Stacy's body?"

"No way." I sat back in surprise. "I didn't go anywhere near the back door."

His thoughtful expression revealed that he believed me.

"I get why you would ask, though," I continued. "Only Sean, Olivia, and I have keys."

Deacon shook his head. "Olivia Chen told us she and Sean gave Stacy her own key a month after she began working for them." He paused, as if debating whether he should share the information on the tip of his tongue. "It was missing from her key ring when we examined her belongings found at the crime scene."

Stacy had her own key? I hadn't known this, but I suppose it made sense for her to have one. "So, she let her attacker into the store, they killed her, and then took her key to lock her back in?" It seemed like an odd series of events, now that I said it.

"It *is* possible Stacy left the back door unlocked while she was working." Deacon ran a hand over his shaved head, beads of sweat glistening across his furrowed brow. "Olivia told us that whenever someone was alone in the store, both doors were required to be locked. It was part of her 'mandated security plan.' Her words, not mine. Yet, it's entirely possible Stacy forgot to do so that morning."

I shivered at the literally fatal error.

"Another thing that's hard to explain is that the lock on the back door wasn't damaged or scratched in any way. Stacy had quite a few keys on her key ring, and many of them looked almost exactly the same. You'd think that whoever took her keys would have gone through trial-and-error trying to figure out the right one to use. But the lock didn't look like it had taken any damage to reflect that at all."

An impressed whistle slid across my lips. "You can tell that from a doorknob?"

"We had a locksmith examine it and give us his professional assessment. It wasn't nicked or scratched up as we would have expected."

I considered his words for a moment. "Which means, unless they got really lucky picking the right one from the start, someone knew which key to use."

"Which leads us right back to you, Sean, and Olivia." Deacon immediately held up his palms in protest. "I mean, not that we think *you* did this."

A surge of worry encompassed me, as my clients were once again being painted the villains by the county crime team. With all I'd learned about Stacy's tumultuous dating life, I tried to think of an explanation for the missing key. Not so much that it was missing, but the fact that someone knew which key would lock the store's backdoor. I considered Charlotte and Jasper to be family, but I had no clue what they kept on their key chains, so it seemed highly unlikely for Rochelle to know what Stacy's keys were used for. While it didn't completely absolve her of my suspicion, it certainly put a major snag in my theory. This left me to consider the baby daddy and Jack. My heart thumped against my ribcage. What if they were one in the same? I hadn't thought about that likelihood until now. Maybe Jack and Stacy had rekindled their relationship, now that he was an unmarried man.

"Why do I get the feeling you're holding something back from me?" Deacon's worried voice interrupted my thoughts.

Despite my pledge to help the Central Shores Police Department crack this case, I couldn't afford to sit on the information I had any longer. If Gavin and Chief McInnis didn't see the value in what my friends and I had unearthed, maybe Detective Forester and her team would. "Here's the thing, Deacon..."

I spent the next ten minutes filling him in on all that we had uncovered over the past day and a half, concluding with Jack Donahue buying Stacy a GPS-enabled car. I left out that I thought Jack was Rochelle Frost's ex because I didn't have proof of that…yet. "Any two-timing skeeze who tracks his mistress every hour of the day has way more means and motive for murder than my clients do." Pride fluttered in my chest. At the drop of a hat, or new evidence coming to light, I'd created a pretty convincing case against Jack Donahue, and he hadn't even been my prime suspect until Deacon had informed me about the missing key mere minutes ago.

The serious look on Deacon's face when I finally shut my mouth told me he was far from impressed by the lengths we'd gone to in order to secure this information. His ears practically steamed.

"Before you yell at me for interfering, I *did* tell Gavin McInnis this information earlier today." I hoped to spare myself another lecture.

He surprised me by remaining silent for a few moments. "You think one of Stacy's suitors would have known which key she used for work?" Deacon's expression revealed just how much he doubted my theory.

"I know what all of Hudson's keys are for on his key ring." Granted, my boyfriend only had three, but I kept that tidbit to myself.

Deacon raised an eyebrow. "You've also been together for over four years. From the sounds of it, Stacy's beaus didn't stick around for very long."

"The one she met before Valentine's Day did. I think he financed her Crestview apartment. That's commitment, if I've ever heard of it." I reminded him of my Instagram findings and pulled up the enhanced pillow image on my iPhone to show him. "She planned to have a family with this guy before she lost her baby. They must have been serious."

"I'm not at liberty to share any of the circumstances regarding her failed pregnancy."

Oh snap. Did this man know how to read minds or something? "I wasn't asking you to share. I'm just pointing out it wouldn't be too unbelievable to assume if they were planning to be a family that they'd know what each other's keys would unlock."

"So, what is the theory you're trying to sell me, Coco?" Deacon challenged. "That Jack Donahue killed Ms. Lockner because she was getting serious with another man? That he killed her because she was pregnant? That he killed her because she wasn't pregnant anymore? Or that some other guy killed her because of the pregnancy?"

My eyes narrowed as he drawled on. "I don't appreciate being mocked. All I'm saying is that there are plenty of other people who have more reasonable motives to kill Stacy than the Chens and I do."

Deacon leaned back on the bench, closing his eyes as he tilted his head toward the sun. "I didn't mean to mock you. You've unearthed quite a bit of dirt on this case." He sighed, making moves to stand up. "I need to head back to the station and fill Harriet in. I appreciate all you've done, but it's not necessary. We can handle this case."

I couldn't resist a doubtful scoff. "A few minutes ago, you were telling me you were up against a dead end."

"Please, Coco. Let us take it from here." Deacon gave me a stern look.

I glanced at my phone. I only had twenty-five minutes before I planned to meet Jasper at the Villas over in Crestview. "Well, then, good luck following up on *my* leads, Deacon." As I walked away, a twinge of regret swept over me at my churlish reply, but I convinced my conscience he had it coming. I wasn't about to let the crime lab team brush me off after all the light I'd shone on their case.

Chapter Twenty-Two

A question simmered in my mind as I drove up the coast. What would prompt someone to take just *one* of Stacy's keys and not the whole keyring?

The detail rolled around my brain, keeping me preoccupied for the length of the drive. Before long, I was winding my way through the ritzy seaside suburbs of Crestview, searching for a spot that didn't require parallel parking. With the red clay rooftops of the Villas in sight, I spied Jasper's Porsche parked along a side road and slipped into the vacant space behind him.

I gathered my things and hopped out of the car to meet my friend as he haphazardly paced the sidewalk up ahead, barking commands into his iPhone.

"I don't care if you have to go to the show in a paper bag! Just get to those runways," he said with a snarl before terminating the call with an aggressive button tap. He heaved a hurricane-strength sigh as I reached his side. "Sometimes, I miss snapping my old flip phone shut in a huff." He mimed a gesture so frequently used during the days predating touchscreen smartphones. "One of my columnists lost her suitcase at LaGuardia on her way to the New York Fashion Week Bridal shows. It's amazing how much handholding these Gen Zers require from me."

I didn't bother to point out that he and I had only missed the Gen Z cut-off by two years, and despite the whole "millennials vs. Gen Z" debate—usually hashed out on Twitter and TikTok respectively—our age groups had a lot more in common than not. But I was still too preoccupied with the mystery surrounding Stacy's keys to defend our younger generational counterparts.

It concerned me that someone would go to the trouble of removing Stacy's store key when it would have been just as easy, if not easier, to take the entire keychain.

Since I'd promised Deacon to keep our beachside debrief on the down-low, I framed my burgeoning question in a blasé, off-handed manner. "Why would you remove a key from a keyring instead of just taking the whole set of keys with you?"

You know, super subtle.

Jasper took a long sip of the Frappuccino he wielded in his other hand. "Well, hello to you, too, sweetness."

"Hello," I rolled my eyes as he delayed answering with his lovable sass. "Now, my question?"

"Ah, yes, your random AF question…" Jasper tapped his chin thoughtfully, his eyes hidden behind polarized Armani lenses. "I suppose there could be a few reasons. One, the person didn't want to have to lug all their keys around. Or maybe they didn't have the pocket or purse space for a decked-out key chain."

Neither of these scenarios seemed like something that would be running through the mind of a killer after they'd just committed murder.

"There's also the possibility this person wanted to go off the grid. Some people have a fob on their keys that they can track via an app if they ever misplace them. Leaving behind their keyring ensures they aren't traced."

My pulse quickened at the implications. "A fob? I thought that was the fancy name for an electronic car key?"

"A sign you never went corporate." Jasper sighed. "It's also the term for a location-tracking security device. Mostly used to badge into buildings. You touch the fob to a special control pad and you're in." He rummaged through the pockets of his tailored blue slacks. "Like this." He pulled out his work ID and showed me a small plastic disc hanging from his lanyard. "But they now make personal key fobs that sync to mobile apps. In case you misplace your keys, the app shows you where they are. Pretty easy to buy one, too. There's a display of them at practically every gas station."

I snapped a picture of the round, little device with my phone. If Stacy had something like this on her key ring, it could be why only the store key was removed. Whoever killed her didn't want the fob being traced by the police. I thought about my options for a moment. Would Chief McInnis or Deacon even listen to me if I told them this theory?

Jasper pulled his shades down so he could stare at me haughtily with his icy blue eyes. "Are you going to tell me why you're asking me about this?"

"As much as I'd like to, I can't."

His foot tapped impatiently, waiting for me to spill. "Does this have anything to do with Stacy? How am I supposed to help you if I don't have all the deets?"

Not wanting to give Deacon or the Central Shores police any more reasons to be annoyed with me, I feigned an apologetic shrug and turned my attention to the sidewalk up ahead. From here, the tops of the Villas' red clay Mediterranean-style roofs sprouted from the tree canopy. The rest of the view was obscured by a huge stucco wall surrounding the impressive property.

Jasper must have realized I wasn't going to crack under pressure, so he gave up and waved a hand to the street corner. "I looked at a condo here last week. The gate faces the main road." He led the way as we walked around the block, his noisy slurping the only conversation between us. Tossing his venti-sized cup into a nearby trash bin, Jasper held a finger to his lips before approaching the fancy iron gate boasting a guard stationed in a tiny hut. I guessed this meant he planned to do the talking.

"Good afternoon." Jasper flashed the security guard a debonair smile. "I was here last weekend looking at a few condos, and I left my planner in the leasing office. Mind if I come in and grab it?"

I shot a curious look his way, confused why he wasn't using our *Divulge* cover story like we'd planned earlier that morning.

His stoic expression told me to trust him.

The guard gave us a once-over and buzzed us inside. "The management office is on the beachfront path."

"Thanks, I remember." Jasper saluted, pulling me inside and down a brick walkway sheltered by a curtain of trees.

"What was that about?" I asked when we were out of earshot. "What happened to our fake *Divulge* tribute piece?"

"I doubt this place would appreciate reporters snooping around and potentially harassing their tenants, so I improvised."

I had to admit, it was a smart move. "Isn't he going to watch us walk to the management office from his little security shack?"

Jasper shook his head. "During the tour I went on, the guide told me the front gate is monitored twenty-four-seven, but there are no security cameras within the actual compound, out of respect for their tenants' privacy."

"Glad you did your homework." I patted him on the back, taking in the beautifully manicured surroundings. It was hard to believe I hadn't left the state and been teleported to some tropical paradise. The developers behind the Villas had planted a ton of palm trees that somehow managed to survive our changing seasons. White sand artistically swirled alongside the stone pathway, with little fountains and "reflection pools," as Jasper called them, stationed all around. I spied tennis courts in the far corner, as well as a one-story building labeled with a sign reading "Sauna" in big, black letters. "Why didn't you get a place here?"

"I'm looking to buy something, and they only have only one condo on the market. It didn't have a good enough view for my refined palate," Jasper said with a straight face.

I sensed I was being baited into teasing him about his high-end tastes, so I kept my lips pressed shut.

He frowned at my lack of reaction before continuing with his tour guide spiel. "This building is dedicated exclusively to apartment rentals." We stopped in front of a five-story stucco-style building, something I would imagine seeing in Santa Barbara, not Delaware. "As you can see, it's 'quarantined' from the rest of the development. During the tour, they only brought me over here to show me how secluded it is and to prove that condo owners wouldn't even notice renters moving in and out."

"Ah, the peasants must be kept out of the way of royalty."

"Out of sight, out of mind." Jasper gazed at the multiple balconies overlooking the yard of reflection pools. "No joke, that's what one of the property managers said when we walked by this part of the compound."

I threw him an offended look. "I didn't realize it was a requirement to have a stick up your butt to live here."

The corners of his lips curled. "A stick dipped in gold, no doubt."

I elbowed him in the ribs, worried the security guard would hear our laughter echoing throughout the complex and come looking for us.

Rubbing his side, Jasper looked up and down the length of the building. "Any idea which floor Stacy lived on?"

I shook my head and walked to the front entrance, doing a quick scan of the bronze buzzers outside the glass door. "Looks like there's a Lockner on Level Four. Apartment 45."

"Excellent." Jasper grinned, pushing the buzzer of a second-floor apartment.

No answer.

"Um, I said she's on Level *Four*." I pointed to the directory once more.

"I heard you. This way, no one on the fourth floor will know we're coming up. We'll catch her neighbors off guard, which means they might spill something juicy." His expression said his reasoning should have been obvious to me. "No one will wonder why we needed to be buzzed in, either. *We* want to be the ones asking the questions, not the other way around. Have you forgotten Journalism 101?"

I believed he was overthinking things, but I let it slide. It had been a long time since I'd been in the reporting ring. While people might think they're one and the same, blog writing is a wildly different ballpark than investigative journalism. I needed Jasper's expertise, so I let him use his roundabout method.

He pushed two more buttons at random before Apartment 26 buzzed him in. They didn't even bother to ask who was at the front entrance.

"How neighborly," Jasper said with a smirk, holding the door open for me.

"So much for high-end security," I murmured as we stepped into the grand foyer.

My nose wrinkled as the harsh aroma of cleaning products blasted me at full force.

"This reminds me of an all-inclusive I stayed at when I was in Mexico." Jasper coughed, his eyes watering as his footsteps echoed across the mosaic tiled floor. "Although, I'm pretty sure this establishment isn't cleaning vomit up in the halls on a nightly basis."

I, too, wondered about the reason for the sterile smell. It ruined the serene oasis atmosphere the rest of the Villas exuded.

Taking the stairs two at a time, we arrived on the fourth floor moments later.

"Remember," I kept my voice low, "we're looking for information that will lead us to Stacy's baby daddy."

"Understood. Any other marching orders?"

I stuck out my tongue at him. "You take the first five, and I'll start at the end."

Nodding, wariness painted Jasper's face. "Be quick about it. That security guard might come around and check on us if we take too long." He raised his hand to Apartment 40 and rapped on the door.

I dashed to the end of the long hall and knocked on Apartment 49. After waiting for a few moments, and counting several dog yaps, I decided no one human was home.

Just as I turned from the entryway, a frazzled, platinum-haired woman whipped open the door with surprising force. "I hope you're here to apologize to me!"

"Excuse me?" I was certain I'd never seen this lady before.

She deflated, the wrinkles on her leathery face falling slack. "Oh, I'm sorry. You looked like someone on the property management team from the peephole." The petite woman looked me up and down, confused as to why she had a visitor. "How dare they accuse my little Pepe of bringing fleas into the building," she grumbled.

Ah, now the aromatic smell of pesticides made sense. "Good afternoon! I'm a reporter for *Divulge*, the society magazine." I seized my opportunity. "I'm doing a special tribute piece on Stacy Lockner. I believe she was your neighbor." I motioned down the hall to the looming apartment door that once belonged to the unfortunate young woman.

"So?"

I stuttered under the woman's frosty gaze. "W-well, I was hoping you might have a story to share about the deceased that we could feature, Ms..."

"DeMayo. Ida DeMayo." She sized me up, and I could only imagine what was going on under that dyed-within-an-inch-of-its-life blond hair. "Can't say that I do, other than I'd like to know where she got all her cute dresses from."

At her lack of common decency, a frown tugged at my lips. "Did you interact with Ms. Lockner much?"

Ida disappeared behind her door, popping back with a fuzzy white ball cradled in her arms. "No, not really, other than the occasional run-in at the elevator. She wasn't a fan of Pepe and usually tried to avoid us at all costs. I don't know what kind of person wouldn't love this handsome little guy." She buried her face in the ball of fur that, to my surprise, yipped in reply.

Catching sight of Pepe's beady little eyes bulging above a flattened nose dripping with snot, I sensed this was a dog that only its owner could love. I took a step back, not wanting the drifting wads of matted hair to latch onto my dark outfit. "During those times you did see her, was Ms. Lockner ever with anyone?"

"No, she was always alone. Why?"

I realized my line of questioning seemed a bit unorthodox to her and scrambled to cover my blunder. "We're searching for other people in her life that could contribute to the article. We don't have much to go on, you see."

"Ah." Ida smiled, revealing tobacco-yellowed teeth. "Eh, it makes sense. That girl kept to herself from what I could tell. She hadn't been living here too long, but she didn't go out of her way to socialize with the rest of the residents around here."

I can't imagine why. I cleared my throat. "Okay, well, thank you for your time, Ms. DeMayo."

She tilted her head. "Have I met you before? You seem familiar."

Oh gosh. I'd completely overlooked that I wasn't snooping around Central Shores, my safe little haven away from the pitfalls of being a celebrity. The last thing I needed was Ida logging onto *Trending Topic* and posting to the world that I'd interrogated her about a murder I had no business investigating. I hastily summoned a plausible scenario, scolding myself for not being prepared for people to recognize me. "My picture is posted under my *Divulge* byline." There was no way I was giving this woman a name she could trace.

Ida sucked on her teeth a moment. "Ah, that must be it." With that, she shut the door in my face, barely muffling her fawning gibberish over Pepe.

"Strike one," I muttered, shooting a disappointed look down the hall. Jasper was nowhere to be seen. I hoped he'd been invited inside one of the apartments and hadn't abandoned me on this potential goose chase.

Chapter Twenty-Three

Immediately regretted knocking on the door of Apartment 48. The dark-haired woman who appeared before me looked like her entire body had just been Botoxed, and she didn't seem pleased to be receiving visitors. Or maybe that was how her face always looked.

"What?" she snapped through a mouthful of chewing gum.

I began my little monologue. "Hi, I'm a reporter with *Divulge* magazine. We're doing a tribute piece on Stacy Lockner—"

"Tribute?" The woman folded her arms with a sneer. "That little harlot doesn't deserve a tribute."

Caught off guard by her venom, it took me a beat to recover. "Really? Everyone we've spoken with has said Stacy was a lovely girl." I'd stretched the truth, of course, but I wanted this woman's unfiltered take on Stacy.

"You haven't interviewed any married women then."

I sensed this woman's insecurities dripping from her plastic-injected face. "Oh."

"Thank the Lord my husband had the sense to see past her tiny skirts and lowcut tops." She examined her one-inch fake nails with disinterest.

I glanced at the welcome mat under my feet. It was one of those customized rubber doormats displaying the household's name. "Well, Mrs. Pickler, I'm sure our readers would be intrigued to read about a darker side of Stacy. Anything you'd like to share?"

Her ballooning lips pursed. "Not that I'd like printed, thank you very much. But I'll have you know, I've slept much easier now the little tart isn't shimmying around this place."

I struggled to keep my expression neutral. With the revelation of the purchased Mercedes, I'd been so focused on Rochelle Frost and Jack Donahue's ties to Stacy that I hadn't stopped to consider another renegade wife might be responsible for her death. Mrs. Pickler didn't look like she had the strength to lift a feather, let alone fatally bash someone over the head with a teapot, but the spite in her voice made me wonder. "Did Ms. Lockner ever approach your husband? Make advances toward him?"

Mrs. Pickler's cheek twitched. "Well, no…but her outfits sure advertised what she was offering."

My gaze flickered to the cropped top covering her clinically enhanced breasts, and I suppressed an eye roll. If that wasn't the pot calling the kettle black. "Did you ever see her with any other men?"

"My husband and I have taken a few vacations recently, so we've hardly been here since she moved in."

I wondered if that was intentional on her part to keep Mr. Pickler away from Stacy's charms. As per the Villas' *highly* unethical classist motto, *out of sight, out of mind.* "I take that as a no, then?" The more she spoke, the more it seemed this woman's dislike of Stacy stemmed solely from her youthful figure and her flirty wardrobe.

Mrs. Pickler managed to lift a stiff eyebrow. "Just because I never *saw* a parade of men coming from her apartment doesn't mean there wasn't one." Her gaze shifted around the empty hall. "Although I'd appreciate that being kept between you and me. My husband doesn't approve when I speak ill of our neighbors."

After promising our conversation was off the already fake record, I said goodbye, relieved to escape her vicious presence. I wasn't about to let Mrs. Pickler know how close to the mark her homespun gossip had been.

A maid answered the door to Apartment 47 and had no helpful information to share. Well, she might have, but since I didn't speak Hungarian and she didn't speak English, it was a bust.

"I'm never going to hear the end of it from Jasper if his experience has been anything like mine," I mumbled as I tapped my knuckles against Apartment 46, my last remaining hope.

I heard shuffling inside and stepped back as the door opened and an elderly white man greeted me. "May I help you, young lady?"

His charming smile and kind blue eyes put me at immediate ease. "Yes. Hi, sir. I'm from *Divulge* magazine, collecting stories for a tribute piece on your next-door neighbor, Stacy Lockner. Were you acquainted with her?"

"Oh, poor Stacy. She was a real sweetheart." A wistful expression spread across his papery face. "Always brought my packages up from the mailroom if she saw any lying around. Terrible, terrible thing, her being killed."

Even though I felt bad for making the older gentleman's eyes water, I pressed on, hardly believing my good luck. Between Ida and Mrs. Pickler, I had yet to really learn anything about Stacy other than her dislike of ugly dogs and passion for seductive clothing. "Did you see her around the apartment complex a lot?"

He lifted a dubious eyebrow. "Well, we didn't exactly hang out, now, did we? She was a young jewel. She didn't have time for an old geezer like me." He rubbed the back of his bald head, his smile shy. I wasn't sure if he was pulling my leg, so I remained quiet. "But she was always ever so nice in passing…even if her gentlemen callers weren't."

Chills danced up my spine. Gentlemen callers? Had Stacy continued to date multiple guys, even after hooking up with Mr. Valentine's Day? What if the guy financing her apartment found out he wasn't the only one receiving her affections? "What do you mean by that, sir, if you don't mind me asking?"

"You know how it is. Young people these days don't know how to treat their elders." My latest informant scowled. "Not that many of them were all that young."

"Would you recognize any of them if I showed you a picture?"

"I might." He started to sound suspicious at my line of questioning.

I knew I was in danger of blowing my cover, but I couldn't pass up the chance to confirm the theory I had bouncing around inside my skull. Pulling out my phone, I brought Jack Donahue's picture up on LinkedIn. "Does this man look familiar?"

He studied the professional headshot, putting on his reading glasses for a clearer look. "I believe this one showed up once or twice. He was always red-faced and in a bad mood when he left."

I wanted to do a victory dance right there in the hallway, but I forced myself to remain professional. "Can you remember any details about any of her other gentlemen friends?"

"There was an old, stately-looking fellow. He came by once. I thought he might have been her grandfather at first, but then he slapped her butt. He looked somewhat familiar, too, but I couldn't quite place him. Given his age, I would have thought his manners would be better, but no." He lowered his voice. "Pardon my language, young lady, but he was a pompous ass."

I choked back a laugh at the man's earnest expression. "You're excused, sir. Do you recall anyone else visiting Stacy?"

"The only other one I can think of was a really nice, middle-aged man who came around a few times. Very polite and always helping her when she needed furniture set up or something like that. He might have been one of those poor sods that gets put in the...what does my granddaughter call it... oh yes, the 'friend zone.'"

"Can you tell me what he looked like?"

A frown burrowed through the gentleman's wrinkles. "Well, now, I usually brag to my bingo club how good my memory is, but, for some reason, I can't really picture him. His polite manners stick out, but that's about it."

I gave him a comforting smile. "No need to worry. You've been helpful enough as it is." For all I knew, it was likely Stacy's father helping her get settled. Goodness knows how often my dad stopped by my condo during my early days of homeownership.

Jotting down a few notes on my phone, I thanked the older man profusely for his time. "I'm sorry, I never asked you for your name."

"It's Truman. Truman Hanks." He held out his weathered hand and gave me a surprisingly sturdy handshake.

I couldn't resist the temptation. "Any relation to Tom?"

He rolled his cornflower blue eyes at me. "Oh, ha ha, like I've never heard *that* before." He cracked a smile.

"It's nice to meet you, Truman. I'm Coco." I took a risk giving my name to him, but I felt like I owed Truman some form of truth after all he'd shared with me. "I really appreciate your help."

"Always happy to assist a lovely young lady with her work, whatever it may be." The twinkle in his eyes suggested Truman had seen through my *Divulge* excuse. "My lips are sealed." He mimed the iconic gesture.

My face warmed at my cover being blown, so I thanked him once more and hurried out of the apartment complex, heading toward the meeting place Jasper and I had designated.

Jasper was already there, tapping away on his phone as he waited beside the reflection pool.

"You will not—"

He cut me off with a *shush* and tapped the face of his imaginary watch. "We need to get out of here before the security guard comes after us," he said in a steely tone.

I followed him with reluctant obedience through the lush gardens to the entrance gate.

"Finally found it in the pool house," Jasper called to the guard as we appeared in his view. Having miraculously pulled a small leather planner out of his sports jacket to make our cover story credible, Jasper made idle chitchat with the guard while we waited for the gate to open. "Thanks again!" He waved with fake cheeriness, urging me to book it under his breath.

"I think we're safe now." I panted as we arrived at the metered parking spots where we'd left our cars.

"Yeah, I think we're in the clear. Good hustle." Jasper wiped a bead of sweat from his brow, but otherwise, looking unfazed by our speedy departure. "All right. What did you turn up? Must be better than what I found out. You've been grinning from ear-to-ear for the past five minutes."

Taking a deep breath, my exchange with Truman cascaded out of my mouth.

Jasper's eyes grew wider with each detail. "Wow, so Jack Donahue *has* paid Stacy a visit since she moved in. All I heard from the neighbors were complaints about how horrible some bug-eyed creature named Pepe is."

I shuddered at the bulging eyes etched into my memory.

"Glad you had more success than I did." Jasper crossed his arms, and I could tell he was struggling to contain his irritation over what he'd been subjected to for the last twenty minutes.

Hoping to derail his focus, I pushed onward. "Truman described Donahue as being angry and upset whenever he left. Maybe he was trying to win Stacy back and she wasn't having it." The more the blossoming idea churned in my mind, the guiltier Jack became.

"It could be that Jack got jealous of Stacy's new love interest and attacked her," Jasper suggested. "Maybe he somehow got wind of her new beau from Rochelle."

"I think the first thing we need to confirm is that Jack and Rochelle were once actually married," I pointed out sheepishly. "I'm pretty confident in my online stalking, but I could be wrong."

"Fair enough." Jasper bowed his head in agreement. "Now, what do we think about Stacy's other two visitors your informant mentioned?"

"Well, Truman thought the nice, middle-aged guy was just a friend. I'm thinking it's probably her dad. The other visitor," I stifled back a snort, "he labeled an old pompous ass. His words, not mine."

"Hmmm, old and arrogant. Who do we know that fits such a description?" From the look on his face, Jasper thought he already had the answer.

"What's your theory?"

"Remember what Claudia Harris let slip about one of Stacy's suitors when we were at the club..." Jasper was going to make me figure this out on my own.

Thinking back to all the secrets that had been shared last night at the country club, I felt like an idiot for not circling back to it sooner. "She said Stacy once implied she hooked up with Mayor Beaufort." I clasped my hand over my mouth, still not believing it could be true. The man was bulbous and decrepit. How Stacy could stand for him to touch her was beyond me. "And from how the mayor has been behaving regarding the police department, I'd sure describe the jerk as a pompous ass."

Jasper rubbed the light stubble sprouting across his chin. "So, the question becomes, was Stacy still sleeping around, or was she trying to tie up the loose ends from her previous affairs?"

"Regardless, if the guy bankrolling her apartment found out or presumed she was cheating on him, he could have killed her," I wagered.

"Maybe the baby wasn't even his to begin with," Jasper countered.

I suddenly became lightheaded from all the information swimming inside my mind. We had drummed up way too many suspects and subsequent theories for me to process. It also occurred to me that I hadn't eaten a solid meal all day, and hunger only added to my frazzled mental state. Caffeine didn't sit well for me on an empty stomach, and I had never stopped by Zaddick's to get a salad to tide me over. "Before we go too far down the rabbit hole, let's head over to the club and get some food. I need sustenance. We can strategize once I've eaten."

Never one to pass up a meal, Jasper showed his agreement by hopping right into his sporty little car. I trailed him in Jolly for all of two and a half minutes, as the Crestview Country Club sat close to the Villas' beachfront property.

Once our cars were under the care of the valet, we strode into the club lobby, indulging in the blast of AC that greeted us. Within moments, a hostess had seated Jasper and me in the dining area of the lounge. As soon as our waiter took our order, I began scanning the crowded room for Rochelle, my mood deflating. It was a gorgeously warm day, so there was a chance she had claimed a chair by the heated outdoor pool, as she was nowhere to be found inside.

My phone vibrated with a text from Hudson.

I just got off the phone with Deacon. He asked me about Stacy's Benz—did you clue him in too?

I quickly typed back. **Yes. I know I said I was only going to tell Gavin, but it felt like the right thing to do.** I didn't mention being hit by tsunami of panic upon hearing that Deacon still considered Olivia and Sean the top suspects.

He told me to rein you in. I said fat chance.

I smiled at the heart emoji he sent immediately after. Charlotte must not have mentioned my tenacity to Deacon if he thought I was going to give up the chase that easily.

Chapter Twenty-Four

Sinking my teeth into the delicious, juicy cheeseburger, I nearly spit out my bite when I caught sight of a bikini-and-sarong-clad Rochelle waltzing into the room from one of the sliding glass doors leading out to the pool deck.

I nudged Jasper's arm so hard that I knocked his buffalo chicken wrap out of his hands. "Look! She just came inside. What's the plan?"

Scowling as he picked his disheveled lunch up from his plate, Jasper gave me a blank stare. "Looks like she's heading to the bathroom, so that counts *me* out."

I took one last bite for the road and dashed away from our table in the direction of the women's powder room. I barely gave myself time to finish swallowing my burger, let alone enough time to come up with a coherent plan. Barging through the doorway, I froze, a stray piece of ground beef lodging itself in my throat. Rochelle stood right in front of me, applying a fresh coat of lip gloss in the wall-sized mirror.

I choked back a hacking cough as I fought to clear my airway and waved in strangled greeting. "Hey, Rochelle," I croaked as nonchalantly as I could muster, averting my watery eyes. I'd nearly suffocated on the remnants of my burger the moment I saw her.

My coughing fit didn't seem to have fazed her in the slightest. Pulling her gaze away from her immaculate reflection, she looked me up and down, and it was quite clear she was having a hard time remembering me, even though we'd spoken last night.

"Oh, hi, you," she gushed with Alexis Rose enthusiasm before the metaphorical lightbulb popped on over her head. "Coco Cline, right?" she said with sincerity this time. "I checked out your Insta this morning. You have good taste."

Her comment sparked a feeble idea, and, considering it was all I had, I ran with it. "You're too sweet. And thanks again for taking the time to speak with Jasper and me last night for the *Divulge* article. Readers will be touched to know Stacy had such devoted friends." I lied through a beaming smile. "Hey, while I have you, I wanted to confirm we had your name right." Pulling out my phone, I pretended to look important by scrolling through my notes. "You see, one of our junior editors thought you were married, and, since I know Frost is your maiden name, I wanted to make sure we ran the right one for the article." I silently prayed to the holy trinity of Gaga, Adele, and Beyoncé that she believed my shaky tale.

The corner of her lip twitched ever so slightly, and my heart skipped. I had made the right call.

"You can use Rochelle Frost for the article," she replied with restrained coolness. "I was married, but not anymore."

"Oh, I'm sorry to hear that. Was it a recent breakup?" I was testing my luck by prying but I figured I had nothing to lose.

"It happened toward the end of last year."

I gave her a sympathetic pout while I searched my brain for another question that would entice her to spill more details.

She continued without my coaxing. "It's totally for the best, though. He got too involved with his work and turned into a completely different person. Since he turned into a total prick, it wasn't all that difficult to get over him."

I snorted at her candidness, and she flashed me a conspiratorial smirk.

"We hadn't even been married that long," Rochelle said as she examined her nails. "We were one of those couples who'd dated since high school and were just expected to get married after a while." She sighed, turning her sparkling gaze back to the mirror to appraise her glamourous reflection. "But I needed more from our marriage, and he couldn't give it to me. So, I set myself free."

"*You* decided to end things?" I'd pictured their marriage ending because

Jack wanted a change, not the other way around.

Rochelle glanced my way. "That's right. And I had to pay a small fortune because of it. Our stupid prenup covered his penniless ass if I decided to leave him."

I held in a low whistle. This conversation continued to throw curveballs at all my preconceived notions. I'd assumed Jack had his own money, given his fancy tech exec title on LinkedIn. But then again, trust fund Rochelle's definition of "penniless" might have been wildly off base from reality. "Well, I'm glad you're free of him. What's his name, if you don't mind me asking?" I leaned in closer, playing the role of an eager confidante. "I want to make sure to alert all my girlfriends to stay away from the dude."

Rochelle picked up her small clutch from the nearby vanity. "He doesn't live around here anymore, but his name's Jack Donahue."

Bingo. I finally had the corroboration I'd been searching for, but I would have to celebrate my investigative triumph later. "I'll spread the word that he likes to lick toes or something," I joked, pleased that it pulled another smile across her face.

"You wouldn't be too far off," Rochelle said with a wink, waving goodbye as she sashayed out of the room. The sound of the door closing echoed off the bathroom's subway tile walls.

"That went a little differently than I expected," I murmured, giving myself a once-over in the mirror. Despite the day's escapades, my outward appearance did a masterful job at concealing the muddled thoughts ricocheting inside my skull.

Jasper's fingertips drummed against the polished wood as I arrived back at our table a few moments later. Two empty plates sat in front of him.

"Hey!" I punched him in the arm. "I was saving my sweet potato fries for last."

"They were mushy. You would have hated them," he replied robotically. "Did you get what you needed?"

I slid gracelessly into the booth, my bare legs sticking to the leather. "Well, Rochelle and Jack were indeed married."

"Why don't you sound excited about this?" Jasper propped his elbows on the table. "This validates your theory that Rochelle killed Stacy because she slept with her ex."

I glanced over my shoulder to the glass windows showcasing the blindingly bright outdoor pool deck. "I don't think so. When she talked about her ex, Rochelle didn't seem to harbor any notion that Jack cheated on her. He got too invested in his job and grew apart from her. She seemed happy to be rid of him."

"Are you sure it wasn't just an act?"

"She'd nab an Oscar nom if that was the case." I reached for my iced tea, since it was all Jasper had left of my lunch. "I think she was telling the truth. The only thing Rochelle seemed upset about was having to pay Jack a chunk of change because of their prenup agreement."

"They had a prenup?"

I nodded. "Yep, and get this. In the event she broke off the relationship, *Jack* would be compensated."

"I guess we can rule out Rochelle killing Stacy over a prenup dispute." Even while sulking, Jasper sipped his sparkling water with regal poise. "Unless there was some stipulation about him cheating. If she paid him all that moolah and then found out Jack cheated on her, that could spell bad news."

"But why kill Stacy? Rochelle's anger would have been directed toward Jack, not her," I pointed out.

"Hmmm. I guess you're right." Jasper tossed his napkin from his lap in a huff. "There goes one suspect out the window."

"Which leaves us with Jack and the baby daddy, if they're not one and the same."

"What if Jack found out Stacy was buddying up to Rochelle?" Jasper proposed. "If there was something in their prenup about adultery and Rochelle connected the dots about the affair, she might have been able to sue Jack for the money she shelled out to him, even after the fact."

My eyebrows met my hairline. "That could be why he went to see Stacy at her Villas apartment. He wanted to confront her about her friendship with his ex." What's more, Stacy might have had the decency to feel at least some remorse over her affair with her new friend's husband, even though it happened before they knew each other. If she mentioned to Jack that she wanted to come clean, he could have killed Stacy to prevent his divorce settlement from being taken away.

Both our phones chirped as a *Taylor's Version* text tone of "Fearless" filled our booth.

Charlotte had messaged our group chat. **That new cop was just in here grabbing coffee. Overheard him on the phone. They brought Donahue down to the station after ur talk with Gavin, Cokes!! But bad news. He has a solid alibi. Cops already released him.**

I felt like my lungs had been punctured. "You've got to be kidding me!" I slapped the table with anger-fueled force.

"Well, doesn't that just rain on our parade." Jasper tossed his phone aside. "What a waste of a day."

A manic storm brewed in my chest. "No, it wasn't." Jasper was just throwing in the towel because he didn't see what was really at stake here. I wasn't going to give up the chase that easily. "We just need to rework our theory, that's all. Maybe Jack hired someone to attack Stacy." My thumbs flew over my phone. "I'll tell Charlotte to float the idea past Officer Riley."

"Gurl, please. You've got that unhinged look in your eyes." Jasper took my trembling hands in his and squeezed them. "This is Central Shores we're talking about. Folks don't hire hits on people here. Come on, we gave it our best shot." He sat back. "This isn't like a Hallmark movie where everyday people stumble into mysteries and solve them just like that. This is real life. And we're glorified gossip columnists, not private detectives."

"But what about Mayor Beaufort?" I snapped back. "We haven't even explored how he could be connected yet."

The pity in Jasper's eyes was almost too much to bear. "I doubt Central Shores's mayor went down to the strip Wednesday morning, murdered his mistress, then called his friend, the crime lab director, and made solving her death a top priority."

Even in my frantic state, I knew Jasper was right about that one. "Well, maybe Rochelle *did* kill Stacy for ruining her marriage?"

"You just said she didn't have anything to do with it. That she was glad to be rid of her lech of an ex."

My top suspects had all but vanished, just like that. Where did that leave us?

"We're done with this," Jasper responded unknowingly to my unasked question.

I grabbed the sleeve of his polo. "But what about Mr. Valentine's Day and the baby?"

"What about it?" He brushed away the wrinkles from where I'd seized his linen shirt. "We have absolutely no idea who Mr. Valentine's Day was. We've already asked Stacy's friends and neighbors. What more can we do?"

I shrunk helplessly back into the booth.

He tossed me a sympathetic look. "Come on, Cokes. It's the weekend. Let's have some fun and forget about this stuff. All this talk of murder has been a drag." He pulled me up from our table and led me to the front door. "How about I pick Charlotte up at the coffee shop, and we'll come over for a movie night? I'll even share my Disney Plus subscription."

"Sure. Whatever." Normally, I would be all for a Disney princess marathon, but all I could think about was Stacy's bloody figure, crumpled on the floor of Once Used, Twice Buy. Her murderer was still out there, walking free. I felt like I had failed her.

A despondent cloud hovered over me as we paid for our lunch and left the club, heading outside to the valet pick-up area.

"Hey." Jasper waved his hand in front of my dazed expression. "You gonna be able to drive home okay?"

"Yeah, I'm fine." I handed the valet a tip before sliding into the front seat of my car. "I'll see you at my place in a bit." I drove off, leaving Jasper staring at me with a worried expression I could see from my rearview mirror.

About ten minutes into my drive, Jolly's speakers rang out, and I answered a call from Olivia Chen.

"Did you hear the news, Coco? We got the store back!" She sounded like she was dancing with joy. "I'm having a cleaning crew come in tonight to erase all the awfulness the police left behind. I'm paying top dollar for it, but I'm hoping it buys us back the time we need to have our grand opening proceed as originally planned next Saturday."

I didn't feel like I was in the best headspace to have this conversation with her right now, but I owed it to my clients to redirect all the energy I'd put into my silly investigation toward their business. "That's great news about the store, Olivia. The police did mention the chance to me earlier, but I didn't want to get your hopes up." In all honesty, I had totally forgotten about it. I couldn't believe how neglectful I'd been as a consultant. I had to do right by CoA and the Chens. I took a deep breath, preparing myself for my next bit of news. "Regarding the opening, though, I still think would be best if we postpone things for now, with the investigation still ongoing and all."

I pictured Olivia tensing up. "Why should we have to postpone?"

"The optics won't look good for you guys, to be completely frank. Your assistant is murdered *in your store*, yet you still throw a big, flashy event ten days after her death? The local news will skewer you, not to mention the internet trolls." One-star Yelp reviews flashed before my eyes.

"I don't think the media will fault us," Olivia clapped back, her voice inching up an octave. "We already spoke to the news crew from WMTG today. We came off as very kind and considerate employers."

My grip tightened on the steering wheel. "Interview? What interview?" I felt like the rug had been pulled out from under me.

"Millie Stabler told us *you* were the one who arranged it. I thought you would have known."

I didn't miss the sneer dripping from her words.

My head throbbed with stress. With everything else going on, I'd completely dropped the ball as the Chens' public relations expert. "Yes, I talked to her earlier this week about setting up an interview with you guys, but someone from the network was supposed to call *me* first to schedule it." My voice gained a defensive edge to it. I know I hadn't missed a call... had Millie decided to take matters into her own hands? Did Hudson know about this? No, he would have told me. This had Millie Stabler power move written all over it. Crap, I should have been there to run interference between my clients and the news team. With me out of the picture, Millie might have been able to get more from the Chens than I bargained for.

"Well, it's over and done with. Sean and I came off as very sympathetic," she assured me.

I rubbed my temples with one hand. "I'm sure you guys meant well, but video editing can be incredibly deceptive." I took a calming breath. "If Millie gets wind that you're pushing onward with your store opening like nothing has happened, she'll make you guys out to be fake and uncaring."

Sean's voice arrived on the line. "I hope you've talked some sense into her, Coco. I've been telling her since the police returned my key that we can't have a grand opening the week after our employee's unsolved murder."

"Goodness, it's not like Stacy was *that* good of an employee, Sean. This is our livelihood we're talking about." Olivia sounded like an overgrown child.

"Funny. Our livelihood didn't seem so important when you decided to blow it on an overpriced tea set."

"It belonged to *the Queen!*" Olivia yelled, as if that made it any better.

This conversation was escalating rapidly out of control. "Why don't I come over at nine-thirty tomorrow morning, and we can discuss the next steps. I think we can still proceed with a soft opening online and not seem disrespectful," I conceded, wanting to disconnect the call before Olivia's shrieking voice gave me a full-blown migraine.

"Sounds good, Coco. See you then." Sean ended our connection before his wife could further assault my eardrums.

The phone call had eaten up my entire drive back home. Not five minutes after hanging up with the Chens, I was in yoga pants, stretched out in front of the TV. Alone with my thoughts, crushing humiliation rained down on me. Who was I to think I could find a viable suspect in a murder investigation? What had I gotten my friends into? Hudson had been right all along. I'd been putting myself needlessly in danger, just for the thrill of playing detective. Not only that, but I'd completely abandoned my clients in their hour of need. I should have been there, coaching them through this PR nightmare. Instead, I'd been off playing millennial Agatha Raisin. I shuddered at whatever footage Millie Stabler had been able to wheedle out of Olivia and Sean without me there to mediate.

CHAPTER TWENTY-FOUR

Three episodes into an HGTV marathon, I heard Hudson, Jasper, and
Charlotte tiptoe into the condo. I ignored their conspiratorial whispers
as they planned how to approach me, instead intensifying my focus on
the redesigned outdoor firepit displayed on the TV screen. Maybe I could
feature the perfect party patio in an upcoming *Trending Topic* post...

"Hey, babes. How are you doing?" Hudson came behind the couch and
rubbed my shoulders tentatively.

Jasper had obviously assembled the troops and informed them of my mini
meltdown at the country club.

Charlotte was far braver than the boys and sat down right next to me,
already in sweatpants. She offered me an open box of Cheez-Its, her face
a mask of sympathy. "Sorry to be the bearer of bad news, Cokes. I think
you really had the police convinced Jack was the killer, though, if that's any
consolation."

I reached my hand into the box and scooped out a handful of cheesy
goodness. "It's not your fault. I'm glad you texted when you did. It saved
me from wasting any more of our time." I stuffed the crackers in my mouth
and sank back into my cocoon of sadness.

She rubbed my arm with sisterly concern. "If it makes you feel any better,
Deacon stopped by not long after I texted you. He said he was pretty
impressed with the intel you dug up, even if it led to another dead end."

"Thanks." I threw a plush blanket over my head, willing myself to disappear.
My failure still felt mortifying, especially in front of my best friends.

"And besides, all hope isn't lost." Jasper patted my head. The couch
cushions shifted as he took a seat on the far side of the sectional. "I ran into
Gavin outside of Brewed to Perfection while I was waiting for Charlotte to
close up shop. He said your tip about Stacy's surplus of suitors has expanded
the scope of their investigation tenfold. With their resources, they might
even be able to track down her baby daddy for questioning."

I peeked over the covers. "I guess that's good." Even if I hadn't found
Stacy's killer, at least I'd provided the police with useful information. It
might not have been justice, but it was something.

Hudson leaned over the back of the couch. I could feel the heat of his lips near my ear. "Nancy Drew would be proud."

Chapter Twenty-Five

As much as my friends tried to pull me out of my funk, I crawled into bed later that night still feeling rotten. I'd let Stacy down by not finding her killer. I'd let the Chens down by not being focused on their consulting engagement. I felt like I'd let my friends down, too, dragging them all over tarnation on a foolish quest.

Sleep didn't come easy, but at least I awoke Sunday morning feeling slightly refreshed and not so disappointed in myself. Jasper was right. I was a celebrity blogger, a social media influencer with a budding PR business. As if I could honestly piece together a murder, even one in a town as small as ours.

With a cup of coffee in one hand and a toasted poppyseed bagel in the other, I was ready to face the day ahead. Today's agenda would be all about my clients and my followers. I'd yet to respond to any of yesterday's comments from my décor post. Polishing off my bagel in a few hearty bites, I grabbed my iPad, ready to go to work, when a text came in from Jasper.

Forgot to confirm last night. We still on for house hunting today?

"Oh, crap." So much for today being all about work. I'd forgotten all about meeting Jasper in Cherry Springs. Deciding a call would get the job done more efficiently than a series of texts, I dialed his number.

Jasper answered promptly. "Yas, Queen?"

"What time are you meeting your realtor? I made an appointment with the Chens to do some damage control regarding their store." I rubbed my temples. "I'm sorry. This totally slipped my mind."

"I'm meeting her at eleven. I didn't feel like encroaching on my beauty sleep with an earlier appointment."

"Oh." I breathed a sigh of relief. "I can definitely meet you there by eleven. I'm heading over to the Chens in like twenty minutes, and I cannot imagine this meeting going all morning."

"Well, if I know you, and I do, if you even think you might be late, I'll get a million messages about it." Jasper chuckled. "Thanks for helping me with this, Cokes. It means a lot."

"Oh my gosh, you never show appreciation for my amazing friendship. Thank you!" I gushed, and we both dissolved into giggles.

Ending the call, I grabbed a peach sundress and headed for the shower.

Leaving a sealed-with-a-kiss Post-It for Hudson, I was in the car exactly twenty minutes later. My hair was still wet, so I rolled down the window to let it air dry, reveling in the sun streaming across the dashboard.

Fortunately, the church traffic didn't slow me down, and within twelve minutes, I was entering Mill Row. As I drove past the luxurious homes, golf clubs and tennis rackets were being loaded into the trunks of sleek cars. The weekend was still well underway in this neck of the woods.

Two houses away from the Chens, I had to slow down to let a group of pastel-clad pedestrians cross the road, likely on route to the residential tennis courts that had been built last summer exclusively for Canopy Cove homeowners. A little blinded by the morning sun, it took me a moment to realize one of the figures had parted from the group. She waved as she approached the side of my car.

I greeted her with resignation. "Hi, Amanda."

"Hi, Coco." Her ponytail bobbed enthusiastically in the breeze. "What brings you out to Canopy Cove? I hope you're not working, are you? Wow, the Chens keep you on a tight leash," she teased.

"You guessed it." I already wanted this conversation to be over.

Amanda stroked her leather Louis Vuitton tennis bag. "Well, make sure to swing by my place on your way out. I'm sure you'll need a pick-me-up, and I had Daphne buy all the ingredients for that special pear sangria of yours. She can whip it up in a jiff."

Not sure who the heck Daphne was, I forced a contrite smile. "Thanks for the offer, but I'm meeting Jasper in Cherry Springs right after this."

"Jasper Hastings?" she parroted. "How adorbs. You guys were always so cute together in high school. I would love to have a best friend like him."

Once again, her new and improved memories of our school days baffled me. She'd endlessly tormented Jasper for his larger-than-life personality and, often, his appearance when we were kids.

"Maybe you and Hudson can come over for drinks before the Chamber of Commerce gala, then."

I studied her with a critical eye. Amanda looked almost desperate for me to say yes. Had Arthur replaced his wife with some fancy, high-tech clone? "Sure. That sounds great." I finally caved in to her request, declaring myself to be the better person. Hudson and Arthur could at least enjoy bro-ing out before an evening of pomp and circumstance. "How about we come over at six?"

"Sounds perfect! Oh gosh, I'm so excited. See you then!" Amanda literally jumped for joy right before my eyes. "Honey, guess who's going to come over Wednesday night before the gala?" she called out to someone who must have been Arthur as she jogged off to catch up with the rest of the group heading for the Mill Row recreation park.

Releasing a breath I didn't know I'd been holding in, I resumed my drive and slipped into the Chens' driveway a few minutes later. No surprise, I arrived a bit early. I killed the time scoping out my Facebook newsfeed. I hadn't been online much these past few days, and there was a lot of celebrity drama to catch up on. The latest Prince Harry and Duchess Meghan drama filtered to the top. Now, there was a duo who needed a skilled PR consultant. I wondered if Hudson would object to relocating to Montecito...nah, the Sussexes' celebrity status was too big for even the likes of me to handle.

At nine-thirty on the dot, I slipped my phone into my bag and rapped my knuckles against the front door.

Sean, once again, greeted me with a grateful smile. "You're a saint." He ushered me through the foyer and into the kitchen. "I'm so sorry to tear you away from your weekend. I hope Liv's hysterics didn't spoil any Sunday morning plans?"

"She didn't ruin anything. I'm here for you guys." After putting the Chens and their needs on the backburner in the days following Stacy's death, it didn't seem professional to mention I could only stay for an hour before scooting out for a personal engagement. I'd just have to find a polite way to extract myself from their presence. "I know it's been a tough week."

Sean did look awfully tired as he nodded his agreement. "Between Stacy and this mess with the Queen's tea set, I'm afraid we're really in over our heads, Coco."

My heart tightened at the sorrow in his eyes. "I'm sorry I haven't been around as much as I should have."

He waved a hand aside. "Oh, please. I know you've had our best interests at heart. I really appreciate your running interference between us and the police. It's kept Liv at bay, for sure. Heck," he managed a small smile, "you even got Once Used, Twice Buy back in record time, even if we can't launch it yet."

I squeezed his arm reassuringly before taking a seat at the long kitchen table, scanning the cluster of papers spread over the glossy, oval top. "Well, I'm glad you and I are on the same page regarding the opening. I feel much more confident in the store's success if we play this safe."

"Agreed. The toughest part of this whole ordeal will be convincing Liv. If we can do that, I'm sure the launch will be a brilliant success." He winked. "Let me go get her. She's been in the study most of the morning."

Sean strolled out of the kitchen, leaving me to my own devices. I mentally prepared myself to face Olivia's ire. Despite her headstrong opinions, I knew Olivia to be a smart woman. I just had to convince her the bottom line of the store would suffer if she bulldozed ahead with her delusions of a grand opening.

As the minutes stretched on, I perused the paperwork laid out on the table. The pages were printouts of the store's inventory, as well as receipts for purchases the Chens had made to bulk up their stock. They'd accrued quite the extensive collection over the last several months.

"Coco, you're here." Olivia finally made her anticipated appearance, her unenthused voice greeting my ears.

"Good morning." I summoned as much cheer as I could muster, but it did little to lessen her deep frown. "Is something the matter?" Other than the obvious, I guess I should have added.

She bit her lower lip as she shuffled through the handful of papers she'd entered the room with. "Well, I'm not sure, I suppose."

That was odd. Olivia was rarely ever uncertain about anything.

"I was taking care of some miscellaneous expenses this morning, and was planning to dip into our rainy-day savings to do it, since we have so much tied up in Once Used, Twice Buy right now…" She tossed the papers onto the table, grabbing another handful and rifling through them with speedy precision.

The same savings that she'd already dipped one point eight million dollars into for a tea set, no doubt.

"…and it's strange. I know the Sandringham china set us back a bit, but I thought we'd have more money left." Olivia frowned, finally making eye contact with me.

Set us back a bit? It took all my willpower not to reach out and smack her senseless for her out-of-touch stupidity. More money left? After spending nearly two million dollars? "It's weird how money works that way." I knew it was rude to backtalk to my own client, but come on…

"I must have underestimated the additional fees or shipping costs or something." She held up an official-looking piece of paper. "On our March bank statement, there's a ninety-five-thousand-dollar withdrawal processed a few days before I confirmed the release of the tea set funds." Her gaze flitted across the document. "I guess it could be for some type of service retainer, but I don't believe this auction house required one."

If I remembered their earlier argument correctly, that meant the Chens had barely one hundred grand left in their emergency savings account. My stomach clenched with worry, with yet more pressure riding on the success of the store.

She thumbed through the papers in her hand once again. "I didn't want to mess with wiring money overseas, so I gave the auction house our bank routing number to allow them access to initiate the necessary transfers. I'm trying to find the tea set receipt before I call them to double-check I wasn't overcharged, but I can't find it."

Her anxiety put me on edge. "It's not on your computer?"

"No. All the emails containing details of the purchase are gone." She tugged at a strand of dark hair. "I must have deleted them by accident when I finally sent the coverage adjustment request over to the insurance company yesterday."

Knowing how flippantly Olivia Chen managed her finances, I was surprised she was so concerned about spending an extra ninety-something grand on a multimillion-dollar tea set. "Well, if you're too busy to talk about the opening right now, I can come back later."

She dropped into a chair, releasing a sigh I'd expect from someone with lungs twice her size. "No, no. It's fine. It will just be one more thing Sean will yell at me for later."

Sean waltzed back into the room. "Since when do I ever yell at you, my dear?" He kissed the top of her forehead, his hand going to her shoulder. "Although, I might get a little testy if you don't see reason and let Coco push forward with an exclusive online launch. Now that we have access to everything in the store, we don't even have to limit our inventory."

Sean made a good point, and it seemed Olivia agreed with him, as well. "Fine. If you think a soft opening will honestly bring us more profit in the long run, then go ahead." She sank further into her chair. "I give up."

Well, that's the spirit. I hid my eye roll before turning my full attention to my clients, who'd been put through the wringer this past week. "I truly believe the only option we have is to postpone the grand opening. It gives the town a respectful amount of time to grieve, and, hopefully, for Stacy's killer to be brought to justice."

"I still can't believe this has happened to us. That ditz ruined everything," Olivia grumbled through pouted lips, her slim arms hugging her body tightly. "I mean, I was on the fence about hiring her in the first place."

My insides tightened at her unabashed malice.

Apparently, I wasn't the only one affected by her harsh words. Her husband cringed as he took a seat next to her. "Come on, Liv. That's not fair to

Stacy. She didn't ask for any of this," Sean reminded her gently. "I mean, imagine how her family and friends must feel about this whole nightmare. It's terrible."

"Well, I suppose they're appalled, finding out she was actually a little tramp," Olivia spat back, shocking both Sean and me. "It's all over the local news this morning. The police are asking any men involved with her to come forward. Did you know she was the resident paramour of this dopey little town? I wonder if she even knew who the father of her baby was."

Her bitterness made me shiver. Where was all this sudden animosity coming from? Had I been wrong in defending Olivia so adamantly to the police? She certainly had enough venom in her voice to give me pause.

"Since when do you feed into town gossip?" Sean gave his wife a stern look. "Stacy was getting her life together, and you know it. She had a good job with us, she was taking business classes, and she'd gotten a nice place at the Villas. She was a good kid."

I turned my attention to Sean. "You knew she lived at the Villas?"

He gave me a funny look, clearly thrown by the curiosity in my question. "Of course. She told us she'd moved there a few months after we brought her on board. We had to change the address on her employee forms because of it. Right, honey?"

Olivia shrugged her shoulders. "Yeah, sure."

Great, so she was completely checked out of this conversation. At least Olivia's despondence was easier to deal with than fighting with her.

I clasped my hands in front of me on the table, ready to grab the reins and steer our conversation in a productive direction. "Okay, now that we've decided what to do about the opening, give me a few minutes and I'll draft some announcements and social media captions for you guys to approve. I'll work on spreading the message around the community that we'll be delaying the launch until further notice."

"Go nuts," Olivia said with a sour expression, not even bothering to make eye contact with me.

Sean fondly squeezed her arm before getting up. "I'll get us all some coffee," he said and walked over to the kitchen counter.

I began clearing the table to set up a makeshift workstation when I heard a slight scraping noise under a stack of papers I'd pushed away. Lifting the stack, I found a familiar-looking key lying on the table. "Is this a key to Once Used, Twice Buy?" I asked.

Olivia nodded. "The police dropped it off yesterday afternoon. We gave them Sean's key to use." She motioned over her shoulder to her husband, who was too entranced by the fancy espresso machine to notice. "I'll put it back on his key ring," she said begrudgingly before disappearing into the hall.

I went to work drafting a press release that the Chens could sign off on so that we were all on the same page regarding the store's status. I would post the statement on the Once Used, Twice Buy website and blog after I got back from house hunting with Jasper. Over the next few days, I'd roll out targeted social media campaigns via Facebook, Instagram, and Twitter announcing the exclusive online event.

Trying to use sincere, but not overly flowery language, I was about halfway through my press release draft when Olivia shuffled back into the room.

"There's already a Once Used, Twice Buy key on your key ring, Sean. Mine's accounted for, too. Where'd this one come from, then?" She held it up from the doorway.

Her husband glanced up from pouring frothy milk on top of three coffee mugs, his forehead wrinkled with confusion. "Hmmm. That must be our spare copy."

Satisfied with the explanation, Olivia placed the key on top of the pile of papers before me and sat back down at the table. I could feel her eyes watching me work, probably wondering why my hand had stopped scribbling notes.

"Olivia," I whispered to her, my brain spinning rapidly, "you gave *me* the spare key to the store, remember?"

Her olive skin paled as she thought back. "You're right. And I just saw mine in my purse. Whose key is this then?"

Time slowed as I replayed the memory of Deacon's smokey twang sharing what I thought to be trivial information in the grand scheme of things. The key. The only keys to Once Used, Twice Buy belonged to Olivia, Sean, myself, and Stacy. Stacy had her own key to the store. *"It was missing from her key ring when we examined her belongings found at the crime scene."* Yet, all four keys could be accounted for within the walls of this house. I had to be staring at Stacy's copy.

The Chens hadn't been allowed in the store until last night, after the police had thoroughly searched the premises and collected evidence, including Stacy's belongings. Stacy would have used her key to get in the store the morning she was attacked. The killer had to be the one who removed the key, using it to lock her body inside. In order for it to be in the Chens' possession now...

"Oh my God." Every inch of my body seized with panic.

"What's wrong, Coco?" Sean's calm, collected voice asked as he placed a steaming homemade latte in front of me. "You look like you've seen a ghost."

Wordlessly, I fumbled for my phone, trying desperately to swipe out of my Facebook app to dial the police. My hands were shaking so violently, I ended up dropping the phone onto the kitchen table. "I'm so sorry. Clumsy me," I managed to say, although I sounded unstable. I tried to reach for my phone again. My fingers lightly brushed the screen before Sean took my hands, his grip firm.

"Coco..." he watched me very carefully. "Are you alright? You're trembling." His once kind eyes were distorted, void of care and concern. Meeting his gaze sent spasms of terror down my spine.

I forced myself to smile and nod. "Of course. I just got overwhelmed for a moment, thinking about all we have to do. I'm sorry. That was completely unprofessional of me. Let me run to the bathroom to splash some water on my face." I attempted to stand and grab my phone once more, but Sean's grip tightened on me, keeping me firmly rooted in my seat.

"Sean, what are you doing?" Olivia looked annoyed and confused by her husband's actions. "Let the poor girl go to the bathroom."

"Coco is going to stay right here and drink her coffee," Sean asserted with alarming confidence.

I looked at the frothy foam. Had Sean drugged it or something? I yanked my arms back, hoping to catch him off guard and make a run for it, but he was way stronger than he looked. I barely rocked in my seat.

"Sean, what's gotten into you?" Olivia reached across the table to knock his hands away from my pinned arms.

"Enough of your incessant nagging, woman!" His explosive shout rang throughout the spacious room. "For once in your life, just shut up."

Stunned, Olivia's mouth hung slack. I, too, was having a hard time reconciling the sweet, charming Sean I had worked alongside these past few weeks with the monstrous man before me now.

"What's going on?" Olivia's voice was barely above a whisper, but she locked gazes with her husband.

Sean just glared back at her, his grip on my arms tightening, tears springing to my eyes with pain as his fingernails pinched my skin.

"Haven't you figured it out, Olivia?" I croaked, my throat tight and dry, as if daring me to drink from the coffee mug before me. "Sean killed Stacy."

Chapter Twenty-Six

"Goodness, Coco. You really are full of it today." Sean's fingernails dug into the flesh of my arms. "Why don't you just zip it, and do as I ask, hmm? Drink the coffee," he seethed.

Tears of pain and panic streamed down my face, streaking through my bronzer. I shook my head defiantly.

Much to my dismay, Olivia continued to sit in her chair, observing her husband. The hopeless expression in her eyes was almost as terrifying as Sean's unrestrained rage.

"Olivia, get help!" I cried, only to receive a slap across the face from Sean. Seizing the opportunity he'd given me by releasing one of my arms, I reached for the coffee to toss it in his face.

Numbed by shock, my own sluggish movements foiled my attempt. Sean saw my assault coming and dove out of the way, the dark liquid splashing across the piles of paperwork. With surprising strength and agility, he was back on his feet in an instant, one arm wrapped around my neck before I could escape my seat.

"Don't do anything you'll regret, Liv," he growled at his frozen wife. "Things will get very unpleasant for the both of you if you move from that chair."

I sputtered, trying to fill my lungs with air as he held his grip firm. "Olivia!" I pleaded once more, begging the indifferent woman to figure out a way to stop her deranged husband.

She watched us struggle for what seemed like an eternity, a shell of her former self. "Is it true, Sean? Did you kill that girl in our store?" she asked at last, her voice limp.

"Of course not," he roared, keeping me rooted in my chair with a headlock. "Coco's lost her mind. The stress of everything has clearly been too much for her."

A blizzard of details whipped through my mind. The key. Mr. Valentine's Day. The baby. The missing ninety-five grand from the Chens' savings account. "Don't listen to him." I gasped, clawing at his muscular arms. "He killed Stacy. He was having an affair with her!"

"How dare you say such a thing to my loving, wonderful wife," the madman hissed in my ear.

"A wife who couldn't give you the child you craved," I bit back, the pieces of Stacy's life falling into place. "You must have been so happy when you found out Stacy was pregnant. You were finally going to get the family you always wanted." The image of the cutesy pillow post on Instagram floated through my mind. Had they bought it together?

"Shut up," Sean yelled, his arm pushing tighter against my neck.

"When you found out she was pregnant, you took a chunk out of your rainy-day fund and moved her into a nice apartment." I now had his wife's undivided attention. "That's why you had less money in the account than you expected, Olivia. Sean never thought you'd actually use the savings account because you always seemed to forget about it. He reminded you about it so much, even I was aware it existed. But once you used the money to buy the Queen's tea set, he suspected you might notice another sizable withdrawal once the fund was drained by the auction purchase." No wonder Sean had been so understanding about Oliva's pricey acquisition. He'd probably already found out about it and just didn't want to draw any further scrutiny to other activity within the rainy-day account. "I bet *he* deleted all your emails, making it so that you couldn't check the actual price from the auction house."

"Coco, I am *this* close to silencing you for good." To make good on his threat, Sean tightened his arm even more around my throat.

Oh God. I was beginning to see black spots.

Olivia's eyes glazed over with a memory. "Sean took over managing all

230

our online bank accounts months ago, but I noticed the March statement from the rainy-day fund on his desk this morning while doing some work. When I read it and mentioned the ninety-five-thousand-dollar transaction to him, Sean said it probably had something to do with the pound to dollar conversion, causing the auction house to take out an additional withdrawal. He told me not to worry about it." She wavered a moment. "His reasoning didn't quite make sense, though. On the date the money was withdrawn, I hadn't even authorized the purchase of the tea set yet. That's why I wanted to double-check the auction house receipts for any hidden fees..."

"He's lying to you, Olivia. Don't you see? He's been trying to blame *you* for the money *he* spent on his mistress." I wished I could turn around and look the murderer in the eye. "What I don't understand is why you killed her, Sean? What did Stacy do to make you bash her over the head?" I coughed, my breath coming in shallow rasps. Maybe if I could keep him talking, Olivia would finally snap out of her trance and get help.

Sean growled like a rabid animal. "I didn't kill her. I was here with my wife at the time Stacy was attacked."

"I was taking a nap, Sean," Olivia replied. "You could have left while I was sleeping."

Hope tingled down my spine at the fire beginning to simmer in her eyes, even though she still sat fixed in her seat.

Sean began to tremble behind me, the vibrations pulsating against my neck and shoulders. Whether he was angry, scared, tired, or a bad mixture of the three, I couldn't tell. His muscles, though, relaxed their hold just a little. "I didn't kill her."

"Was it an accident?" Maybe a different approach would work. With his loosening grip, I was able to take deeper breaths, although he still had me pinned to my chair. "The police have gotten it all wrong, haven't they? Stacy wasn't murdered in cold blood. It was an accident, wasn't it?" I used the softest, most feminine tone I could muster under such circumstances.

Even though I couldn't see his face from the angle I was at, I heard him sniffle a couple of times. I was getting somewhere. "You didn't mean to hurt her. You never would have hurt her intentionally. You loved Stacy, didn't you, Sean?"

More sniveling before I heard his throat catch. "Yes, I loved her. I loved her so much. She made me so happy. Happier than I've ever been." He cried freely now, his tears falling onto my hair and shoulders. "It was love at first sight. Back in December, when we interviewed her to help us launch the store, I knew I was in love. God, the connection between us was electrifying."

Olivia's face crumbled as her husband confessed his feelings for another woman, but still, she sat glued to her seat. Why in the heck wasn't she running to get help?

I couldn't afford to focus on her and lose this opening with Sean. "When did you start seeing each other?" I cooed, slowly inching closer to the back of the chair, the gap between his arm and my neck widening by the second as I distracted him with memories of the past.

"Well, we began fooling around in the store pretty much the week after she was hired. But after the new year, things started getting more serious between us...we were so happy."

Stacy's most recent Instagram pics cycled through my thoughts. Her smile. Her sparkling eyes. She was the epitome of a woman basking in the warmth of new love. No wonder Stacy hadn't wanted her event planning job at the Crestview Country Club back; she thought she'd found her bliss working alongside Sean.

He gurgled through his emotions. "Then we found out we were pregnant. We were going to have a baby."

I caught Sean's reflection in the large glass windows overlooking the sprawling backyard. His toothy grin was maniacal and terrifying.

"I gave her the money to lease a nice apartment and treat herself well, away from her parents...her friends...this gossipy little town. Somewhere we could enjoy each other's company without having to worry about prying eyes."

Knowing the Villas prided itself on its exclusivity and privacy, Stacy had made the best choice in the area. "You provided for her." I hoped he believed my false praise.

"I did. I promised to take care of her and the baby." Sean's reflection revealed his smile growing bigger. "Once the store opened and we made back some of what we'd put into it, I was going to leave you, Liv, and go raise my child with Stacy."

I flinched at the casual way Sean inflicted such emotional devastation on his infertile wife. From the blank stare Olivia gave him, I couldn't help but wonder if she was used to this kind of torturous, psychological abuse.

"What happened to the baby, Sean?" I asked softly, slowly sliding my right arm out from being pinned between my body and the chairback.

"I knew Stacy had a lot of boyfriends before we met," he answered, "but she said she'd stopped seeing them all after we started dating. I believed her. I still do. But one of them cornered her at her new apartment. His wife had left him, and he thought he could win Stacy back. But each time, she said no. The last time he came around, he got real angry and roughed her up a bit too much. She…she lost the baby because of it." Sean took the arm that wasn't around my neck and wiped his eyes. "Why she waited so long to tell me, I don't know. I guess she was worried about how I'd react." The sad irony of Sean's statement was clearly lost on him. "She sent me a cryptic DM to meet her at the store Wednesday morning. I had a special Instagram account so we could communicate without fear of being caught. If Liv ever got suspicious about our affair, there'd be no text messages for her to trace."

I thought back to Stacy's profile. I wondered which private account belonged to Sean Chen. Maybe, if things went south here, the police would dig more into her social media apps, find that incriminating conversation, and connect the dots.

"Once we were back from the doctor's and Liv was asleep," Sean continued, "I drove over, and she told me what happened."

"And you were upset, of course, when she told you. As was your right." I nearly gagged on my own twisted words, but I had to make Sean think I was on his side. I was so close to getting him to reveal the truth.

"Yes, it *was* my right to be upset." Sean sounded like he fully believed every word coming out of his mouth.

I pressed his psyche further. "You had to show her how angry you were, that's all. It only proved how much you cared for her, right?"

His sobs were his only response.

"Why did you take her key, Sean?" I wanted to keep him talking, hoping he'd drain himself of his remaining energy and finally let me go.

"I'd left my keys in the car, and I needed to lock up the store. We always keep Once Used, Twice Buy locked," he said robotically. "I removed Stacy's key from her keychain and used it to lock the door behind me. I knew, if I locked her in there with her key, the police would narrow it down pretty quickly that she was attacked by either you, Olivia, or me. There would have been no room for any other suspects to emerge."

I trembled at the detached way he explained the thoughts running through his mind, as he'd let the woman he loved bleed to death on the break room floor.

"I meant to throw it away," Sean said with a shake of his head, "but I left her key on the side table in the entry hall after I returned home to clean myself up. I forgot all about it until Detective Forester came by later that afternoon to question us and asked for a key to the store. Liv saw the key I'd left on the side table, and, thinking it was mine, gave it to the detective. I nearly had a heart attack over Liv's carelessness, but in the end, it didn't end up mattering. Those idiot police never even realized they'd had Stacy's key all along."

Liv's carelessness? I gritted my teeth together, anger boiling within me at Sean's cruel, patronizing attitude. "Was Stacy still alive when you left her? Or did you make sure she'd never get back up?"

"She deserved to be punished for ruining everything! She deserved to feel the same pain I felt in my heart, knowing I'd never get to hold my child." He paused, as if picturing the vengeful moment in his head. "If she hadn't been such a tramp before I met her, none of this would have happened. *None* of this would have happened! I would still have the love of my life. I would still have my little baby..." Sean openly wept in the middle of his picturesque kitchen.

"And now, you truly have nothing, Mr. Chen."

My gaze snapped to the far corner as Chief McInnis entered the room, his gun drawn. Deacon and Detective Forester appeared on the other side of the hall, blocking all the kitchen exits.

"Let Ms. Cline go, Sean. Time to turn yourself in." The chief's voice was uncharacteristically warm and reassuring, expertly trained to coach criminals like Sean off the ledge, more so than I had been. "No one else needs to get hurt."

"Come on, Mr. Chen. That's it now." Detective Harriet Forester's sharp features contorted into a delicate smile.

With my captor momentarily distracted by the new visitors, I kicked at the leg of the table, forcing my chair to tip backward. Caught off guard by my body tumbling to the floor, Sean leaped back and released his grip. Able to finally breathe freely, I gasped at the blissful air.

In the chaos, Deacon and Harriet both lunged forward, tackling Sean's flailing frame to the ground.

"Sean Chen, you are under arrest for the murder of Stacy Lockner," Detective Forester recited the Miranda rights as she handcuffed my client. "You have the right to remain silent. Anything you say can and will be used against you in a court of law..." her voice trailed off as she and Deacon escorted the disgraced man out of his storybook home and into an awaiting police car.

I was still sprawled out on the floor, trying to catch my breath, when Chief McInnis's towering frame loomed over me. "I guess there's a benefit to working with the county team. I can let them do all the heavy lifting."

I couldn't resist a laugh, although I was sure my frayed nerves had something to do with the vigor in which I responded to the chief's lame joke. He helped me up off the floor, looking me up and down. "You all right, kiddo?"

Massaging my sore neck, I nodded. "I'll be fine." I released a sigh of relief. "No thanks to her, though." I shot a withering look at Olivia Chen, who still hadn't moved from her seat. From the haunted look on her face, I wondered if she even realized her husband was no longer in the room.

Chief McInnis motioned for her to stand up. "We're going to need you to come down to the station for a few additional questions, Mrs. Chen."

Gavin McInnis appeared in the doorway, sizing up all the clutter. With paper strewn everywhere, spilled coffee, and a fallen chair, it didn't look like a room that belonged in the Chens' normally pristine house.

With a wordless command, the chief ordered his lieutenant to remove Olivia from the premises and take her down to the station.

As Gavin helped her up from her chair, she finally spoke. "I'm sorry for everything, Coco. I really am."

My neck still burned, and I imagined the ugly bruising left by my attacker. I didn't have it in me to offer my immediate forgiveness.

She hung her head at my silence and followed Gavin out of her home.

I turned to the chief, my mouth agape. "You arrived just in time. How on earth did you know to come here?"

He snorted, stroking his five o'clock shadow. "Well, it seems you're not allowed to be a few minutes late without your friends raising the alarm."

I must have looked as confused as I felt.

"Your buddy Jasper phoned the station, saying you were supposed to meet him in Cherry Springs at eleven, and since it was currently eleven-o-*three*, he was concerned. He told me you had gone to the Chens' house for a meeting earlier in the morning, and because you weren't answering your phone, it was the best place to start."

I decided right then and there I would rename my blog *Coco Worships Jasper* as tribute to his incredible friendship...for a few hours.

"We weren't entirely too thrilled about dropping everything and meeting his demands." The chief walked across the kitchen to where my phone lay on the table. He studied my phone a moment and, for some reason, touched a finger to the screen before tossing it over to me. "But then Gavin and every other person in Central Shores—hell, maybe even all of the U.S.—received some Facebook notification touting that 'Coco Cline is now LIVE.'"

I barely managed to catch my phone. "What?" I was still dazed and reeling from what I'd just witnessed.

"Well, you know, I really don't like all that techno stuff, but somehow you launched your camera from your Facebook app, and it started broadcasting everything going on here. All we saw was the ceiling, mind you, but we heard enough to get our butts over here in a jiffy." He raised a bushy, gray-speckled eyebrow. "You might want to work on your camera angles next time."

I turned my phone over in my hands and unlocked the screen once more. Indeed, it opened up onto my Facebook camera, which, fortunately, was no longer live streaming. Chief McInnis's actions a moment ago while scoping out my phone now made sense. He'd ended the stream. I must have brushed the LIVE button while Sean and I struggled, unintentionally filming this whole ordeal for my online connections to witness. I shuddered to think what would have happened if I hadn't. I had never been so grateful for social media as I was in that moment.

"Do you want me to take you to the hospital, Coco?" the chief asked, his expression back to business. "We don't need an official statement just yet because, well, you kinda already gave us one." His concerned gaze flickered to the phone and back.

I shook my head. "I'm fine. Shaken, but fine. I'm feeling better by the minute, knowing Stacy's killer will be behind bars."

He nodded his consent and escorted me to the front door. "You did good, Coco. I listened to you piece it all together in that video on the drive over here. I'll never admit to it to anyone else, but you're pretty darn good at playing detective." He paused, clearing his throat as I grinned madly at him. Little did he know, I would cherish those words for the rest of my life.

As we walked out into the bright, warm April sunshine, the chief grunted. "One of your friends here has offered to drive you home."

Inhaling the glorious spring air, I gazed out happily across the lawn, expecting to see Jasper or Charlotte.

Instead, a beaming Amanda Highgrove waved from beside Jolly.

"On second thought, maybe I should go to the hospital," I murmured, my triumphant bubble deflating into the pit of my stomach.

Chief McInnis was well aware of the bad blood between Amanda and me. Back when he was a spry, young deputy, he'd been the one to respond to the reports of Amanda and her cronies trashing my parents' front lawn with rotten squashes, an ode to my "Gourdy Cordy" moniker. Now, the chief patted me on the back and watched with veiled amusement as Amanda raced up the porch steps to gather me into a tight hug.

"Oh God, Coco. I was glued to the whole thing on my phone. At first, I thought you were doing some kind of role-playing, but then when we heard him threaten you? What was happening? Was he strangling you or something? The camera angle was awful."

I didn't have the bandwidth to answer her barrage of questions and wordlessly walked down the gravel path to Jolly. With one final look back at the Chens' front door, I settled into the passenger seat of my car.

"Oh, and Coco?" Chief McInnis grabbed my car door just as I leaned over to close it.

"Yes, sir?" I hoped he planned to save me once more from the torture I was about to endure.

"I told you it was one of the Chens." He winked as he shut the door in my face.

I don't think I've ever rolled my eyes harder.

Chapter Twenty-Seven

"No offense, but you don't look so great, Coco. Are you sure you don't want to swing by the hospital? I don't mind."

Amanda's genuine concern had me wondering if I'd been sucked into an episode of *Black Mirror*. From Jolly's passenger seat, I twisted my head in her direction, wincing at the stiffness growing in my neck by the minute. Was this really the same woman who'd made me cry nearly every day of sophomore year before I'd learned to tune out her insults?

"I'm fine, Amanda. I just want to go home."

"You really are something, Coco Cline. I would be a mess in your position. A hot mess, but a mess nonetheless."

I managed a snort at her little joke. Self-deprecating humor suited her.

Silence settled over us for a time as Amanda drove, but soon, she removed her hand from the steering wheel and reached for my left hand. "I'm glad you're alright." Her throat bobbed, like she wanted to say something more. Was she finally going to acknowledge our bitter past? Had it taken a near-death experience to get her to own up to her being a bully?

I waited with bated breath, but instead of an apology, Amanda rescinded her hand and continued the drive toward my home.

It was in this quiet moment that I finally realized life was too short to hang onto a high school grudge. And that maybe, in her own special way, Amanda had been apologizing for her behavior all along. "Same here."

She smiled and nudged my arm. "Have you talked to Hudson yet? You may want to give him a heads up before he gets wind of Sean's arrest or sees your Facebook story." She shuddered at the thought. "Your being attacked by an insane madman probably shouldn't come from anyone but you. Besides, that awful co-anchor of his would probably find a way to make the incident all about her. Did you see her throwing herself at every guy under fifty during the WMTG fundraiser? Absolutely no class. How does Hudson put up with her antics?"

I giggled at Amanda's evident disdain for my new nemesis. Maybe there was more common ground between us than I thought. What's the saying? The enemy of my enemy is my new bestie? "Where do I even begin? I doubt, **Hey, babe! My client tried to off me because I realized he'd had a torrid affair and ended up killing the girl. Fun times** would go over well."

Amanda grimaced. "You should probably keep the more gruesome deets to yourself until you talk to him at home."

She was right. I couldn't risk Hudson driving recklessly after learning what had happened to me.

I still hadn't finished drafting my text to Hudson by the time Amanda parked Jolly in the garage. Sean's deranged face blurred my vision as I attempted to vaguely summarize what had transpired at the Chens' house. Every time I tried to push past the memory, a lingering, phantom grip tightened around my neck. Maybe I *should* have gone to the hospital. Considering I asked Amanda to stay with me while I waited for Hudson to arrive, I was definitely more traumatized than I realized. But being alone with my thoughts seemed like an even worse alternative.

It took some teamwork to craft a suitable text message that would alert Hudson of a serious development without scaring the daylights out of him.

Hey, babe. You'll never believe it—I cracked Stacy's case and the police nabbed the killer. I really need you home, though, so please come as soon as you can.

It was actually quite funny, because Amanda and I had been watching Hudson film a live promo for the upcoming Stacy Lockner tribute segment while finishing up the noontime Sunday news when I finally sent the text. I didn't realize Hudson kept his cell phone at the anchor desk, or I would have waited to send it until after they'd finished filming. On live TV, he did a doubletake at his desk, and the next thing we knew, rising star

Hudson Caruthers dropped everything and hurried off set, yelling that his girlfriend had singlehandedly thwarted Stacy Lockner's killer. Despite Millie's immediate displeasure over his unprofessionalism, the afternoon ratings skyrocketed, breaking the station's record for the time slot. It didn't take long for Hudson's wild exit to become a trending clip on YouTube and Reddit. In that moment, much to my ego's chagrin, my boyfriend became a household name across America.

My Facebook LIVE session made the rounds across the country as well, although, for the integrity of the investigation, the Central Shores police requested that Facebook remove the video as quickly as possible. Little did poor Chief McInnis know that when you asked the internet to bury something, it did the exact opposite. My footage had already run on every major network news program by the time they erased it from the site.

The media attention didn't stop there. Without the Facebook video at their disposal, news networks began running soundbites from my three-year-old *Today* show interview with the caption, "Tech Industry Icon and Social Media Influencer Coco Cline Cracks the Case" among other mind-blowing variations. Me, an *icon*. Before I turned thirty. All because I had accidentally swiped left and turned on my smartphone camera.

"Coco!" Hudson called my name as he ran up from the garage, signaling his arrival home after his spontaneous departure from the station.

I greeted him at the door but didn't have the chance to say anything before his mouth encompassed mine and he'd scooped me up in his arms.

"I'm dating the millennial Miss Marple. I can't believe it," he said through a kiss that turned into a laughing smile.

"Miss Marple?" I giggled against his lips. "Can't I be someone svelte and sexy, like Phryne Fisher?"

"I'll let you two lovebirds have the place to yourselves," Amanda interrupted meekly, waving goodbye. "Arthur's here to take me back home."

Surprising even myself, I broke away from Hudson's protective grip to give her a bone-crushing hug. "Thank you, Amanda. I really appreciate your being here."

She looked like she might cry with happiness as she disappeared down the walkway to where her husband's Tesla was waiting.

"Your text told me you discovered Stacy's killer and that the police arrested him." Hudson looked between me and the empty doorway. "You didn't say you'd brokered peace in the Middle East, too."

I shook my head, feeling loopy. "Would you have believed me if I told you?"

Later that night, after the marathon of police interviews had ended, and the shock of my narrow escape ebbed away, Jasper and Charlotte arrived at my front door bearing gifts of champagne, cheese, and cured meats.

"No better feast, if you ask me." I celebrated by popping a bottle open on the back deck, the stars twinkling overhead.

"Hear, hear!" Hudson, Charlotte, and Jasper all raised their empty glasses, ready for them to be filled with the sparkling pearly liquid.

I felt warm and fuzzy, tucked under Hudson's arm in a lounge chair, and not just because of the two drinks I'd already tossed back. Chief McInnis's praise still echoed through my head. I had done a pretty good job getting to the bottom of things, after all.

"I can't believe sweet Sean Chen killed Stacy," Charlotte murmured once silence had settled over our little group.

"I can't believe we didn't think of him sooner." Jasper pouted. "At the Villas, Truman Hanks said a kindly, middle-aged man was always hanging out with Stacy. We totally dismissed that guy as a threat."

"Sean had us all fooled. I thought he was so devoted to Olivia." I sighed, knowing I couldn't go back and change what had happened over the past few crazy days. I'd inserted myself into Stacy's murder investigation because I wanted to prove my clients innocent. That need eventually morphed into wanting to get Stacy the justice she deserved. Who knew that to do one, I'd shoot a torpedo through the other?

"What's going to happen to the both of them?" Charlotte asked me.

I stroked my champagne flute, the glass cool between my fingertips. "With everything that came to light this morning, the police have more than enough evidence to take Sean to trial for second-degree murder and assault. Chief

CHAPTER TWENTY-SEVEN

McInnis told me he could get a life sentence."

Jasper and Hudson released low, simultaneous whistles.

"Leaving poor Olivia to pick up the pieces of her shattered life, once she's released from the hospital. She was taken there after being interviewed at the station." I sighed. "Her doctors informed the police that she was in shock due to victimization, which is why she didn't make any effort to help me escape."

Hudson's grip tightened protectively around me. I'd never seen him so emotional as I walked him through what I had survived, being Sean's hostage. I didn't realize until I shared my experience with him how close I'd come to being seriously hurt or worse, and both of us had shed ample tears at the horrific outcome that might have been if not for my Facebook LIVE mishap.

Seeing my friends' expectant faces, I continued, "Sean had been emotionally *and* physically abusing his wife for years because of her failure to conceive. Often, victims can struggle fighting back against their abusers, even if given the chance." I felt awful about the whole situation, cursing myself for never picking up on the subtle ways in which Sean belittled and hurt his wife. All those tender squeezes I'd witnessed had actually been harsh, controlling touches in disguise. He'd masked it all so well, but Olivia still had the bruises hidden under her clothes to prove it. "Olivia asked to see me, so Hudson took me to the hospital earlier this afternoon to hear her out, once I was done with the police." I looked between Jasper and Charlotte. "She apologized for not helping me, and I've forgiven her. As for Once Used, Twice Buy, she's going to sell the building and the store's entire inventory is going up for auction. She plans to donate the money to battered women's shelters around the area."

"Well, that's something, I guess," Jasper said with a scoff. Clearly, he wasn't as compassionate toward Olivia and her situation as I had been.

"Hopefully it helps her heal," was all Charlotte offered.

"Tell them about Jack Donahue." Hudson nudged my arm, coaxing me to share more of the unfolding drama.

"What about him?" Jasper and Charlotte asked in unison.

"He confessed to pushing Stacy over the back of her couch when he came by her apartment two weeks ago. He said he went to try to win her back again, and they argued. According to Jack, Stacy attacked him and he 'simply defended himself.'" I used air quotes to highlight my disbelief. "Whatever the case, he's the one who caused the miscarriage."

My friends' hands flew to their slack mouths.

Charlotte's eyes filled with tears. "Poor Stacy."

I nodded my solemn agreement, hoping the troubled young woman was finally at peace now that her killer was behind bars.

With the help of two more bottles of champagne, we were a much merrier group an hour later at the beach, happy to have all the unpleasantness that had befallen our little town behind us.

"Cheers to Coco for being basic enough to confront a murderer with only her phone for defense," Jasper called out to the crashing waves, downing his fifth—or was it sixth?—glass.

Charlotte laughed, hiccupping a few times as she tried to catch her breath. "Cheers to Coco for being so neurotic about being on time that she's made us all neurotic as well!"

"Cheers to our very own amateur sleuth." The alcohol made it extremely hard for Hudson to say "sleuth" without spitting all over my cheeks.

My heart glowed at their adoration. "Cheers to my three best friends who stuck with me through it all. This victory is just as much yours as it is mine," I said, feeling generous.

"Oh, no way. You will not lump me in on this. I will never, ever associate myself with anything remotely related to Facebook LIVE," Jasper snapped with his legendary sass. "I'm more of a TikTok betch, *betch*." He burped out the last part.

Our laughter floated out across the beach, mingling with the radiant starlight.

Chapter Twenty-Eight

"This stuff is amazing. I can't believe you came up with the recipe yourself," Amanda gushed as she took another sip of my Party Pear Sangria from her crystal wineglass.

"Now, remember what Coco said, Mandy? It's got quite the kick, so don't drink too much before we head over to the gala," Arthur reminded his wife for the eighteenth time since we'd arrived. "I'd like to be able to dance with you after the awards are all doled out."

Amanda rolled her eyes, and it was the first time I'd ever seen her sass her adoring husband to his face. "Please. I could waltz my way through a rosé-filled swimming pool."

Hudson and I chuckled, catching each other's gazes as laughter filled the grand sitting room. Surprisingly, I had been enjoying the pre-party drinks with the Highgrove-Bushmans, although it helped that Jasper, Charlotte, and Deacon were here to break the ice.

Deacon and Charlotte looked like they were on their way to a movie premiere, not a small-town event. His dapper tuxedo was so shiny I could see my reflection in it, and Charlotte looked simply divine in a floor-length crimson dress. She reminded me of Jennifer Lawrence during her first Oscars red carpet.

Jasper wore a sharp navy, pinstripe suit, refusing to conform to the traditional expectations of a black-tie dress code. He'd snagged a last-minute invite to the Central Shores Chamber of Commerce gala, as the offer he'd secretly put down on a Sunny Shores condo had been accepted the previous morning. Even though I teased him mercilessly about it when he finally told me, Jasper had helped save my life by calling Chief McInnis, and I was ecstatic my oldest friend would be living only three empty houses down from me.

I noticed the watchful eyes in the room darting between Hudson and me and occasionally, glancing at the bare ring finger of my left hand. Charlotte had been certain Hudson was going to propose the minute she and Jasper left Sunday night, but we'd just slept under the stars. As much as I wanted Hudson to ask me to marry him, it felt wrong to assume a run-in with a crazed murderer would prompt him to get down on one knee. He would ask me when he was ready, although I hoped that would be sooner rather than later. He was my person, and we belonged together. Looking at him now, with his clean-shaven face and sexy new buzz cut, he could have been wearing a garbage bag and still looked like a million bucks. But his Tom Ford suit didn't hurt. I couldn't wait to take it off him once we got home.

Our hosts, Amanda and Arthur, looked like the charmed, one percent darlings they were. Arthur's slim figure was made bulkier and more muscular by the cut of his PRADA tux, and Amanda's pink A-line Calvin Klein gown was truly breathtaking. Not three minutes after we arrived did she mention to Charlotte and me that it had been custom made.

Catching my reflection in a nearby mirror, I decided I had cleaned up nicely, too. Since it was her afternoon off, and I had no scheduled CoA engagements, Charlotte and I had gone dress shopping yesterday at the outlet mall near Rehoboth Beach. I'd snagged a stunning Michael Kors gown on clearance. It felt amazing against my skin, the minty green satin hugging my curves in just the right way. Dangling diamond-encrusted hoops borrowed from *Divulge's* fashion department glittered from my earlobes to complete the look. I felt like a princess. However, the stiffness in my neck reminded me that my dress also served as a shield. Its high neckline covered the nasty blue bruises Sean's grip had left behind. *Out of sight, out of mind.*

"Well, shall we head over and make our grand entrance?" Our hostess surveyed our empty glasses. Amanda had sent town cars to collect us each from our homes, as she and Arthur had arranged for a large black Escalade to chauffeur us all from their estate over to the public library, the only place in Central Shores with enough room for, well, the whole town.

"Remind me again why we hate her?" Jasper whispered out of the side of his mouth. He, of course, didn't need reminding of our childhood bully's exploits, but even I was beginning to warm to this new "Mandy" Highgrove.

Twenty minutes later, our group tripped over each other as we cascaded out of the limo in the library parking lot.

"Wow, that sangria hit me fast." Amanda stumbled, grabbing her husband's arm for support. "Deadly stuff, Cokes."

I shot a raised eyebrow at Charlotte and Jasper, who both had heeded my warning about the drink's strength. They'd helped me come up with the recipe for *Trending Topic* in the first place, so they knew I wasn't overestimating its potency.

"Cokes? That's *our* name for you," Charlotte hissed with a joking pout.

"I doubt she'll remember anything about this evening past our arrival at her front door," Jasper muttered as we entered the elegantly lit library and followed a genuine red carpet up the stairs to the second floor.

During regular business hours, the second floor was littered with study tables and cubby desks. Since the building had become Wi-Fi enabled, folks occasionally brought their laptops and tablets from home to use the faster bandwidth, but usually, it sat empty for most of the week.

Tonight, round banquet tables had replaced desks, and there were long buffets lining the walls, overflowing with deliciously smelling food catered by the local restaurants in the area. An open bar was in full swing at the back of the room, opposite a stage and a large dance floor. A snazzy jazz band played music as guests arrived, dressed to their version of "the nines." Considering the varying levels of wealth throughout the community, you had people dressed in right-off-the-runway looks or designer items, as well as folks sporting their best ensemble from department store clearance racks. Regardless of the price tag, everyone looked lovely.

Friendly faces frequently stopped me on my way to my seat, begging me to rehash my harrowing tale of escape. I'd been asked so many times to recite the whole debacle I'd memorized a Chief McInnis-approved blurb. Sean Chen's trial wasn't scheduled for several weeks, and I needed to keep the messy details to myself as much as possible for now.

It was a feat easier said than done. With my Facebook LIVE appearance becoming national news and Hudson's WMTG clip becoming a meme, we had both been overwhelmed with unwanted attention from the press. The endless attempts to get us to comment about Stacy's death or Sean's upcoming trial brought flashbacks of the media frenzy around the LiveIt acquisition. The dark side of celebrity. But together, Hudson and I weathered the chaotic media storm, mostly by silencing our phones and emails and tucking ourselves away in our condo safe haven. Our fifteen minutes of fame only lasted a few days. At least, on the nationwide scale. We got bumped off the nightly news by an iconic Hollywood couple announcing their shocking divorce. In Central Shores, Hudson and I were very much still a hot topic of conversation, but then again, we had been before all this crazy stuff had happened.

Breaking free from my clamoring fanbase, I rushed over to hug my mom and dad, happy they had decided to attend the gala. I hadn't told either of them I was an award recipient this evening, but I'd enlisted Thea to help me convince them that they needed a night out on the town. Mom looked foxy in a navy-blue gown with pearl accessories, and Dad cut an impressive figure in his steadfast tan suit, which I thought he may have worn to their wedding.

"Nice outfit, Dad," I said with a chastising tone, and I caught my mother rolling her eyes in agreement.

She threw me an exasperated look. "I told him to buy something from this century to wear."

"If it fits, why bother?" Dad looked genuinely confused by the fact we were making fun of his nearly forty-year-old suit.

Despite the smiles on their faces, fresh strands of gray showed in their hair. I had sat down with them Sunday afternoon between visiting the police station and going to see Olivia Chen at the hospital. As I told them about my encounter with Stacy's killer, they seemed to age before my eyes. I was happy Thea and I had been able to convince them to a night out. They deserved it.

"I'm so glad you guys made it." I gave them each another hug for good measure. My brush with death had certainly made me more unreserved with my affections of late. "I'll swing by your table in a bit. I'm seated up near the front for some reason." I shrugged my shoulders, playfully pretending to be confused as to why I was so close to the stage.

Fending off the eager crowd as I waltzed my way through the sea of people, I relaxed as I settled in my chair next to Hudson, with Jasper taking the seat on my right.

Lacie Burbank joined us moments later, giving us each a kiss on the cheek in greeting before sitting down next to Jasper. Then Amanda and Charlotte arrived, having gone to use the ladies' room before the start of the ceremony, and Deacon and Arthur brought the table a round of drinks from the open bar before settling in.

Our dashing host for the evening, Deputy Mayor Roger Sullivan, asked everyone to take their seats, his voice blaring over the microphone. Usually, it was Mayor Beaufort's role to play the Master of Ceremonies, but I'd heard through the grapevine this morning that he was stepping down from his position. While I wasn't sure if the rumors were entirely true, word on the strip was that Chief McInnis confronted the mayor, accusing him of purposely trying to run the police department out of town. Whatever else the chief had said prompted Beaufort to hand in his resignation immediately following their conversation. After having shared everything I'd learned about Stacy Lockner with the chief, I couldn't help but wonder if Chief McInnis had investigated my unproven theory that our morally sound mayor had had an affair with her, and unearthed the evidence I'd failed to obtain. Whatever the reason for Beaufort's sudden departure, I was glad. Our town deserved better than that slimy politician.

Speaking of the police department, Center of Attention had just signed Chief McInnis and his team as its newest clients. With my skill set, I planned to boost their social media presence, allowing the police department greater community outreach potential now that they didn't have to worry about the mayor closing up shop on them. The Director of the Sussex County Crime Lab had been quite impressed with how our small-town department managed Sean Chen's arrest. At a recent press conference, the director praised the chief, stating that Lloyd McInnis's steadfast direction was one of the reasons the police had apprehended Stacy's murderer so quickly in the first place. I'd kept my mouth shut and let the chief enjoy the small victory. I'd requested for my involvement in the case to be described as simply being at the right place at the wrong time when Sean was arrested. No one besides the chief, Gavin, and Deacon needed to know the lengths I'd gone to beforehand to dig up information on Stacy's case. I had an image to maintain for my fanbase, after all, and I wasn't ready for that to change. Since we weren't breaking any rules or risking the integrity of the prosecutor's case, Chief McInnis was happy to keep my clue finding to himself.

My request for anonymity worked to everyone's benefit. Director Morrison was so pleased with the chief that he even granted McInnis's request to have a few crime lab techs relocated from County to train and work alongside the Central Shores officers for the foreseeable future. This had Charlotte over the moon as well, as Deacon had been the first to volunteer. Now, her beau would be able to visit her during his lunch breaks every day.

At the front of the room, Deputy Mayor Sullivan ran a hand over his slicked-back hair and cleared his throat. "My dear friends," he began, clinking his glass for silence, "I thank you on behalf of the Chamber of Commerce for joining us in celebrating the achievements of our wonderful town. Over the past year, we've had a lot of change in our community, but never once has the spirit of Central Shores faltered. Tonight, we honor the business leaders and volunteers who do so much to make this little slice of heaven the jewel of the East Coast."

The room laughed at his exaggerated praise, but as I glanced at the faces around me, I realized our deputy mayor was telling the honest-to-goodness truth. There was a reason I hadn't moved to New York City or L.A. or Miami once I'd made my mark on the online world. Central Shores had something none of those places could hold a candle to: the love and support of the best people I'd ever known.

I squeezed Hudson's hand under the table, suddenly overcome with emotion.

"Everything all right, babes?" he asked, his handsome face full of concern.

I kissed his cheek. "Things couldn't be better."

Acknowledgements

I am beyond grateful that *#FollowMe for Murder* has made it into your hands, dear reader. This little story has gone on quite the journey since I first started writing it in 2017. Writing a book is openly sharing a part of yourself with the world. There are so many people who have influenced who I am today, and thus, this book, that it is hard for me to thank them all.

I'd like to start off by recognizing all the hard work my agent, Dawn Dowdle, put in to making this book possible. Without her support and championing of this series, I wouldn't have made it to this moment.

A big thank you goes to my editor, Shawn Reilly Simmons, and everyone at Level Best Books who gave Coco the space to find her place in this big world. The Level Best team was willing to take a chance on us, and I couldn't be happier that Coco and I found a home with them.

A special thanks to my sounding board, Evan Grant. Evan has been with me through it all. He always goes above and beyond the call of friend duty to help me through my writing roadblocks.

In today's world, we often forget the importance of being kind and just how big an effect kindness can have. Without the simple kindness of J.C. Kenney, I don't know where I would be today. It's amazing how one bit of advice can change the course of a person's life. And lastly, thank you to Tina Crossgrove and Bettye Underwood, two people who shaped my writing more than they'll ever know.

About the Author

Sarah E. Burr lives near New York City. Hailing from the small town of Appleton, Maine, she has been dreaming of being Nancy Drew since she was a little girl. Since Sarah wasn't stumbling across any crime scenes in corporate America, she left her career in healthcare technology to write mysteries of her own.

Her novel #FOLLOWME FOR MURDER, first in the TRENDING TOPIC MYSTERIES, shines the spotlight on a social media PR expert after she discovers a dead body in her clients' store, forcing her to untangle a web of secrets in her small, beach-side town.

Sarah is also the author of the Court of Mystery series and the Glenmyre Whim Mysteries. She is a member of Sisters in Crime, currently serving as the New York Tri-State Chapter's social media guru. When she's not spinning up new stories, Sarah is off seeing Broadway musicals, reading up a storm, video gaming, and enjoying walks with her dog, Eevee.

SOCIAL MEDIA HANDLES:
Facebook: https://www.facebook.com/authorsaraheburr
Instagram: https://www.instagram.com/authorsaraheburr
Twitter: https://twitter.com/SarahEBurr

AUTHOR WEBSITE:
www.saraheburr.com

Also by Sarah E. Burr

Glenmyre Whim Mysteries:
  You Can't Candle the Truth

Court of Mystery series:
  The Ducal Detective Mysteries
  Paradise Plagued
  Burdened Bloodline
  Sovereign Sieged
  Crown of Chaos
  Harrowed Heir
  Ravaged Reign
  Innocence Imprisoned

www.ingramcontent.com/pod-product-compliance
Lightning Source LLC
Chambersburg PA
CBHW020719130726
47899CB00011B/502